The Sailmaker's Daughter

Also by Stephanie Johnson

Belief: A Novel

The Sailmaker's Daughter

STEPHANIE JOHNSON

ST. MARTIN'S PRESS ≋ NEW YORK

www.stmartins.com

Library of Congress Cataloging-in-Publication Data

Johnson, Stephanie, 1961–.
    [Heart's wild surf]
    The sailmaker's daughter / Stephanie Johnson.—1st U.S. ed.
       p. cm.
    Originally published with title: The heart's wild surf.
    ISBN 0-312-30693-8
    1. Plantation life—Fiction. 2. Mothers—Death—Fiction. 3. Influenza—Fiction. 4. Girls—Fiction. 5. Fiji—Fiction. I. Title.

PR9639.3.J62H4 2003
823'.914—dc21   2003040639

First published in New Zealand under the title *The Heart's Wild Surf*
by Vintage/Random House New Zealand Ltd.

First U.S. Edition: July 2003

10 9 8 7 6 5 4 3 2 1

$\mathcal{C}$ o n t e n t s

Pronunciation

b, which represents *mb*, as in me*mb*er
d, which represents *nd*, as in Mo*nd*ay
q, which represents *ng+g*, as in fi*ng*er
g, which represents *ng*, as in si*ng*er
c, which represents *th*, as in fa*th*er.

$\mathscr{A}cknowledgements$

$\mathscr{T}$hanks are due to my great-uncles, Len McGowan and the late Eric McGowan, and my great-aunt Emsell McGowan, my brother Bruce, Dr Ahmed Ali, Consul-General of the Republic of Fiji in Auckland, Margaret Patel at the National Archives of Fiji in Suva and the Simpson family of Savusavu Bay. Also heartfelt thanks to Theresa Koroi and Jane Cooper for their Fijian and French, respectively, and to Donogh Rees, Joan Livingstone, Dave Giddens, Pam Mayo, the *Spirit of Adventure* Trust, Dick Scott, and the staff at Auckland Public and Grey Lynn Libraries, especially Manjula Patel, for their assistance. Gratitude also to the Alexander Turnbull Library for their kind loan of microfilm of the 1918 *Fiji Times*. The author gratefully acknowledges the assistance of the QEII Arts Council of New Zealand (now Creative New Zealand), without whose generosity this book would not have been possible.

I am also indebted to Claudia Knapman for her history *White Women in Fiji 1835-1930: The Ruin of Empire?* (Allen and Unwin, 1986); Peter Downes for his *Shadows on the Stage* (McIndoe, New Zealand, 1975); Martin McDonnell for his thesis "Wai-me-gere: A History of a European Plantation on Taveuni" (Auckland University). Other books that proved useful are the *Cyclopaedia of Fiji 1907* (reprinted by the Fiji Museum, 1984), *At Home in Fiji* by Constance Cumming (Blackwood, London, 1882), *Islands Far Away* by Agnes Gardener King (Sifton Praed, London, 1920), *The History of the Pacific Islands* by Deryck Scarr (McMillan, Australia, 1990), *Tales From Paradise* by June Knox-Mawer (Ariel, London,

1986), *The Violence of Indenture in Fiji* by Vijay Naidu (University of the South Pacific, 1980), *My Twenty-One Years in the Fiji Islands* by Totatram Sanadhya (Fiji Museum, 1991).

The poem in chapter nine is "One Day" by Rupert Brooke (1913). The sermon in chapter eighteen is from *The Nature of Holiness* by John Wesley, compiled and edited by Clare George Weakley Jr. (Bethany House Publishers, Minnesota, 1988). Agnes Perkins-Green's description of Suva in chapter two is from *Islands Far Away* by Agnes Gardner King. The advertisement for Wood's Peppermint Cure is from the *Fiji Times*, 1918. The text for the advertisement for *Aladdin* is from *Shadows on the Stage*.

Many thanks also to my mother and especially to Tim.

This book is dedicated with love to
the memory of my grandmother,
GERALDINE FRANKHAM.
b. Suva 1905 – d. Auckland 1993

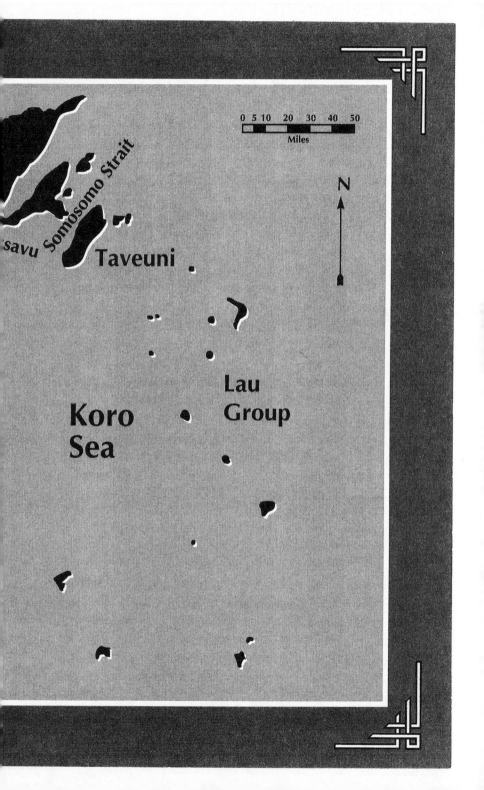

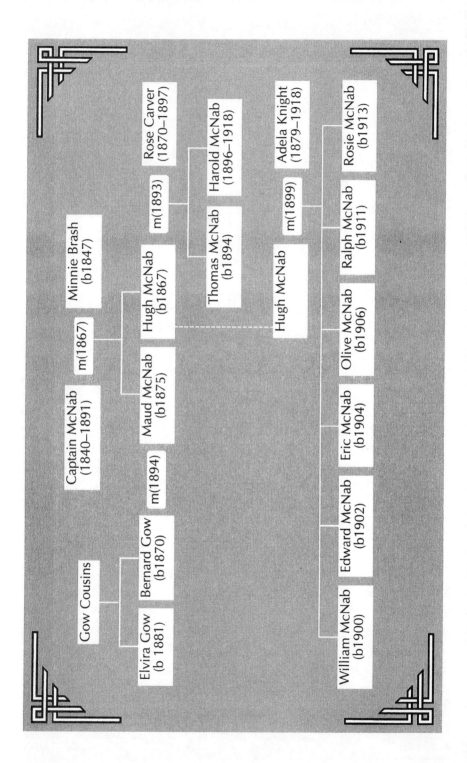

Usually a person seeking an island
craves simplicity and glories in a world
that is still incomplete and therefore full of possibilities.
PAUL THEROUX

History is impossible to penetrate,
and that is its great richness.
RYSZYARD KAPULCINSKI

They say that the Dead die not, but remain
Near to the rich heirs of grief and mirth.
I think they ride the calm mid-heaven, as these,
In wise majestic melancholy train,
And watch the moon, and the still-raging seas,
And men, coming and going on the earth.
FROM "CLOUDS" BY RUPERT BROOKE,
THE PACIFIC, OCTOBER, 1913

There was once a girl who lived in a village
high in the mountains of Taveuni, beside a lake.
One day her mother spanked her for playing
when she should have been doing her chores.
The little girl ran away, crying, and became entangled
in a vine where her tears turned to blood.
As each drop fell upon the ground it turned into
a beautiful red flower. From thenceforth,
the vine was named Tagimaucia.
FIJIAN LEGEND

$\mathcal{P}r\,o\,l\,o\,g\,u\,e$

$\mathcal{A}$t the bantam's first cry, Olive McNab was dreaming she could fly and that, as she could, she did, rising high above the garden where Elena the ayah was hurrying from her bure to find little Rose standing at the back door of the house, rubbing her pale-blue eyes in the sun.

Olive twirled in the smoke rising from the kitchen chimney where Champak stoked the range for her father's oat breakfast. Porridge, with a sprinkling of salt, a dollop of soured cream and a mouthful of malt on the side: it was the same breakfast Hughie McNab had eaten all his adult life. In the smoke whirled phantoms of cinnamon and cumin, coriander and turmeric, fenugreek and fennel, small clouds of Champak himself mingling with the wood smoke, dissipating in the air.

Like a diver Olive left the pitched roof of the bungalow, rising high above Suva Harbour and the already busy steamers and cutters, skimming the masts of the wrecked schooner *Expansion*, slowly breaking up on the reef week after week, past the bay where her father's little yacht *Vai* rocked, around the south of Viti Levu to Ovalau, the tiny rocky island with the old beachcomber's town of Levuka held steady by the cupped hands of the cliffs. Hovering in the air, blown by the glassy wind off the Koro Sea, she heard the French clock of the Sacred Heart strike the hour twice. It was the bantam's second cry.

Olive turned, arms akimbo in her aertex vest and pants to fly across the sea to the southern tip of Taveuni Island. And there below her were Aunt Maud and Uncle Bernard, doing the tango on a dance floor jutting out into the Somosomo Strait. Aunt

Maud's fashionable handkerchief skirt flapped in the breeze, her tiara glittered in the dawn. Uncle Bernard, one eye brown and one eye blue, the progeny of cousins, danced with his head back, his great shaggy head and terrifying laugh frightening Olive so she flew on to Savusavu on the southern rainy side of Vanua Levu. There she looked down with fondness on the multi-coloured Molloys going about their early morning on the copra plantation. Florrie was boiling the copper with the steam rising above her tawny head. Her baby, Lily, as dark as her name was not, played among some fallen nuts. There were the three old Molloy men, as alike as triplet lemons, dour and sour. The rivers gleamed, the bush shone and the mop heads of the cocoa-nut palms scrubbed at the pristine sky.

The bantam cried for the third time, his clarion call finding Olive's wind-blown ears one hundred miles away as the seabirds fly. Olive tumbled backwards, somersaulting over the coral-reefed islands, circles within circles, green and blue, fantastical breakfast eggs, riding the currents of the air back to Suva, and dropping like a cocoa-nut into the garden, where she flew in the back door. In the corridor she passed her father rapping on the bedroom doors of her brothers Tom and Bill, Eddie, Eric and Ralph. Through the thin walls she heard her mother's dry cough.

*O*live's eyes open. The smell of porridge is in her nostrils. She springs out of bed, pulls on her cotton dress and drags a comb through her tangled hair. From her dressing table she takes her Lucky Lunaria, Gem of the East, and puts it, as always, deep in her pocket. She steps out on to the grass mats of the corridor, soft beneath her bare feet, and turns towards the dining-room. It lies at the heart of the house, windowless and dark, and beside it lies its twin, the bedroom of Grandmother. Within that dim chamber lies the sleeping, sweating bulk of Minnie McNab, the only one of this island-scattered family still asleep on this glittering, dazzling, morning.

CHAPTER ONE

Leaving Suva

Halfway to the dining-room, Olive remembered she should have put on her church frock, because today they were going on a voyage. Not the usual voyage on Dad's little yacht to Nukulau Island for a picnic, but a trip on the steamer to Taveuni. Taveuni was where the Toffs were, and you had to dress up for them. It was seeing Dad that reminded her, going in Grandmother's door. Olive stopped and looked in.

There was Dad, standing at the foot of Grandmother's bed.

"Wake up, Mother," he was saying. "Boat leaves at ten."

Grandmother's bulk didn't shift. Perhaps she's dead, thought Olive, hopefully. That would mean they wouldn't have to go, because there would be a funeral to arrange and she'd have to stay and help Dad because Mother couldn't; not while she was still so sick.

"Mother?" said Hughie again. He was holding the cuff of his white jacket to his nose, Olive noticed. Always there was a strong smell in Grandmother's room. Peppermint for her "snuffle" and another sweet, cloying smell that seemed to come from Grandmother herself. It was at its most acrid in the morning because Grandmother had been in there all night, and there were no windows to let in the air.

"Mother!" Now Dad was irritated. "I know you can hear me, Mother."

Grandmother groaned. She wasn't dead then. If she suddenly reared up and caught a flash of Olive, there would be trouble. "Lurking", Grandmother called it. She didn't understand that often it was the only way of finding things out. Grandmother's answer to "Trust in Providence". Olive did that as well, and very often Providence showed her some very queer things.

Olive stared at her bare toes, then her fingernails. They still bore traces of dirt from her turtle's box. She'd cleaned it out last night and laid in a store of live flies. Stanlake had eaten them all at once, of course, even though she'd explained to him that she was going away. He most likely hadn't understood. After the last fly was snapped up in his hard, pale-pink mouth, he'd blinked at her, let out a soundless, dry kind of turtle burp, drawn his head into his shell and gone to sleep.

Grandmother groaned again and sat up. Quickly, Olive walked backwards, counting, one two three, the number of steps it took to go round the corner from Grandmother's room into her brothers' room. Eddie had already gone down to the Sailroom to open up and the younger boys would be eating breakfast. There was only Elena, packing a trunk.

"There you are, Miss Olive," said Elena. "I've put your frock out on your bed."

Olive scowled and pretended she hadn't heard the ayah. Elena's strong, heavy arms shook out a shirt.

"Have you eaten your breakfast?"

"I don't want any," said Olive. She crossed the room to the open window, passing between the big bed shared by Ralph and Eric and the narrower one that was Eddie's. The sheets of the big bed were peeled back. Ralph had wet the bed again. Olive pointed.

"Have you told Mother?" she demanded.

But the ayah didn't answer. She was pairing socks.

"You should tell Mother. He's seven now, you know."

Elena was counting the pairs.

"They won't need that many socks. We're only going for a few days — until Mother is better."

Elena's dark head remained bowed over the chest of drawers.

"Elena!" Olive was shouting, but she couldn't help it. She didn't want to go to Taveuni with Grandmother and Ralph and Eric. She wanted to stay in Suva and help Dad. Soon Mother would be well enough to visit. Her horrible, frightening, shuddering coughs would ease, and Olive would be able to go in and sit on the edge of her bed as she'd done in the early days when Mother was first ill, before she'd caught the influenza, when it was only the new baby making her sick. Soon Mother would be able to tell her stories again, stories about when she was a little girl in a cold, damp place called Auckland. Stories of when she was a famous actress — Adela Knight, Bernhardt of the Colonies — and how people would want to touch her hand, or the stuff of her skirt . . . Elena had lifted her face and was staring at her. Olive saw something that made her heart leap, something that frightened her more than when she'd scaled the cliffs with the boys, just like the real soldiers at Gallipoli, and she'd slipped and fallen twenty feet to the beach below. Elena's eyes were full of sorrow.

Olive climbed through the window on to the verandah. On this side of the house most of the verandah had been closed in to make a room for Harry and Tom, her half-brothers. That was why there were no windows in Grandmother's room or the dining-room. The door stood open and the room was empty. Tom's bed was a rumpled, sweat-yellowed mess. Pages of the *Fiji Times* lay crushed and muddled through it. There were smudges of grey on the sheets, which may have been ink, or perhaps ash. An overflowing ashtray sat on the bedside table. There was a sticky glass leaning up against the picture of Tom and Harry in their uniforms, with a background of palm fronds. It was the studio portrait they'd had taken just before they went away.

Harry's bed had the blankets folded at its foot. The striped, ticking pillow lay undented at its head. Harry would never sleep in that bed again.

Tom had come back though, back from France, his shoulders hunched, his eyes never meeting Olive's. Sometimes she played a kind of game with him, shifting her face, hoping his gaze would fall on hers. If that would happen just once, then it would be as good as if he'd said hullo. It seemed to Olive that the last thing Tom had said to her was "Goodbye", three years ago, when he'd boarded the troop-ship.

There he was now, out in the garden with a cigarette, dragging the smoke down as if someone had dared him to. He's so thin, he caves in, thought Olive. He's like an old man.

Circling Tom's feet was the bantam, the one who'd roused Olive from her dream. The bird never liked his territory invaded, especially first thing in the morning when he was showing off to his wives, and least of all by the mournful, smoke-puffing spectre that was Tom. Olive loved Banty and she knew the workings of his tiny, fevered mind. Tom wore singlet and pyjama pants, his feet were bare and his bony toes were perfect bantam targets. Flying from the edge of the verandah just as the bird made a lunge, Olive was in the nick of time to kick Banty in his green-feathered side. She hauled to a stop in front of Tom, whose eyes, resting momentarily on the top of his sister's head, registered mild surprise. He'd hardly noticed Banty's presence, despite being his victim many times before. Olive knew that since he'd come back from the war, Tom had difficulty remembering things.

"Tom, come with me."

She took him by the hand and dragged him unresisting down the path, around the lily pond, to the cool, shaded corner that was Stanlake's.

"Can you feed him for me? While we're away? And my iguana and mynah bird?"

Tom nodded. He dropped the butt of his cigarette, took tin and papers from where they were tucked into the waistband of his pyjamas, and rolled another one. His sadness rushed over Olive like a wave at the beach.

"Why don't you come too, Tommy? To Taveuni?"

Tom gave no answer but a gentle smile. He glanced up as high as Olive's knees and down again.

Olive sighed and knelt by Stanlake's box. She lifted the lid off. The turtle was still asleep. It was Dad who'd named him, after the head of Suva Police.

"That's about the pace he goes," he'd laughed, watching the baby turtle crawl along the grass.

Olive rapped hard on Stanlake's shell.

"Hullo, hullo, anybody home?"

The shell may as well have been empty, like the polished ones Dad bore home from the Bowling Club as trophies, for all the signs of life it gave.

"Olive?" It was Dad, calling from the verandah. Olive took Tom's hand again, but this time he pulled away.

"Off you go."

Olive went. The mynah in the cage on the verandah post was shrieking.

"My giddy aunt!" said Dad, when he saw her. "Look at you. Go and change before you say goodbye to your mother."

Olive stood on tip-toe by the mynah's cage. "When will he learn to talk, Dad?"

"Please Olive," said Dad, in that new, tired voice he had. Olive hated it, it made her spine go stiff with rage, not at Dad, but at whatever it was that made him like that. Or *who*ever. It was Mother. Mother was the reason Dad was tired, and she was the reason they were going away. Mother's perpetual illness, the baby and the flu. Olive looked up at her father and wondered if he knew that she knew about the baby. He was turning now, walking purposefully ahead of her. Olive wondered if he was looking forward to them going away. He liked peace and quiet, she knew. In the evenings he liked to sit on the verandah, with his cigarettes and Scotch. Mother used to sit with him, but lately, Olive had taken her place. She knew not to talk, at least she knew to try not to. Sometimes Dad would laugh at something she said; sometimes he would take her hand and they'd watch the evening come on in the town below. Lights would be set twinkling in windows, the Indian horse drivers would be turning their nags into the paddock below the house, or coming for rested horses and fixing lamps to the open carriages.

Now Dad's head was down and his hands were clenched at his sides, below the cuffs of his jacket. Something was on his mind. Olive longed to ask him what it was, but he'd already turned in at the back door.

Say goodbye to your mother, Dad had said, in that flat voice. On the table outside Mother's room there was a little bottle of eucalyptus oil and a clean, folded white cloth. Olive picked up the bottle and sprinkled it on the cloth. One or two drops flew on to her church dress, white linen with cotton broderie anglaise trim. She hated it for its tell-tale colour and absence of pockets. She hated the stockings more, the sweat and prickle of her legs. The feeling in her legs was worse now. Perhaps it wasn't just the stockings. At their core, inside their bones, her legs were as heavy as cast iron, as if they wouldn't walk anymore, especially not into Mother's bedroom. Behind her the dining-room door clicked. It was Dad coming out into the hall. With the cloth held to her nose, she took a deep breath and edged into the room, around the tallboy.

Mother's eyes fluttered and opened. It was as if they'd sunk further into her head, as if her head itself had shrunk, but maybe she just appeared that way because they'd cut all her hair off. Her hair had been dark and curly before, but now in the dim, shaded light, it was silver and straight. Her thin, long hands lifted from the mound that was her stomach.

"Olive — is that you?"

"Yes, Mother."

"Are you leaving now?"

"Yes. They will be waiting for me."

"I can't hear you."

Olive took the cloth from her nose and mouth. "How are you, Mother?"

Her mother didn't reply straight away. She laughed, in a quiet, hoarse sort of way. Then she said, "You sound so formal. So grown up."

"I am grown up, Mother, I'm nearly thirteen."

"So you are."

They were quiet again. The eyes in the pale, round face were turned on Olive. The mouth in the face moved again.

"Well, goodbye."

"Goodbye, Mother." She turned, in her hard, uncomfortable boots, on the soft grass mats. Beside her on the tallboy, almost at eye level, among Mother's silver-backed hairbrushes, were Mother's favourite photographs and daguerreotypes. There was the wedding portrait: Mother, a bride of twenty, and Dad so much older. There was a picture of Mum and Dad, soon after he brought her back to Fiji. The boys were in the picture, too, Tom was five and Harry was three. The photographer had caught the bewilderment in Tom's face and the bliss in Harry's as they had held their beautiful new mother's hands.

The third picture was Olive's favourite: Mother holding her as a little baby, Dad's first daughter after five sons. After Olive there had been another son, which was Ralph, and then little Rosie. Little Rosie was everyone's favourite. It made Olive's heart ache to think that Rosie had to stay behind in Suva with Elena. Dad said she would be too much for Aunt Maud.

Suddenly Olive turned and flung herself back on the bed, her face pressed against Mother's hard, round tummy with the baby inside it. The bed linen still held her perfume, a whiff of violets

7

under the overpowering eucalyptus oil and sour smell of Adela's laboured breathing.

Under Olive's cheek the baby moved. Her mother drew a long, halting breath. Was the weight of her head hurting her, Olive wondered? She lifted herself up to see her mother was crying. There had only been one other time she'd seen her mother in tears, the time Olive had surprised her with Elena, sorting out little clothes.

"There's going to be another baby," Mother had said, her cheeks wet but pretending to Olive that she was pleased, and Olive had become a shadow, drifting back, back out of the open bedroom door, skidding on the mats in the hall to turn and run as fast as she could out to the garden. This time she wouldn't run away.

"Mother — what is it?"

Mother's hand, the long, cool fingers, was soft on Olive's forehead, and her eyes were half-closed. She didn't reply. Outside the Chandler sounded its horn. With the eucalyptus cloth, Olive dabbed at her mother's tears. She kissed her cool, wet cheeks. There was no powder on them anymore, Mother was so different now.

"Mother? What's the matter?"

Adela shook her head and the movement set her coughing. She turned away, her hand falling from Olive's cheek. The Chandler honked again.

"Olive!" It was Dad, calling from outside.

"Goodbye, Mother." Olive bent over and kissed her mother again, and the cheek that met her lips was hard, tensed with the effort of coughing. Now Olive was running, across the slippery mats, down the hall, across the verandah, down the steps and into the waiting car.

CHAPTER TWO

The Voyage to Taveuni

On the gangway it had seemed to Olive that another arm had sprouted from the mildewed folds of Grandmother's pungent mourning. Grandmother had kept a grip on her Gladstone and all three of the children. But after they'd waved farewell to Dad and Little Rosie in the crowd on Suva wharf and the island steamer had begun to slip past the raintrees along the harbour's edge, Ralph and Eric had slipped into the mêlée of Fijians and Indians, goats, chickens and even a sheep, its eyes rolling and tongue lolling with the heat.

"Downstairs," said Grandmother, her fingers pincers on Olive's arm. "Downstairs we go."

"I'll just find Ralph and —"

"I don't want you ruining your stockings." Grandmother pushed Olive ahead through the narrow cabin door. "Or your dress."

"All this for Aunt Maud and Uncle Bernard," thought Olive. Aunt Maud goes round all tizzied up like a queen, even when Uncle is away and there's no one to see her but the natives. That's what they said about her in Suva.

Olive sat down in the empty cabin beside her grandmother. Grandmother wheezed, put a Peppermint Cure in her mouth and reached for a *Fiji Times* from the top of her Gladstone. Olive shifted opposite so she could read the back pages. All she could make out with the roll of the steamer was the advertisement for the dentures that had been there for months and months. Olive imagined her grandmother with two shining rows of white teeth and a broad smile.

"You should get some of those," she said. "Those teeth."

Grandmother's teeth were nothing but rank black stumps.

The old woman flicked to the back page and felt a stab of outrage. Under her skirt she was itching like mad. It was as if some creature had taken up residence in her most private parts and every now and then gave her a sharp nip. The fiendish climate encouraged this kind of female malaise and modesty prevented ladies, such as herself, from consulting a doctor. She rolled the newspaper, thinking to give Olive a smack with it, but the arrival of another lady prevented her.

Olive stared. The lady's face was a map, two red fields bearing flora and fauna of moles and spots, separated by a jagged mountain range of flesh. Olive wondered what could have befallen the poor lady, what terrible tropical scourge left one with a serrated nose.

"Mrs Stone," said Grandmother, peering. "How are you?"

"Very well, thank you, Mrs McNab, and yourself?"

"Mustn't complain." Grandmother ate another Peppermint Cure, put the newspaper flat on her lap and gave herself a surreptitious scratch beneath it.

Olive, sharp-eyed, saw and noted, and wondered why. The rattle of Grandmother's hand against the underside of the newspaper became more frenetic, but Mrs Stone didn't appear to notice, engaged as she was in bringing forth from an enormous tapestry bag a pair of knitting needles. She dug around and found some more of the dark-blue wool.

Memories of her arduous time in the Rewa crowded Mrs Stone's mind, being tipped out of the long open boat on her way to visit one of the lady knitters, the river flooding into her bedroom there, the heavy rain that filled the scow on the return journey, deeper and deeper, until it was as if she reclined in a clammy, tepid bath.

Sometimes it hardly seemed worth it for a pair of socks, even if they were socks for the Prince of Wales. Mrs Stone reassured herself with the thought that when the socks were eventually parcelled off to London the letter would bear her name. She pictured it now in her best copperplate: "To H.R.H. Prince of Wales, with love and kind wishes from the Ladies of Fiji," then in brackets, perhaps, in the corner, perhaps, "(Mrs B.Q. Stone, Organiser.)" It gave her a twinge in her belly to know that He would look upon her name and perhaps think of her when He wore them.

She began casting on for the second sock, this one to be knitted by the ladies of Taveuni and Vanua Levu. She may as well press on. No time like the present. The first sock, wrapped up in greaseproof paper, was tucked into her petticoat top for safe keeping. She could feel it there, glowing regally, against her bosom.

Grandmother McNab fastened her eyes upon the flashing needle tops. She licked her lips.

"Mrs Stone," she said, in her best Sunday voice, her fingertips picking up ink as she folded the newspaper, "I haven't yet knitted my row."

Mrs Stone cast an eye around the steamy cabin in order to roll it at someone. This kind of impertinence was hard to bear alone. She considered she'd been very generous in extending the honour to ladies of much lower status than herself — Mrs Austin Roy, the Suva piano-tuner's wife, for example, and the launch mechanic's wife, Mrs Agnew. But at this woman, this Mrs McNab, she must draw the line. Scraps of that woman's history still blew about the town of Levuka: tales of her wild beauty and drunkenness; of her lovers while her husband was away at sea; of her cruel snobbery from middle-age on. Everything Mrs Stone had ever heard about Mrs McNab conspired against her worthiness to knit a row of the Prince of Wales' socks. Two other ladies had come into the cabin and seated themselves. Neither of them were looking her way.

"Ahem, Mrs McNab, have you not?"

"No," said Mrs McNab, popping in a Peppermint Cure, straightening her back and extending her hands to take the needles.

"Well then . . ." said Mrs Stone, at a loss. She gazed around again. Who the newcomer was with the large white hat seating herself by the cabin door she couldn't fathom, but surely the other lady, the enormously fat one, was Mrs Jamieson, the Somosomo Methodist minister's wife. She was turning the pages of a small, red book, her forearms, big as Christmas hams, resting on the jutting black shelf that was her bust. Great drops of sweat ran down Mrs Jamieson's face and soaked into the top of her dress. A globule slipped from her forehead, flew past her eyes and soaked into the opening line of chapter six: "'My cheeks burn even now when I recall my first dinner and first evening at the Dragon Hotel.'"

Mrs Jamieson silently cursed her rubber corset. Perhaps she could have taken it off for the voyage, had a holiday from it. The truth was, it hadn't occurred to her. Every morning, rain or shine, hurricane or flood, Mrs Jamieson squeezed herself into her rubber tube, just as her husband squeezed himself into his. They wore their corsets like wedding rings, suffering in silence their twin torments, the agony of copious white, moist flesh flattened and inflamed. Their eczema was what kept them apart at night, when, like rotting fruit, they finally peeled themselves free of their rubber skins. She renewed her concentration on the page.

Mrs Stone strained her flinty eyes — Her Mad Month, by Mabel Barnes-Grundy — then longed for assistance, but the round eyes in Mrs Jamieson's sad, saggy, red face remained riveted to her open book. Grandmother's hands settled back to her lap like broody chooks to the hen-house perch.

Olive sat up, sensing tension and the possibility of entertainment. In a single, impatient move, Mrs Stone dumped the needles and wool into Mrs McNab's hands. She would unravel the row later, she decided, relieved to have thought of a solution. Mrs McNab made a stab into the first stitch.

"Are you going to Taveuni, Mrs Stone?" asked Grandmother. "I presume it is stocking stitch and the right side facing?"

"Yes to the first," sniffed Mrs Stone, "and to the second it's a rib. One pearl. One plain. And I presume you are acquainted with the circular needle."

Grandmother worked hard on her Peppermint Cure. Olive watched her lizardy mouth suck in and out.

"Have you missed a stitch Mrs McNab?" That's the ticket, put her off, thought Mrs Stone.

"I don't think so," said Grandmother, crossly, peering in the gloom at the dark wool. "No I have not."

"Oh, I am sorry." Mrs Stone sucked in her mouth as if she too had a sweet and fixed Olive with her eye. "Is this young lady Olive, your granddaughter?"

"Yes," said Grandmother, intent on the knitting.

"And hasn't she grown. I haven't seen her since the Christmas pantomime, last year. Very tall. And is there Spanish blood in your family, Mrs McNab?"

Grandmother looked up sharply. By Olive's estimate she'd worked five stitches. She was no knitter. There wasn't much call for it in Fiji.

"No. English. All pure English blood except for my husband who, as you remember, was a Scotsman — "

"Actually, I don't remember at all, Mrs McNab. It's just that Olive is so tanned. You should watch that, my dear." Mrs Stone leaned across and tapped Olive on the hand. "Wear a hat from now on. Even in the shade. And gloves. Just as your dear grandmother does."

"There could of course be Spanish," said Grandmother loudly, "in her mother's family." She looked momentarily nervous, as if she'd put her foot in it. She opened her mouth to continue, but Mrs Stone was too quick for her.

"Well, yes, of course there would be. An actress! Anything, anything from the four corners of the globe in that one, if you ask me."

Mrs McNab pursed up her lips and glared at the sock. Mrs Stone laughed and looked around the cabin. Neither of the other ladies joined in. Olive sighed. There was a fly buzzing in the cabin, which made her think of Stanlake. If she had been allowed to bring him with her she would have caught the fly for him, for his lunch. Thinking of Stanlake brought Olive to thinking of the bantams and to hoping that Tom would remember to drop the odd worm into the lilypond for the carp and goldfish. And there was also her rare, prize, Fijian iguana who lived happily under the eaves of the verandah but appreciated the odd, still-wriggling fly held out on a pin. She hadn't explained that to Tom, she hadn't even told him where the iguana lived, and she'd forgotten to tell him the mynah needed not only food but company especially if he was to talk, which he didn't, yet. He just yelled, like a colicky baby. She was beginning to fret about her menagerie. Something was needed to take her mind off it. She decided to stare at the lady in the white hat. Grandmother often scolded her for staring, but this time she wouldn't notice. She still had her tongue out, straining over the knitting.

Lodged in the nostrils of the lady with the white hat was the distinct smell of rubber. And something else. Yeast? She was sure the rubber came from the fat lady opposite. It turned her stomach, although goodness knows, she'd smelt worse since her arrival in Fiji. There were so many smells here and so many of them associated in some way with putrefaction. Agnes checked her bag, her "tent" she called it privately, as a joke. It was canvas, gargantuan, commodious enough for her three-legged stool, her paintbox, her sketchpad, her pencil case, various notebooks and a change of clothes. Packed away in the hold was a box, bigger still, which held a kettle, a teapot, a saucepan, a tartan rug, a hammock, a bedsheet, a pillow, a nightgown, a curtain for privacy, toiletries, a spare skirt, two petticoats, two pairs of bloomers, a bathing dress, two towels and a mosquito net.

Agnes Perkins-Green, Artist and Unaccompanied Lady Traveller, prided herself on travelling light. *Unaccompanied and Unencumbered*, that was her motto. The legend was written in her perfect copperplate on the inside cover of her notebook. She wondered now what was happening on deck. A confinement of twenty hours, or thereabouts, on board a steamer would be a fine opportunity for sketching. The natives, she thought, standing, are always so very picturesque.

Agnes was tall, taller than most white men, and definitely too tall to attach a hat to her head inside the cabin. She bent her knees to lower herself away from the ceiling, but it was no good. The hat slipped forwards and there was a titter from that woman in the corner — Mrs Stone, the old lady had called her. What a face, thought Agnes. Ugly, as they say, as sin. She pushed her hat round to the back, gathered up her tent, and made for the door.

On the steps she made way for Reverend Jamieson, a man of immense proportion like his wife. He and the canvas bag squeezed and popped. Agnes Perkins-Green, her grey eyes steady on his, smiled. The Reverend was unnerved. This stranger has the look of a woman of the world, a woman who has seen things a woman shouldn't, a woman who has indulged in discreet but carnal relations with men, thought Reverend Jamieson. Further, he imagined, the recipients of her affections were more than likely the husbands of her globally scattered hostesses. His face impossibly redder, the Reverend Jamieson got by and opened the cabin door.

Agnes Perkins-Green, thirty, a virgin, passed up the stairs into the sunlight and wind.

Mrs Jamieson, who had recognised her husband's footfalls on

the stairs, tucked her secret Mabel Barnes-Grundy back into her reticule and retrieved instead a volume of Wesleyan prayer.

The Reverend winked at Olive as he sat down, forcing a fresh gust of rubber odour into Olive's corner. Grandmother had her tongue out and was on her eighth stitch.

"Grandmother," said Olive, plaintively. She pulled her lace hanky from her pocket.

"What is it?" A little stream of peppermint spit sucked back from the corner of Grandmother's mouth.

"I feel sick."

"And what do you propose I do about it?" asked Grandmother, beginning her ninth.

"Could I go up for some fresh air? I promise I'll go quietly."

Grandmother dropped the ninth stitch and took a quick squint at Mrs Stone to see if she'd noticed. She hadn't, being at that moment ensconced in conversation with the Reverend.

"I do believe," he boomed as he did on Sundays, forgetting for a moment that he was in a tiny cabin, ten foot by ten foot, "that cattle, pigs and turtles should be made the official martyrs of the Christian Fijian Church. They slaughter them in their hundreds and any excuse will do for a meke —"

Mrs Stone tut-tutted. "Well, I do think the clergy have made a mistake, if you don't mind my saying so, Reverend. You're all far too lenient these days, you allow the natives dancing and singing and all sorts, instead of encouraging them to leave all that behind on their way to civilisation. Not like when I was a girl."

"Grandmother?" said Olive.

"Oh, if you must," said Grandmother, knitting on. She was beginning to feel sick herself, the boat was rolling more. They were through the reef.

"Excuse me," said Olive, pushing past the six knees of Mrs Stone, the Reverend and his wife. "Excuse me."

As she came out into the light a gust of wind caught Olive's frock and wrapped it tightly around her legs. The little steamer had passed into the open sea, and the Fijian crew were busy hoisting the sails. Olive blinked in the leaping sun and held fast to the rail. There, on the lee side of the boat, was the tall, pale lady who hadn't been able to get her hat on below decks. The hat was now firmly attached with a huge white scarf. She had taken a little stool from her bag and was sitting on it, sketching. Olive sidled closer and peered through the tiny gap between the lady's hat   and shoulder. On the white expanse of the sketch pad a charcoal pencil charged about like a cane train.

Olive straightened, looked to where the lady was looking, then back at the page. It was the coastline, sort of, with the Devil's Thumb slipping from view. Heavy clouds clustered in smudgy pencil around the hills. The lady was sketching in the sun now, leaving gaps for the white to shine through, where the sun hit the water.

"Hullo," said Olive.

The lady craned her head around, the brim of her hat catching Olive under the nose.

"Good morning," said the lady. "I see you've escaped."

Olive blushed. "Yes."

The lady smiled and went back to her drawing.

"Are you going to Taveuni or further on?" asked Olive, coming round to stand in front of the lady.

Agnes Perkins-Green took in Olive's lanky frame, the white dress heroically smudged.

"Taveuni. And you?"

"We're going to stay with Uncle Bernard and Aunt Maud," said Olive. "Mother is sick."

"Influenza?" asked the lady, her grey eyes wide.

Olive nodded. The lady made a few more lines on her sketch-pad then licked her finger. She smudged and blurred, then held up the pad critically. Olive stared. The lady was beautiful. She had such very white skin. Agnes sighed and held out her hand.

"Agnes Perkins-Green," she said, "from London."

"Olive McNab, from Suva."

The lady put her sketchpad back in her bag.

"Have you come to live in Fiji?" asked Olive.

"Good gracious, no!" said the lady. It seemed to Olive she found the idea absurd. "I'm here on doctor's orders."

"The doctor told you to come to Fiji?" asked Olive, incredulous. Usually ladies left Fiji on doctor's orders.

"Yes. A sea voyage and a complete change," said Agnes, pulling a small reticule from the canvas bag. She opened it and took out a packet of Capstan Tailor-Mades. She put one in the corner of her mouth, like a soldier, thought Olive, and asked Olive from the corner of it, "Where do you live in Suva?"

"Waimanu Road," said Olive, proudly. Grandmother always said it was a high-class street.

"Can't say I know it," said Agnes Perkins-Green, struggling to get the cigarette lit in the breeze. "Damn thing."

Olive couldn't remember ever feeling so excited. The lady not only smoked, but swore as well!

"Here," the lady was saying, "take this down to the poop deck and light it for me, will you?"

She handed Olive the cigarette and a box of matches and watched as the child went out of the wind.

"Mind you don't set yourself on fire," she added, as an afterthought.

Olive didn't hear her. She bore the cigarette and matches as precious as jewels, down on to the poop deck. Miss Perkins-Green would see from the way she lit up that she was also a budding woman of the world. She and Eddie and Eric sometimes pinched cigarettes from Ming Lo the houseboy, or Dad, or Fred at the Sailroom, and practised the draw-back.

The cigarette glowed. And she hadn't even coughed.

"Thank you," said Agnes, on her return. She exhaled an

emphatic volume of smoke and said, "Suva! I have to say I'm glad to get out of the place."

"Why?" asked Olive. "Because of the influenza?" She sat down at the lady's feet. Grandmother was likely to burst her phoo-phoo about the dress, but it was worth it. She blew out as the lady blew out.

Agnes Perkins-Green held up one finger. "One moment!" She dived into her canvas bag and this time produced an exercise book, very battered, with teacup rings on the cover. She flicked through it.

"These are my sincere responses," she told Olive, "gathered late at night in my hotel in, as Wordsworth said, tranquillity . . ." Finding the page, she read, ". . . 'very English, crowds of commonplace, new, ugly houses.' And further on, 'a town hideously close and airless'. And here 'a stuffy, dead alive hole.'" Agnes Perkins-Green snapped her notebook shut and took another pull on her cigarette.

"Oh!" said Olive. She looked up at the lady, not so sure about her now. "I quite like Suva."

Agnes's grey eyes widened, making them appear even larger, sort of sticky out, thought Olive, like Stanlake's.

"I think," said the lady, slowly, "that if your horizons were just a little broader you would find Suva as I find it. Have you travelled at all?"

"Only around Fiji," said Olive, counting on her fingers. "I've been on picnics to Nukulau Island, I've been to Levuka and I've been — "

The lady wasn't listening. She was standing, looking into the bow of the boat. Loud shrieks issued from that direction. Olive stood too. It was Ralph, stumbling among the crates of supplies, the Fijians sitting with their bundles of dalo and baskets of food, avoiding an enraged goat, which was trailing a thick rope. It lowered its head and charged, this time meeting its target in the back of Ralph's shorts. He shot head-first into the arms of a Fijian lady,

19

who laughed and patted his head. An old Fijian man picked up the rope and glared at Ralph.

"nGone ca," he said, hauling the goat in.

Ralph sobbed, rubbing his bum. The old man adjusted his sulu and squatted, the goat standing under his protective arm. Agnes Perkins-Green tossed her cigarette into the tide and waved her arms.

"Olive, I must sketch that old man. He is so very picturesque with that grey frizzly hair. Mind my bag."

Olive watched as the lady stepped nimbly in her shiny, brown boots up to the old man.

"Sa yadra," said Agnes Perkins-Green, loudly. She pointed back along the deck to her stool. "Will you pose for me?"

The old man raised his eyebrows and sucked on his teeth. Agnes presumed he hadn't heard her.

"Sa yadra!" she said again, shouting this time. "Will you sit for me?"

The old man looked at Ralph for help. Ralph translated.

"I-lavo?" asked the old man.

"He wants to know if you'll pay him," said Ralph.

Agnes bit her lower lip. She hadn't struck this before. The natives in Suva were delighted to pose for no remuneration. She remembered her first subject, a small boy she'd had sent up to the Club Hotel. He'd posed so stiffly in the bright, hot verandah that it had been no surprise to her when he fainted. He'd rallied quickly enough though and stood for a further hour and a half before leaving with a small copy of the portrait under his arm.

She decided against the old man, flapping a disparaging hand at him before turning back to Olive and her stool.

By two o'clock, when the Chinese cook struggled up on deck with the midday meal for the Europeans, Agnes had sketched the Fijian crew at work: Inoke at the wheel, Mosese hauling the sail and Jo attending the steam box. The cook, his face shining with the heat of the cook-house, rang a small bell to attract the Europeans down the poop deck where he had set up a small table. Olive fancied she could see its legs bowing with the weight. It bore roast beef, potatoes, pumpkin, silverbeet — enough for all eight white passengers.

The ladies, except for Agnes Perkins-Green, took their meals back to the stuffy cabin. On her three-legged stool, Agnes finished what she considered to be a splendid repast, lit a Capstan and felt happy. Her nightmarish four months at the Front, doing what her Pappa called her "Florence Nightingale" seemed as far away in time as they were in miles. She heaved a huge sigh of contentment. The people she had arranged to stay with on Taveuni were childless, and for this she was grateful. Children, she knew, were fascinated by her, sensing her thrilling freedom. It had proved difficult to shake that sun-crisped, long-limbed, awkward child, Olive. It was the grandmother, dragging her back to that ghastly cabin to eat her lunch, who had saved her from further questions. Fijian children now, she didn't mind. They were so enchanting, delicious, dusky, little mites. There was one on board with its mother, as dark as India-rubber. Perhaps the mother would let her sketch it.

Agnes made up her mind to sleep that night on deck, under the stars. She would get one of the crew to haul up her box, spread out her bedding and then, she was sure, she would have an utterly clear, refreshing, healthy, outdoorsy kind of sleep. The afternoon was clear and calm, the air caressing, warm and soft as another woman's hand on her brow. All indications were that the voyage would be a smooth one.

At eight-thirty Grandmother fell asleep, heavily, against Eric. On her other side Ralph snoozed, his little pink mouth moist and squashed against Olive's arm, his mousy boy-smell close under her nose. Sleepless, she hooked the arm around him and leaned back in the hard seat. Opposite her, the Jamiesons sat, shoulder to shoulder, Mrs Jamieson's face a mass of sleeping folds. Her husband dozed in fits, dropping each time into the state that encourages snoring, then emitting a loud burst from the nose, following that up with a sawing drawback in the throat. With each burst Ralph startled, then settled. The rhythm of it grated on Olive.

Eric, concertinaed against Grandmother, felt his lower rib scrape his hip bone. On the elbow trapped under Grandmother's steaming bulk, a mosquito bite pulsed and flared. Grandmother began to snore. She and the Reverend together made more noise than the Suva String and Brass Bands combined.

"Agnes Perkins-Green," thought Olive, "is avoiding all this."

At sunset, Miss Perkins-Green had asked Jo to rig her hammock on deck. By the time Grandmother had come up for air and to drag them all below decks, Agnes was reclined in her hammock, wrapped in her mosquito net and executing the sinking sun in watercolours.

"Goodnight, Miss Perkins-Green," Olive had called.

In reply Agnes had raised her eyebrows, intent on her tiny brush.

"Who is that woman?" asked Grandmother. "The one you spoke to just then?"

"Agnes Perkins-Green," Olive said, proudly, "an Artist and Lady Traveller."

"Stay away from her," Grandmother had said. "She looks loose."

Eric pulled himself free of his grandmother, who fell back against the seat, her mouth open. He stood at the same time as Olive, waiting while she carefully laid Ralph's sleeping head on Mrs Stone's knitting bag. Mrs Stone, who in her waking hours would have considered this an act of immense disrespect, had slumped forward as far as her boned corset would allow, her knife-edged nose dipping and scooping inches away from the bosomed Prince's sock. It seemed to Olive, as she and Eric slipped towards the door, that they were moving through a silvery mist of sweat and breath.

Agnes woke to the creaking of the wheel rope. In the tiny light the binnacle lamp cast on deck, she could see Inoke's strong feet bracing and slackening with the slip and thump of hull on sea. The hammock, Agnes decided, was playing havoc with her back. As she had discarded her corset at the Front, this new discomfort must have to do with the way one's body, when slung in a hammock, imitated the shape of a banana.

In the stern of the boat two figures emerged. It was Olive and one of her brothers. Their clear voices carried above the gently flapping sails to the ears of Agnes Perkins-Green.

"When will we go back to Suva, Sis?" the boy was asking.

"When Mother is better. After the baby is born."

There was a long silence while the children looked out at the stars, the distant mounds of islands. The boy, thought Agnes, was almost a man, tall and gangly like his sister and ungainly in his short trousers. The boy spoke again, his voice breaking.

"I don't think Mother will ever get better." He disappeared into the shadows.

Olive stared down into the streaming wake of the steamer. Tucked into the elastic of her bloomers was her Lucky Lunaria. She took it out and held it in her hand, rolling her fingers over its milky, warm, smooth surface. Perhaps Providence would send a sign, a vision of what would happen, of how long it would be before they went home. She waited, but there was nothing. Her heart felt as heavy as a bucket of water, but it would do no good to cry. Just in case, she pulled her handkerchief from her sleeve and held it to her face. Eucalyptus. It was the cloth from outside Mother's room, she'd brought it by mistake. The sharp perfume rushed from her nose to her heart to her eyes, and she was crying. Sitting beside Dad that morning in the Chandler, she was sure she'd seen tears at the corners of his dear, pale, crinkly eyes. It wasn't babyish to cry, not if Dad did too.

CHAPTER THREE

The Lily that Strayed

~ Adela McNab ~

James Pollard had fifteen children and he put them all on the stage. I can say now, though I wouldn't have dared to back then, that not all of them were entirely suited to it. In 1889, when I joined Pollard's Lilliputians, the youngest was my age. Isobel was ten but small in stature — dumpy, perhaps might be more accurate, although crueller. The manner of description suits its subject as like to like, cruel to cruel. I remember her pale, twisted mouth to this day. I, too, was ten, tall, and the grace that later endeared me to audiences was evident already.

The other day — was it yesterday? I am puzzled by time now more than ever: it is the heat, the heat without and the heat within; within this dark room, within my darkening frame. It is like the dengue, this fever, and the doctor is perplexed. It seemed that one day I was recovering from the influenza, and the next aching and thrumming like a taut string. Whatever — perhaps it was yesterday, perhaps it was last week — I asked Hughie to open my drawer in our bureau. It is my special private, drawer and in our eighteen years of marriage he'd never opened it once. Such is the love and trust between us that the drawer has become an emblem of our mutual respect. Hughie's dear hand trembled as he slid the yakka drawer out with a squeak.

"Lift the whole out, my love," I'd said.

There was a finality about it, Hughie lifting the heavy wood with his thin, wiry arms and laying it beside me on our bed, on his side of the bed. The finality came from knowing Hughie will never lie there beside me again, and that these hours looking through the drawer together will be our final intimacies.

Hughie plumped my pillows, and I laid my aching arm along the ridge of the drawer, dipping my hand to retrieve a photograph, a dried flower, some feathers, a yellowing, crumbling printed accolade.

"This," I said, showing Hughie, "was my first major role. I was no longer just a part of the chorus."

And there I am, sixteen years old, sepia toned, upstage from Isobel but dominant just the same. I'd caught the photographer's eye. The play was *Uncle Tom's Cabin* and we were in bedsheets in New Zealand, in Napier. *Uncle Tom* was all we could do, having lost everything in a fire the week before in Palmerston North. The roaring of the fire called us from our beds in the First Commercial across the square, all of us youthful thespians in nightgowns, gazing, horrified.

Robes and wigs, curtains and drapes, chests, trunks, the piano, the organ, Aladdin's lamp, Widow Twankey's falsies, Alibaba's mushroom dell backdrop, all burning and cracking. We heard the sizzle as the fire found our grease-sticks, the hiss as it plunged its orange hands into the powder pots. For a moment a flaming angel's wing, just one, its partner having dropped off in the ascent, hung far above our heads. It frizzled away to nothing, like a feathery fire cracker.

There was a light rain falling, miserable and penetrating to us, but having no effect whatsoever on the hellfire destruction of the Theatre Royal. The Brigade arrived in a mass of gleaming helmets and buttons that spurted gold in the whirling light. The horses bucked with terror, showing the whites of their eyes, upsetting the water tanker, which discharged its load over the railway lines, into the mud. The firemen yelled and swung the hose about, dry though it now was.

A warm arm encircled me, drawing me aside, finding my beginning waist.

"See, Adela. Look around you. Look. Look. Look!"

"I am, Alfred. I am," I'd replied.

"I want you to remember their faces. *That* is terror. *That* is awe."

"There is not much call for that in musical comedy," I remember telling Alfred, James Pollard's eldest son.

He told me then, a square hand cupping one of my thin-gowned buttocks, that I had a future as a great tragedienne, although tragedy was currently out of favour.

Isobel, her true nature being exposed as both cruel *and* cowardly, was hiding behind dear Mrs Pollard. That kind lady was mother to Alfred, fourteen younger Pollards, twenty-two others and our organist besides. I studied Mrs Pollard's dear face, which could only be described as frozen. Isobel's face, a pale rosette to Mrs Pollard's quailing breast, was luminous, her eyes two glowing, terrified orbs.

"Remember, dear Adela. Remember and imitate."

When Isobel, Georgina and I woke in our bed the following morning, the pillows were damp and smutty, tears having coursed our faces and blackened the linen. All of us feared for our futures.

Was I to be returned to the bleak life that had been mine in damp Grafton Gully? My mother would not welcome me, I was sure. My wages, sent by Mrs Pollard from wherever we were, helped to feed and clothe my six younger siblings. The post-marked envelopes, from Queensland, Sydney, Melbourne, Tasmania and all parts of New Zealand, papered the kitchen wall.

I was not returned, of course. I belonged to the Pollards, body and soul. I stayed with them until my marriage.

" *Uncle Tom's Cabin!*" said dear Hughie, laying his warm, dry hand over my damp and trembling one, steadying the photograph that shook about like a photodrama at Suva's Universal. "Look at you, my dear. You are the lily that strayed."

Hughie stroked my image, pale among the cast in blackface. I started to laugh, which brought on the coughing and the catarrh, and how my chest ached. Hughie opened the window further, hoping the germs would fly out, windborne, to drop as far away as the Suva Reef. And I hoped the same. Dear Hughie, I thought, he shouldn't be in here.

The window ushered out the particles of disease but was an open invitation to mosquitoes. At the first drone, Hughie replaced the photograph in the drawer and lifted it from the bed.

"Tomorrow," he said. "Tomorrow you can show me more." He tucked the mosquito net in around the bed. "You must sleep now."

His eyes, crowsfooted from the Fiji sun, the blue bleached pale beneath eyebrows the colour of sand, rested for a moment on my stomach billowing out of the bedclothes like a topsail. I could have told him then, but I daren't burden him further, that this child, my seventh, has scarcely shifted its limbs since the influenza took hold of me.

Hughie took my hand and waited for me to sleep. But I was sweat-soaked, full of the past, and sleep evaded me.

I fell to remembering the last meal I cooked for all the family, in early November. You had wanted beef, and as Champak's religion forbade him to cook it, I rose from my sickbed. Ming Lo had bought the most enormous wing-rib I'd ever laid eyes on. I needed help to lift it to the roasting pan, and Olive, who seems to have an allergy to aprons, was nowhere to be found. Elena helped me though, with the "bulumakau", and once it was cooked I cut off a large chunk for her to take out to the bure.

Then we sat up with all our children, and I saw in your face how you wished your older sons were there. If I had not seen Rose's likeness, taken soon after your marriage to her, I would

27

never have known what she looked like. Tom and Harry were as alike as twins and replicas of you.

Still, sitting in that dark, windowless dining-room, with our four sons and two daughters and me in my place, you carved and served from the head of the table. Your mother sat at your right and tried to look pleased that I'd risen. Olive, located minutes before by Elena, handed round the plates. Her long fingers, curled around the edges of the china, left a lot to be desired in terms of cleanliness, but there was festivity in the air and we were pleased to be together. The younger children were excited and chattered, having to be reminded to keep silent. My eldest, my sombre Bill, even managed a smile at some wisecrack of Olive's. The younger boys and our little Rosie gazed at their plates, the green cassava, the glistening brown meat and pale golden Yorkshire pudding. The summer had just begun in earnest, and I swear that if we had left our plates and returned to them an hour or so later their cargo would have been much the same temperature. Although, of course, the flies would have got to them.

Champak was fetched in from his room to operate the punkah while we ate, thus cooling us and disturbing the wheeling blowies at the same time. He came with very bad grace, I remember, and gave the cord one or two too-sharp jerks before you asked him to steady.

There was a moment, when you spoke to Champak, that we could all have been aboard a great flapping ship and Champak a sailor reckless with a sail. Looking up into the gloom of the ceiling, observing the punkah slow and swing on its pulley, your eyes narrowed and peered as they must have in your sailing days, when you surveyed the broad ocean. And picturing you as a young man brought me to picturing Tom on the deck of his ship on his way to the War, waving to us on the wharf on July the third, and how he must've turned away once the ship passed through the reef. Perhaps he sat somewhere with Harry and they imagined what it would be like "going over the bags" and debated what they would do should they come face to face with a Hun, or Foch, or Fritz, or whatever they're calling those misguided Austrians.

Now he has returned he sits with me sometimes, Tom, but he never talks of the War, nor of poor Harry.

The door opens, cautiously, with a soft rasp on the grass mats. It is Hughie. It is you.

"Would you like to sit with your things?" you ask, going to the drawer.

You bring it to me, and sit down, not meeting my eyes. We were such honest lovers, you and I, never fearing to look well into one another's soul, never fearing what we may find there. What is it? Are you certain I will die? And what of the child? This morning, on waking, I felt a little flutter much like the quickening. There has been nothing like the sturdy kicks of our other children, such bonny babes, all of them.

Sit closer. Sit here. Today I am too weak to retrieve even the tiniest piece of memorabilia. You will have to do it for me.

A yellow, faded gardenia, lifted from the folded programme for *La Poupée*, 1899. We were a real company by then, the Pollard Opera Company, none of this "Juvenile" or "Lilliputians". We opened in Auckland on the twelfth of June for nine nights. The theatre burst at the seams. The tenor and baritone parts were sung by men, no longer the girls, the audience cheered us and we did encore after encore after encore . . . the night we met. Do you remember, Hughie?

It was as glittering an occasion as Auckland could manage. The sparkling bodices and fantastic hats of the women drew the eye away from their muddied hems and boots. Outside the dark was shifting and wild, the wind whipping in from the south with sleet on its breath. That was the night we met. Remember it for me, Hughie, you tell me the story.

"You were nineteen and had the voice of an angel. When you

entered the stage that night at the Royal, for one moment I forgot the terrible cold, which I wasn't used to . . ."

I entered from the right, which never felt comfortable. Mr Pollard had me make my approach so close to the footlights I feared for my life. He wanted shadows on my face, so that while I sang "The Candle Song" my cheeks would appear sunken and starved like the streetling I was supposed to be. But I have a round face and it was hard for the shadows to find the merest gully. They only added to my nerves, those footlights, as I stood in the wings, watching them gleam. My nerves, Hughie, were colossal, and it was never until I was firmly placed and singing that they left me. Alfred was the only one from management who suspected, and he would join me in my waiting. Sometimes he would hold my hand and once or twice he kissed me, knowing that the Rule of Silence imposed on us backstage mummers would allow him this stolen intimacy. What is more, he understood. The younger Pollards wore two hats, being both our employers and colleagues.

"So I waited with my brother and Aunt Lettie till afterwards. Aunt Lettie wore that night an enormous corsage of gardenias. I asked her for one of the flowers, and she told me to go ahead and pluck one. Maybe she'd had one too many ports, I don't know, but she laughed and carried on like a larrikin while I pulled the bloom from her dress."

Hughie looks at me and I urge him with my eyes — continue. Go on. I'm almost back there.

"So I waited with Bert and Lettie, and you came in with that Alfred fellow, and by Jove you were even more of a cracker down on the level with us than you were up on the stage. That Alfred fellow was acting all proprietorial, putting his arm across your bare shoulders, even putting his honk in your hair. You didn't look like you were enjoying it much. You'd sort of laugh when he did. He'd come straight from the table and had a napkin tucked in at the neck. It had a dirty great splash of gravy down it. You kept looking away, but then back at him. You had a little sore, a small boil, at the corner of your mouth, which you kept licking. There was a bit of a press on, but I ended by standing behind you, watching that pink tongue — lick, lick, lick, the little point of it wet as a fish. I stood behind you with Lettie's bosom flower and felt like a ham sandwich at a Jew's picnic . . ."

You trail off, looking at me again. You've told me this story before, you know Hughie, the night before Ralph was born. You didn't mention my pimple, and you made much more of Alfred. You were jealous. I hadn't realised before. What you must've wondered then, if you didn't wonder later . . .

"I'd sort of decided to shove the damn thing in my pocket and splash off home when you turned around. Your eyes. I'll never forget the way . . ."

"My love. Oh, my dear Hughie —"

Elena's voice breaks suddenly into the room.

"Rosie! Rosie!"

There are the light, rapid footsteps of a child on the grass mats of the hall, then a thudding as Elena follows. But she is too late, and Rosie is in the room. She is small, like you, and moves like greased lightning. She runs straight to you. You lift her to your knee and kiss her brow.

Now it is I who am consumed with jealousy. How I would love to hold her. Perhaps I would get better immediately, cured by her sweet child's scent, her smooth, plump-armed embrace. You carry her from the room, her wide eyes over your shoulder. At the door she is handed to Elena and whisked away.

I breathe again. And cough. You wait until the spasm is over, holding your handkerchief over your mouth and nose. Ming Lo is summoned to sprinkle eucalyptus oil from a tiny bottle over the floor and furniture. He is frightened of contracting the disease and moves quickly, making a curious panting noise as he goes. At the door you take the bottle from him and for one moment my breast fills with dread. Lately, the *Fiji Times* has featured cures for the influenza and you have been keen for me to try them. I don't think I have recovered from that episode a week ago, when you induced me to take a mild solution of Condy's Fluid up the nose. I snorted and choked and my heart beat at twice its normal rate . . . it is a miracle that I am still alive!

You douse my handkerchief with oil and hold it close to my face. The scent is soothing. I breathe more easily.

You sit again, take my hand and we gaze out at the hot, uncomfortable day. A male honeyeater, tiny as a hummingbird and gaudy as Cakebau's fabled crown, swoops at the orchid below the window. He hovers, wings blurring, and dips his long, curved beak into the yielding, white flower. A tremor runs through your hand, then your head is on my breast, and you are crying as if your heart will break.

Around us the house falls quiet. Ming Lo has told Champak who has told Elena who has told her husband that Saka McNab is crying. I lift my hand to your hair, the comb marks still standing in it, and rest it there, until you ease and stop. If I wasn't ill, Hughie, we would draw the shades, shut the door and love one another.

When we were first married, when you first brought me to Fiji, our bedroom was my refuge. Everything beyond it seemed so bewildering at first: your two, motherless sons; the heat; the startling natives; the desperate Indians and their broken-down wives; the mean-spirited white women; the brutish European men; the peculiar smells. Our room, with the dim, slatted light, our fervent bodies within it, and our sweet young sweat was balm to my soul. At first, you seemed surprised, even a little shocked, by my appetites, my desires. Your Rose had taught you nothing of how to ensure a woman's pleasure. Perhaps she didn't know herself — how could she — a haberdasher's daughter? In our bedroom I was still an actress; the only theatre left to me. I guided you through damp tempests, spoke wordless soliloquies and knew by your pale eyes I had chartered new depths. And

32

you, the chandler, put your strong sailmaker's hands to silken folds, marvelled at the delicate appliqué of nipple on breast, the thews and sinews of my arching back. You set your sweet lips to tasting the small, salt island of my ecstasy. You learnt to take your time. And, afterwards, we lay rippling, two sails to the same mast, taking our breath from one another.

I am still curious about Rose, despite the loyal silence you have maintained. I would like to ask, did you attend her the way you've attended me in this sickness, or previously, in childbed? Did you bring her small gifts, the string of beaded seeds from a Samoan stall, the spiky seashell from a trip to Kadavu, a green tail feather dropped by a kula, an orchid or hibiscus bloom?

How can I be thinking these things? Guilt consumes me — not only for my jealous inanities, but also for my sense of distance. It is as if I am withdrawing and my actress's mind allows me to observe this process in order to duplicate. Duplicate for whom? Does heaven have a theatre? Perhaps it does, and perhaps the great mystery of sex that occupies us is for them dwarfed by the great mystery of death.

"How did we come to be here?" the actors ask. Perhaps even now Bernhardt and Ellen Terry are playing to immense audiences of dead soldiers, your dear Harry among them, competing for the most tragic and intoxicating death, now they have something real to base it on. It is an amusing idea.

"What was that? You laughed!" Hughie lifts his head and gazes at me, perturbed. His fine brown hair, dashed with grey, is rumpled, his eyes red-rimmed and wounded.

"Never at you, my love. Never at you!"

But he is standing, wiping his eyes with the sleeve of his white duck jacket, going to the bureau for a comb. The mirror, he notices, is gone.

"I had Ming Lo take it out. I had no need for it."

"Where did Ming Lo take it? It was my father's mirror."

I am coughing again. Your handkerchief goes to your mouth and nose, your eyes are wild above it, and you are gone.

My coughing wakes me, and darkness has fallen as if by magic. Champak has brought me a kind of spicy soup and left it to grow cold. Despite the catarrh I can smell its perfume. It is so dark here though. I am afraid to reach out in case I knock it over. Besides I have no appetite.

My earlier light spirits have left me. I listen for the children, for Olive. Then I remember — she and Ralph and Eric have gone to Maud. Tom will be in his room, his head still full of trench horror. Perhaps Bill and Eddie are asleep. Certainly Rosie lies dreaming and in Elena's warm arms, not mine. And Hughie? Where is he?

Ah. From the verandah there is the clink of a whisky glass. And another. And the gurgle of the bottle.

Around us, Suva, once a rattling rambunctious town, lies silent. The lorry that bears the dead down to the wharf under the cover of dark occasionally rumbles by. Sometimes the keening of the natives needles the night air. The authorities commend the Indian practice of cremation for its hygiene, but at dawn the smoke of the pyres hangs in my curtains. I think of the dead who have gone before me, the ones I took soup to, before my illness. At first it was only the Europeans, then conscience took hold of me and I attended the natives as well. If not for that I should never have conquered my fear of them, let alone mourned for them.

It is a long road, this dying, and I am travelling it in company. My audience with Saint Peter will be with my last child in my arms, I am certain of it.

CHAPTER FOUR

A Flea in Your Ear

~ Grandmother McNab ~

All the fat people want to be lean
All the lean people want to be fat
It's hard to know what we mean
Or where we all want to be at.
But despite the dissension that holds
One decision of all will endure
That the very best treatment for colds
Is Wood's Great Peppermint Cure

I'd tell you, if you bothered to ask, that by the time we anchored at Vuna Point, I had an ache that threatened to break my head. What started it was that bitch Stone giving me a chewing over about Ralph sleeping on the Prince of Wales' socks. I'd already given him a good whack, which had sent him howling up on deck. Ralph, I mean, not the Prince of Wales. I wouldn't mind giving that Austrian Crown Prince Willie a flea in his ear though. What was the latest news? Gets about in his woollen underwear while he plays the violin. I ask you. I knew a few Germans during my time in Samoa, never liked them. Didn't much like Samoa, don't much like Fiji either.

Anyways, that sanctimonious toad Jamieson "stilled my

hand" when Olive appeared in the cabin covered in salt black from the deck. Silly little tart. Too much like her mother. One of life's tragedies when Hughie's first wife died, Rose. I liked her. She did what I said. Adela has too much knowledge of the world. While we were rowed ashore I let Jamieson have it. Told him to check his wife's reading matter. That fixed him.

"Mabel Barnes-Grundy," I told him.

His eyebrows lifted their load of sweat.

Maudie and Bernard met us with the Packard and a coolie to cart the bags. Skinny, pathetic looking thing. Still, if Maudie can't see the sense in bringing one of her carthorse Fijians I can't help her. Bernard looked florid, as usual. Too much sunburn and too much whisky. Ruddy, I've heard Bernard described as. Red face with one eye blue and one eye brown. Different men shine out of those eyes. As Maudie discovered after she married him.

"Minnie-mine," he's saying, his face too close. "Good sail?"

"Steam through the reefs, clear sail between."

Bernard wrinkled up his nose.

"What's that? Good God, a sheep!"

No more discussion of the voyage then. Bernard's not like my boys who have brine instead of blood. He's more interested in the sheep, carked over, under a bush by the Custom House. It's panting as they do in the last stages of a lambing, but as I can see the pale, shining, fuzzy goolies from here, it's a ram.

Hooves. I follow the line of heads to see the horse come into view. Didn't hear the hooves myself — in my day you could box children's ears. I boxed mine, my mother boxed me. Fearsome strong, my mother was.

Torte. Sozzled. Half out of his mount. Someone tittered. He reared round, hauled up and dismounted, like a gentleman. Always can pull himself together, Torte, when it comes to the crunch. So could anyone after thirty years of marriage to Hortense. Old Horte Torte. Don't suppose he forgets I was the first nag he rode, and I gave it to him free. Only ever expected payment once, and I wished I hadn't. It was a kind of rule in Levuka: never ask the Tortes for money. Save yourself the embarrassment, tighter than a fish's arse, the lot of them.

There's old Torte, yelling at the natives. He rips off his shirt and gives it to the nearest Fijian who races down to the water's edge and soaks it. Torte, more concerned than ever he would be over a dying coolie, bathes the ram's brow and whispers into its ears. The ram froths and shows its whites.

There's Olive, holding Ralph's hand, his face all blotched over with his crying. Maudie puts her arm through mine, smelling sweetly of rose water. Forty and smelling like a girl. Scarcely a line on her face. Kept indoors has my girl, took my advice. Never had no choice when she was young, under lock and key in Levuka.

"Where are those damn boxes?" I ask. A sheet of sweat drops down the backs of my legs. The fiendish itch bites and burns.

"Your sheep, Torte?" It's Bernard, pushing through the natives. He's a good size, Bernard, even if most of his height is in his head.

"Mother, don't swear," says Maudie, gently.

Torte doesn't answer. He's consulting with Sitiveni, his son, some say, and they say it often enough for it to be true. He's no paler than the other natives, but I'd say he sports the Torte overshot jaw. Sitiveni nods, gets on his father's panting nag and kicks it off through the trees.

"The second ram," says Maudie. "This is what happened last time. They'll bear it back on a litter. He needs it for a breeding scheme."

I cackle. "They'll have to be quick!"

"Don't laugh like that, Mother," says Maudie, gently.

I go to sit in the motorcar, where I can have a good scratch as long as the driver doesn't look backwards. Through the window I watch that trollop Agnes Whatsit come down the gangway. Fancy sleeping all night in a hammock with the *natives*. Disgusting. Who knows what went on. The crew looked pleased with themselves this morning. I know that look in a man. I've seen that look in a lot of men, even Bernard after he jumped the fence in Levuka. I couldn't watch her all the time.

My eyes are deceiving me! Maudie going up to the lady traveller — and kissing her! Now they're talking, their lips are moving. I open the Packard door but I can't hear anything.

The Fijians keep unloading the boat, one box every five or ten minutes and far too much laughing and carrying on. The other white passengers, a small knot of them, stand around with helpless expressions on their faces. You see that expression a lot on white faces in Fiji. Like at the last New Year Dinner at the Grand Pacific. Cooked, the dinner was, splendidly by an Indian and his Chinese assistant, but never delivered to the table. The waiters, native recruits, never showed up. Hughie and Adela went, they came home and told me. Hughie laughed till he cried. Some of the women had jumped up, Adela among them, of course, got the food on to the table.

"Thank God for the women," Hughie had said.

A bang in the back of the Packard. At last. The first box. The coolie goes back for the second one.

In the midst of the Europeans a lady faints. It's that Mrs Jamieson, crashing to the dust, narrowly missing a native child, her rubber corset too much for her. The Reverend loosens her gown at the neck, then he and two Fijians lift her to the church landau, packing boxes around her to prop her up. The Reverend himself looks pretty steamy.

Sitiveni reappears on horseback, a litter under his arm, two poles and bit of old sail. They set about loading the sheep on to it. Suddenly, there's Bernard, leaning in at the chauffeur's window.

"It'll be a bit of a squash," he's saying. "I'll drive. You walk, Vishnu."

The servant gets out of the motor, shutting the door after himself just a little too hard. He sets off up the incline, a haze of dust hanging in front of the nut trees, a little man in a peaked cap. His maroon sash announces to all comers that he's the property of Bernard Gow.

It's Maud.

"You must've met my mother on the boat," she's saying, "Mrs McNab — Miss Perkins-Green, who is staying with us."

Just now it's lovely looking at Whatsher Perkins.

"And the children, too?" she's saying, trembling. Obviously one of those females that's allergic to children. Maybe she's a virgin after all. Yes, I'd say by those eyes that she's untrammelled and untravelled and that children are a poison to her. Still, better that way than to long for the little devils like poor Maudie.

"Ralph! Olive! Eric!" Bernard's yelling would wake the dead. Big head, big voice. One promotes the other.

𝒲e set off, slowly. As soon as we're round the corner, past the Custom House, we get stuck behind the overladen landau. And there's the damn ram behind us, with all its attendants. The landau is hard down on its wheels with the weight of Mrs Jamieson and half-a-dozen native women. It shudders and groans along.

The ram, being borne on foot with old Torte bringing up the rear on his horse, drops behind. We come to a hill and the landau crawls. Mrs Jamieson looks corpselike, slumped among the boxes.

"Poor Emily," Maudie whispers to her husband. "Just look at the poor thing. What a dreadful colour."

At the top of the hill, the ram catches up again and the landau nearly loses the old walrus head-first. She's saved by a quick-thinking native who hauls her back in and wedges her among the trunks and dalo and cassava. So relieved are they at saving the Reverend's wife that at the crest of the hill they burst into song.

"O! For a heart to praise my God, A heart from sin set free . . ."

Olive gets the giggles.

"You want the back of my hand?" I ask her.

Whatayacallit rears away from me, her pale lip sneering.

"*A heart that's sprinkled with the Blood —*"

Bernard is joining in, his great booming voice beating us round the ears. Maudie puts a hand to her head, her fingertips resting on an eyebrow. The natives hear his voice above the motor and wave, singing on, "*So freely shed for me —*"

"Cut that out Bernard or Maudie can drive and you can walk," I say.

Bernard stops. The back of his neck is as red as his face. He can't think of a reply.

$\mathcal{M}$audie's place is looking beautiful as usual. Flowerbeds all trimmed, lawns, the rest. I organise gin and tea to be sent up to my room and retire. Might as well enjoy it. Done my duty.

About four there's a ruckus outside my window. Half-cut I look down on them from my bed. It's Miss Perkins-Green. She wants to sleep in one of the servant's bures and Bernard will have none of it.

CHAPTER FIVE

Taveuni
November 8th, 1918

~ *Agnes Perkins-Green* ~

I had my way in the end. I write in my bure, a coolie is bringing me my things directly. Apparently, he had already carried them upstairs, which makes my heart sore for him. They are surprisingly strong though, those little chaps.

The inside of the bure walls are well smoked. This I am glad of, having learnt to my cost in Samoa how our insect friends thrive in new native houses. How sweet this is, this little gathering of dwellings. Not a true village, of course, but servants' quarters. Still, the house is not visible from here. A stand of banana trees takes care of that.

The coolie came with my bags. I tipped him, feeling gay and continental. Now my hammock is rigged, my curtain fixed to the door, my blanket airing, my kettle boils merrily on its dancing fire tended by a young native boy with eyes so meltsome they are impossible to describe.

All my thoughts are concentrated on my soon-to-be meeting with Constance Prime-Belcher. I will quake in her presence I am sure. It will take some time for her even to hint at approaching my hidden depths, because of that, my quaking. Oh, how oft have I heard her described? Her pith helmet, her serge, thirty-pocket suits, her magnifying glass, tartan rug and omnipresent thermos flask? She is older now, approaching fifty, but to gaze upon her eyes, thus to gaze upon by proxy the vistas they have gazed upon — ah, my travels shall be all the richer for it. I intend to propose that she travel with me. She is an old lover of Fiji and may, near a quietening, darkening village, with our tents luminescent on the shore, want once again to bathe in a limpid, tepid lagoon. This is the memory of Paradise that I shall take back with me: warm, silky currents fingering my thighs and rendering my breasts weightless. At every opportunity I swim in the dark.

How glad I am now of this falling light. I hear the tickle of the sea nearby.

*A*fter my tea I settled to my journal. I have been invited to the house for supper and surprise myself by looking forward to it. They are a kind of self-appointed nobility, Maud and Bernard Gow, despite Maud being sprung from the loins of that dreadful old woman. The house is grand in tropical style: spreading verandahs; English flower beds; out-houses in both European and native style. I couldn't help noticing though, as I passed through the hall, a kind of dankness, or despair in the air. On entering the hall, Maud's shoulders perceptibly dropped. Her mother's barked commands to the houseboy and her husband's insane, braying laughter seem to bear down heavily on her. To witness another unhappy marriage is to relish once again my solemn vow against union of that type. I have witnessed so many. In this part of the Empire the women wane and wilt, the men take up with native women for brute solace. "Mat fever" I believe they call it over gin in the Planters' Clubs. I thank the Lord for his preservation of me, even though it has cost me dearly and cost dear Johnny his life. But I am breaking another solemn vow! That is, never to think of Johnny, much less to write of him.

Being desirous of a wash before supper I follow a small knot of native women to the pump for water. Just nearby I notice two peculiar structures: long, low to the ground and so flimsy I can't imagine them being able to stand up in a stiff wind, much less a hurricane. I enquire of one my companions as to their name and function.

"The Lines," she replies. "Those are the Lines. Where the coolies live."

Between where we stand and the Lines there is a grove of guava trees. Bright lengths of cloth festoon their branches and the guavas shine among them like yellow lanterns.

"Beautiful," I tell my companion. "Like Christmas trees."

"Sega," she says, shaking her head, looking at me strangely. "Not beautiful, Marama."

I could explain to her that I meant the coolies' drying laundry is beautiful, not their dwellings. No one in her right mind would think the Lines themselves are anything other than slums of the tropical kind: hastily erected, poorly maintained, they would better accommodate pigs than people.

One of the women takes my canvas bucket from me and fills it. I return to my picturesque bure, retire behind my curtain and dress for supper.

CHAPTER SIX

Aunt Maud's Bat

It seemed to Olive, as she came around the corner of the verandah, that Aunt Maud was excelling herself. No tiara to be sure, but she wore a fox fur as she sat alone at her afternoon tea. As Olive approached around the side of the house, the fox blinked its little eyes at her over Aunt Maud's shoulder. Olive blinked back.

The other day, the carved dragon on the Chinese mirror above Mother's bureau had done the same, sighed, blinked its mother-of-pearl eyes, rattled its spiked wooden tail. Olive had smiled at herself in the mirror, as she smiled now at Aunt Maud. Aunt Maud's lower lip trembled. Most adults, Olive knew, were unnerved by her, though she didn't know why.

Now the leaves of the banana trees, the grove that stood between the Lines and the house, chattered and whispered to her, "Sit with your aunt, sit with your aunt. Lonely face. She has such a lonely face."

"Olive, dear," said Aunt Maud. "Sit with me."

Olive gazed out over the garden; the thirsty, drooping roses, to where Ralph passed through the banana trees, flickering through the shadows to the Lines.

"Anil Anil Anil," said the banana leaves.

The fox nuzzled Aunt Maud's neck as Olive sat down. White teacups flared and bloomed on the tray.

"When I saw you come off the boat, dear, I thought how lovely to have another woman in the house. Look at you, dear." Aunt Maud smiled, her smooth white face creased sideways. She toasted Olive with her cup. "Old enough to have tea with me." Olive wriggled. The fox held her eye. Aunt Maud leaned forward conspiratorially.

"We will be six for dinner tonight. Dressed fish, Fijian-style. For our visitor."

The fox bent its little head to watch the jewelled rings glitter from fat valleys in Aunt Maud's fingers.

"Help yourself, dear," said Aunt Maud.

Olive reached for the teapot and poured carefully, without spilling a drop. There were things to eat, too, a plate of melting moments. Aunt Maud would have made them herself. She had a cook that let her into the cookhouse, unlike Champak at home. Once Champak had chased Olive out with a knife after her piglet had done its business on the kitchen floor.

"Your uncle's gone up to Torte's. To see the new sheep, with Eric."

Olive bit into the sweet biscuit. Her tongue tingled.

"Just us girls," said Aunt Maud, sighing.

Olive shifted her gaze from the fox to her aunt. Dark shapes of perspiration lay on her voile blouse. Aunt Maud always had such puffy eyes, as if she'd been crying, thought Olive. The pale McNab eyes faded into the wet, surrounding pink. Strange, in a grown-up who always seemed so calm and unruffled.

"Apart from Pepepeli," Aunt Maud went on. She kissed the fox on the top of its small flat head, before leaning back in her wicker chair. At the risk of being squashed, it crept round to Aunt Maud's shoulder and hung there. Olive saw it was a bat and felt cheated.

"Your mother. How was she when you left?"

"In bed," said Olive. "The baby hadn't come."

Aunt Maud startled. "You know about the baby?"

"Yes," said Olive. She sipped her tea. It burnt her top lip and tasted strange, bitter. Cup met saucer with a clatter.

"Your mother told you?"

"Immm," said Olive.

Maud's heart throbbed suddenly. What would she have told her daughter, had one of them lived? How would she have come broadside to the subject? Ah, they would have sorted the tiny clothes together. She would have come to it softly.

"A little one. Another little one . . ."

"She was crying," Olive offered. "I came home from school and she was in the bedroom with Elena. We had to unpack the clothes."

"Clothes?" said Aunt Maud, startled. The child was fey.

"The ones she'd packed up. For the European Ladies Hygienic Mission."

"Ah."

The bat chirruped, like a bird. Or was it a bird? Beyond the banana trees a pair of skinny, dark legs tore through the grass. Ralph's legs, heavier, followed.

"Ralph's over at the Lines," said Olive. "He's gone to see Anil." She licked the crumbs from the corner of her mouth.

There was something in the child's manner Maud didn't like.

"He'll be all right," she said. "The Indians are working — away over at the copra shed." It was safe to let the boys play. Only the children remained behind, the older ones looking after the younger. Ralph could come to no harm.

"Has Grandmother got gin?" asked Olive. Grandmother wasn't allowed gin at home, or very rarely. Even the cooking sherry was kept locked up by Champak.

"No," said Maud. Good heavens, she'd lied to the child.

Olive put down her cup and narrowed her eyes at her.

"Thank you for the tea, Aunt Maud."

Then the child was up and running across the grass towards the bures. Maud hoped she wasn't going to bother their lady guest. She stood to call her back then thought better of it.

The tea had grown cold. She rang the bell for Ah Jack and gazed over the trees, the three small graves, to the sea. For months, after they'd buried the last child, a son, she'd taken her tea inside. Then, one day her sad, swollen feet led her out to the verandah. She'd sat in her wicker chair and realised she felt better with the three of them in sight, Gerald and his sisters. The first daughter was monstrous, so malformed she hadn't seen it. Doctor Ricketts whisked it away while the chloroform still worked its little death. The second daughter came four months ahead of its time so that even if its pale, crooked limbs had been straight, the odd bulbous head its natural shape, the ears shaped humanly instead of how they were — thin, translucent as petals and pointed and primed like a bat's — even if she had bided her time she would not have survived. Maud remembered the size of her, smaller than a cane toad.

The third, the son, she'd borne to full term. The birth was swift and easy. She'd not sniffed at the Twilight Sleep but pushed the nurse's hand away. Bernard was called in as soon as the child was clean and had watched him nuzzle at her breast. The boy's eyes though, open and watchful, bore the mark. That should have been the first fateful clue: one eye darker than the other, the new-born slate grey promising one day to bloom one to blue and the other to brown like the father's, or blue and green like the aunt's. Gerald's limbs were straight, his torso sturdy, but even then, even so, he'd only survived long enough for the sun to sink and rise again. By noon the following day his breathing was sparse, by three o'clock he was growing cold. Doctor Ricketts returned to sedate her and they'd taken the boy from her arms. No more, he'd told Bernard. He knew of the emerging science of genetics in Europe, he knew the consanguineous history of Bernard's family, he put the blame at Bernard's door. A time would come when Doctor Ricketts would defend Maud's erratic behaviour.

"She was cheated of the fruits of marriage," he would tell the court at Somosomo, years later.

After Gerald's funeral, with the Fijian gravedigger still leaning on his spade, Maud knew with terrible clarity why he had died. It wasn't to do with a weakness of constitution, but of mind. Had Gerald survived he would have been like Bernard's sister Elvira, madder than a two-bob watch. He died because for a moment he forgot his own existence, thought Maud, he forgot to breathe. Though there was nothing amusing about this revelation, laughter had come then, like the rains, tumultuous gusts of it billowing her about, tossing her to the ground, filling her mouth with the rich Taveuni soil.

They had carried her inside and given her a powder. Even now the laughter threatened, livid, wild, a cruel sun behind the moist, masking clouds of her daily demeanour. Was it Bernard who'd done this to her? She didn't know. For months, she'd taken her tea in the dim parlour.

Maud let her eyes rest for a moment on Gerald's stone angel, its bowed head gentle against the blinding sea. She rang the bell again for the solace Ah Jack would bring.

*T*en minutes later, Olive stood behind Agnes Perkins-Green's bure and peeped under the roof. Water slapped gently at the sides of the canvas bucket as Agnes dipped a flannel. She applied it to her armpits and sighed. Droplets spotted her silk chemise. A pale curl snaked damply on her paler neck. Her eyes closed with the ecstasy of the cool water. Olive felt a small thrill.

Now Agnes was bending to her thighs and splashing water between her legs. A shower flew to land on the crumpled mound of skirt and petticoat, flung on the mats beside her.

Olive crept away, back to the house, running when she reached the verandah, up the dark staircase to her room. On her bed she huddled face down, a strange, new excitement swelling her veins and filling her mouth with saliva.

CHAPTER SEVEN

Six Diners and a Dressed Fish

~ Maud Gow ~

At six, Mother comes down from her room and the house-boy guides her to a chair on the verandah. Bernard is holding forth about the War — he says it's over, that an Armistice has been signed, that this gem of information was given over to him by Torte while they gazed at the ailing sheep. It is as likely as the sheep surviving this heat wave, besides I hear Fiji's own hero, Captain Faddy MC is returning, and why should he bother if there's no War to go to. Bernard is waving his arms about, his blue eye glittering with wild excitement.

"So, you've missed out, my boy," he's saying to Eric. "You'll have to wait till the next one."

Mother fixes him with an evil glare and holds her glass out to Vishnu for more whisky.

"Good evening!" It's Agnes Perkins-Green, striding across the lawn. "I hope I'm not too early?"

"Not at all!"

Bernard and I lean out from the verandah to greet her. If I no longer love anything about Bernard, I can still appreciate his love of a party.

"A Scotch, my dear?" he's saying to Miss Perkins-Green. "My best malt."

"With water," Miss Perkins-Green responds.

Vishnu steps forward from the shadows with the tray: Scotch in a flask, water in Waterford crystal. Miss Perkins-Green and Bernard raise their glasses to their lips.

"You're not joining us, Mrs Gow?"

"Well, I'm in and out of the kitchen, you know."

"Leave Kalessar alone," says Bernard. "The man is such a namby-pamby, he's continually letting you interfere. You're damned lucky you haven't got a Champak."

Because of the presence of Miss Perkins-Green I blush. Bernard and I blush easily, a pair of Collared Lorys side by side on the verandah rail. At the mention of Champak, Mother startles. Once Champak chased her clear up the kitchen steps, across the grass to the privy, yelling Hindi curses as he went. Mother has never forgiven him.

"And how are things at Waimanu Road, Mother?" Bernard asks. "Running smoothly?"

"Adela is dying, you goat," says Mother, malevolently.

Miss Perkins-Green studies us all keenly and chucks Pepepeli under the chin. Another writer. Rupert Brooke was here once, five years ago. I used to worry he'd write about us, but at least we'd be cloaked in verse, disguised somehow. I heard later he hated Fiji. No doubt we will all be quoted verbatim in Miss Perkins-Green's tea-stained notebook. I have often planned to keep a notebook too, a journal. Mine, however, would not be besmirched with tea, but tears. I draw Miss Perkins-Green aside.

"We are eating native-style tonight," I tell her, "fish, cassava, yams —"

Miss Perkins-Green interrupts. "Really? Shall we sit cross-legged and eat with our fingers?"

"Oh, the natives had forks," interposes Bernard, "long before we did. Don't be deceived by their appearance. Despite a few nasty habits, our natives were an advanced civilisation."

"What have you been reading, Bernard?" asks Mother. "I never heard such bosh."

"Not reading, Minnie, but listening. Sitiveni, up at Torte's, he's quite a scholar."

"He's nothing more than a clever monkey."

Miss Perkins-Green raises her eyebrows. She affords me a small smile with her full lips.

"And the children — have they already eaten?" she asks hopefully.

"Ralph is eating now, in the nursery. Olive and Eric will dine with us."

"Nursery? But I thought —" begins Miss Perkins-Green, before her virginal mind remembers itself.

"Never given up hope, have we Maudie?" Bernard slings his arm around my shoulders. I long to shake it off. Such a lie. After Gerald I began locking my door at night. There was no point in suffering his attentions any longer.

"Ring the bell for dinner, will you, Vishnu?" I ask, and sweep ahead of them into the cool dining-room. Since afternoon tea I have been hard at work with Ah Jack, wreathing the walls with hibiscus and streamers, in honour of our guest. If the Armistice is truly signed, when we see it in the *Fiji Times* in black and white, we will have a huge party, it will be expected of us, if the Tortes don't get in first with the invitations.

I set native fans at every place and check that the orchids have water. The gong booms outside. Olive's footfalls sound on the stairs. Eric is first in from the verandah, his hair greased and slicked back. Bernard, Mother and Miss Perkins-Green follow. While they sit up I go round to the kitchen to organise the chokras and kitchen-hands.

The heat in that room is inhumane. I remain at the door, fanning myself. Two walls of the kitchen are windward, the room being at one corner of the house, but the evening is so still that the room is full of steam. Our youngest chokra, a new recruit from the Lines, stands behind the others, snivelling.

"What is the matter with Aiyaz?"

"Nothing at all, Memsahib," says Kalessar, slipping the dressed fish, a giant beauty, on to the serving plate where it swims in a lake of cocoa-nut milk. My stomach is rumbling.

"But he is crying," I persist.

"Perhaps he misses his mother," jeers Mohan, himself not much older than Aiyaz.

Although I should scold Mohan for impertinence I keep silent. Time is the essence. I look over their uniforms. All is in place. The maroon cummerbunds divide the gleaming white of their shirts from their dark, pressed trousers.

"I will return to the dining-room," I tell them. "We will expect you with the first course in a few moments. Keep that fish hot, Kalessar — I think you may have served it out a little too soon."

*T*he servants arrive with a huge, steaming tureen of consommé. Vishnu ladles it out while Mohan and Aiyaz settle the plates in front of us. All the while I can feel Miss Perkins-Green observing us and it worries me. Perhaps this is not how they proceed at Home, but their servants are possibly more adept with soup plates. Perhaps it would be more correct for the chokra to move around the table with the tureen, rather than ladle it out at the chiffonier.

But it's not that. Her eyes are fixed upon Aiyaz, whom I note, as he lays my soup in front of me, has a large ringworm on his neck.

"Olive, would you say grace, please?" I ask.

Olive has not changed for dinner. She sits in her smudged white dress, her face still bearing evidence of a long journey and a hot day.

"For what we are about to receive, may we truly give thanks," she mumbles. "Amen."

Miss Perkins-Green keeps her head raised. Surely she's not an atheist, in addition to her other eccentricities.

"Good soup, Maud," says Bernard, who is compelled to compliment me on everything that comes from the kitchen.

"Have you ever thought," says Miss Perkins-Green in the tone of one who is about to suggest something earth-shattering, "have you ever thought of serving the soup chilled, as they do in Spain?"

"Spain?" I ask. It's a beef consommé, peppery and good.

"When I was in Spain, I sampled gazpacho — chilled tomatoes and cucumber — delectable in the extreme."

"Really? You must give Kalessar the recipe."

"Have you ever been to Spain?" asks Miss Perkins-Green.

I shake my head as Bernard breaks in with, "Neither have I. Torte, of course, has a Spanish ass."

"A Spanish ass?" Miss Perkins-Green raises her spoon, a quizzical pucker to her face.

"For the breeding of mules," says Bernard. "The natives find 'em easier to handle than horses." He gives one of his sudden guffaws.

The laugh startles not only Pepepeli, who claws my shoulders, but also Miss Perkins-Green, who drops a little soup on to the damask, where it seeps out, spreading across the fibres of the cloth. It has taken the shape of a map of Spain. Or Viti Levu.

The soup finished, Vishnu and Mohan slide forward to take away the plates. The youngest chokra remains behind, a small shadow against the wall.

"Pour some water, Aiyaz."

I regret the command as soon as I've issued it. He struggles around with the pitcher, half as big as he is. Water splashes on to the table, the map of Spain at Miss Perkins-Green's elbow dissolves.

Eric has impeccable manners. He ignores Aiyaz as he comes to his place, shifting only imperceptibly to let him at the glass.

Olive, however, gazes at Aiyaz with pity. As he comes to her she pats him on the back. Aiyaz takes such a fright he drops the jug and it smashes to a thousand pieces, water and crystal coursing about our feet like surf. I am up and at Aiyaz's side before I know what I'm doing, a piece of crystal leaping to my hand before I strike him. He cries out once, feebly like a kitten, his fingers cup his cheek, and I see I have cut him. Maroon blood trickles over his delicate nails.

Bernard takes me by the shoulders.

"Pull yourself together, Maud. Go to your room."

I do not turn back to see the open-mouthed horror of Miss Perkins-Green, nor the malevolent half-grin of my mother. Sometimes I am more like her than I care to be.

Moments later, from my room, I hear the car being brought round to the carriageway at the front of the house. From my window, I watch Miss Perkins-Green climb in, cradling Aiyaz, the side of his head bandaged, while Bernard takes the wheel. Surely not . . . but they are . . . the car turns left at the gate, heading away from Vuna Point to Somosomo, to Doctor Ricketts'.

Miss Perkins-Green has talked Bernard into this excursion, I'm sure. Previously Bernard has regarded injuries to coolies like wounds to cats — coolies heal themselves.

In the moonlight my hands tremble and my jaws slacken with shame.

$\mathscr{B}one$

$\mathscr{I}$t was that night, the same night that Maud Gow committed an offence that would see her stand trial in the Somosomo Court, that Olive contemplated her own death for the first time.

She watched Aunt Maud leave the room, her usually soft shoulders tensed beneath the voile, then looked across at Agnes Perkins-Green. Agnes's eyes bulged.

Uncle Bernard took Aiyaz out to the kitchen, and shortly loud shouts of outrage issued from that direction.

"He must see a doctor!" Miss Perkins-Green tossed her napkin to the damp damask and left the room swiftly.

Eric said softly, after she'd gone, "There will be trouble in the Lines tomorrow."

"What made Aunt Maud do that?" asked Olive.

Eric shrugged. Olive knew he would've answered her if Grandmother had not been listening.

The door swung open again. It was Vishnu with Mohan, bearing the fish and its accompaniments.

"Sahib instructed me to bring you the meal," said Vishnu, laying the fish on the chiffonier.

The McNabs sat quietly while he and Mohan dealt out the food and handed it round. Steaming bowls of yams, taro and cassava were set in the centre of the table. Mohan and Vishnu bowed and began their exit.

"Vishnu!" thundered Grandmother. "Serve a meal for Memsahib and take it up to her."

Vishnu froze. He did not turn around.

"Vishnu. Do you hear me?"

"Yes, Memsahib. I hear you."

"Then do as you are told."

Vishnu returned. He served out a vast amount of fish and vegetables on to a plate. From the chiffonier he took a tray, loaded it, and handed it to Mohan. Mohan nodded, and with a tiny bow he took the giant meal out. A moment later his footsteps sounded lightly on the stairs. Grandmother's eyes were fading so she had not seen what Vishnu had done. Even if she had, she may not have understood its message, as Olive did. By the size of the repast Vishnu was telling the memsahib she was no better than a sow. He followed Mohan from the room. Grandmother caught Olive's eye.

"What are you gawping at? Eat your dinner."

From the front of the house came the sound of the car, the slamming of its doors. Then the engine reverberated, retreated down the drive, and died away along the road.

It was only at about the third or fourth mouthful of fish, Olive was sure she'd eaten hardly anything, it was about then that a sudden, zig-zagging pain tore through her throat. She gasped and clutched at her gullet.

"What are you doing now?" asked Grandmother. The child's pranks were tiresome.

Olive tried to answer, but couldn't. The bone slipped lower, embedded in flesh, bridging her oesophagus, both ends glowing.

"She's swallowed a fish bone," said Eric, pushing his chair back, coming to her. "Open up, Sis."

Olive did as he said, but the dropping of her jaw only served to increase the pain.

"I can see it," said Eric. "It's a long way down. Can you swallow it?"

Olive shook her head and groaned. This degree of discomfort was new to her.

"Blast you!" said Grandmother. She remembered she'd only got out of bed to get another look at Perkins-Green. She wished she'd stayed put with the gin bottle. At the foot of the stairs she yelled up, "Maudie!"

There was no answer. Maud had taken a powder and retired. The crash as Olive left her chair and fell to the floor brought Grandmother back to the dining-room.

"Get up," she said.

Olive coughed. A gobbet of blood landed on the tongue and groove. Eric took off, running.

"I'll go and get Sitiveni," he called.

Grandmother heaved a huge sigh. After a moment she came to Olive and knelt beside her. Olive heard her knees creak and looked up into her face. Something approaching tenderness shone from her eyes. Eric's running feet crunched on the gravel beyond the open front door.

Grandmother laid her hand on Olive's forehead. Suppose the child died? She'd heard of it happening before, with a fish-bone. Years ago, in Levuka, a native child had died of a poisoned throat. There had been a child in Suva, recently, died of asphyxiation.

Olive's eyes rested on a ball of dust under the table. It rolled with every draught from the hall. Her nose filled with the close proximity of Grandmother's peculiar smell. Yeast, mildew and peppermint odours fell from her stroking sleeve. Olive tried to swallow.

"Sitiveni will take you to the doctor," said Grandmother. "You're a brave girl."

Olive's eyes filled with tears, more from this unexpected tenderness from Grandmother than the pain in her throat.

The house was quiet. Grandmother heaved herself into a chair and waited.

$\mathcal{A}$s Eric ran, darkness fell. The Torte's grand driveway was lit on either side by iron lamps. Cattle loomed among the nut trees of the plantation. Eric passed a racecourse, stables. Torte was the biggest of the Taveuni lords. A pot hole — Eric stumbled, picked himself up and ran on. Ahead of him the house glittered, lit up like one of the Union steamships at night.

Sitiveni was sitting on the verandah with another man. They were smoking cigarettes and laughing. As Eric drew nearer, he could see it was Torte himself, the old man.

"Sitiveni!" yelled Eric.

"Who's that?" came Sitiveni's voice. He lifted himself from his chair and came down the steps.

"Young Eric? What do you want?"

"It's Olive. She's swallowed a fish bone. You've got to come quickly —"

Sitiveni was already running for his horse. Eric had the stitch. He clasped his side and bent over double. A glowing cigarette end landed by his boot. Old Man Torte hauled up from his chair and went inside, shutting the door after him.

It was only on the homeward ride, clinging bareback to Sitiveni, that he remembered the Tortes had cars. Two of them. Why had the old man not offered a car? Eric wished he was older than fourteen. The adult world teemed with resentments, oaths and feuds. There would be a reason, known only to the adults, why Torte didn't offer help. There were reasons for everything if only Eric could think of them. Why Mother was ill. Why Sis was so tricky. She wasn't like girls are supposed to be. It was because there were too many brothers. It seemed strange already, only the three of them cut adrift from the cloth of the family. Maybe Sis would get maternal about Ralph. Eric wished she didn't have to be so tough all the time. Harder than nails. Harder than Grandmother, sometimes.

Grandmother said to Olive, "It'll be Sitiveni that comes, on horseback. Torte won't lend the car. Said it before and I'll say it again — tighter than a fish's arse."

Ordinarily, Olive would've giggled. She spat out blood and tried to sit up, but gravity hauled the bone earthwards. She lay on the floor again, sweating. Perhaps Grandmother would fan me, she thought, perhaps she could work the punkah.

Grandmother sighed again and picked up one of the native fans. Olive heard her skirts rasp as she leant forward and took it from the table. Then, with a steady beat, a slow bird's wing blurring in the corner of Olive's eye, she cooled her own powdered cheeks.

Feet pounded in the hall, heavy and light, dull knockings at Olive's floor-pressed ear. Sitiveni carried her out to the horse.

"You mustn't fall," he said, "put your arms around me."

Olive pressed her face into his broad back and breathed him in for safety. The horse trotted out of the gate, rising to the gallop on the road. In Olive's throat the bone jagged and tore. Her arms felt as sinewless as cloth. They sagged round Sitiveni's waist. The regular lines of the cocoa-nut plantations were giving way to bush, trees blurred and rushed. The night's hum rushed into her head from ear to ear and out again. She tipped her head back. Maybe the bone would dislodge before they got there.

Stars loomed and faded, the moon was Grandmother's face, she was back in the dining-room at Aunt Maud's, then Sitiveni called out, "You're slipping!"

The horse careered away from the road and they were on a bush track leading up into the hills.

"Where're we going?" Olive whispered. She wiped her mouth on the back of Sitiveni's shirt and felt ashamed. It had been clean. It smelt of cotton and soap.

"Somosomo is too far. We'll go to the village."

Had she fallen? If she had she couldn't remember. Perhaps Sitiveni had lifted her down, perhaps they had both fallen. Her throat burnt, her legs and arms felt numb.

Olive opened her eyes. She was lying on a mat, inside a bure. A ring of dark faces peered down at her, brows drawn.

"She's awake," said Sitiveni, who sat closest to her.

An elderly woman squatted down, pushed her liku between her legs and extended a hand to Olive's throat. Her fingers closed around the flesh above where the bone had lodged and pressed and kneaded.

The pain was searing. Olive cried out and struggled to sit up. Sitiveni pushed her back, gently.

"Lie down," he said. "Don't move."

Olive's mouth filled with blood. The old woman pushed and prodded, the surrounding heads of the villagers pulsed and flared.

I am going to die, thought Olive, as the squeezing at her throat went on and on.

There was a sudden respite from the pain. The old woman had taken her hand from her throat. She held a finger an inch away from Olive's mouth, drawing it back, willing the bone to come away. Olive coughed up more blood.

"Wai," said the old woman.

A younger woman knelt now, with a half cocoa-nut shell of water. Sitiveni held Olive up.

"Gunu wai," said the old woman. "Drink."

The water splashed down Olive's front as she struggled to swallow. The bone was perhaps looser, perhaps it was coming away.

"Has it gone?" asked Sitiveni.

Olive shook her head. They lay her down again and the pressing and rubbing continued. Some children crept between the adults and peered at her. They whispered and giggled until the old woman hissed at them to go away.

Once again Sitiveni held Olive up and the old woman held her forefinger just beyond her lips. She drew her finger backwards. The bone shifted, scraped, one end lifted towards the roof of Olive's mouth. She was going to be sick. She held her dress out from her lap and heaved. The bone came away. It lay on her white church frock, sticky and speckled with blood. The old woman patted her hand.

"Vinaka," whispered Olive, "vinaka, Marama."

The younger woman brought her more water to soothe her throat and settled beside her. The villagers had faded away, the children and Sitiveni too. Olive lay down on the mat. From outside, Sitiveni's laughter boomed.

Exhaustion leapt up at her like a dog, weighty and damp. Olive fell to it and lay still and hot until the morning.

CHAPTER NINE

The Day
of Rest

$\mathcal{W}$aking beside his wife in a pool of sweat, the most immediate matter on Bernard's mind was the impending visit of the Government official. Then a slow, easy sensation filled his groin and he remembered the dawn's sweet pleasures. They were all the sweeter for being unexpected.

Climbing the stairs on his return from Doctor Ricketts', he'd turned in the direction of his own room, over the corridor from that of his wife. She'd woken early and was crying. He'd looked at his watch — Ah Jack would not bring the tea for three hours, but still Bernard could have peace in his own room. He wouldn't be able to hear her from there. But the instant his hand cupped the door handle, the sobbing redoubled. He paused, turned heavily and opened Maud's door.

At first he could scarcely make her out. The bed was a jumble of sheets and Maud in her white nightgown was camouflaged among the pillows. He sat on the slipper chair, the fruit bat clinging to the curtain rail above his head, until one mound, heaving and sobbing, identified itself as his wife.

"Cut it out," he said, eventually. It was when Maud carried on like this that he was relieved there had been no children. Children of a certain age cry all the time and nothing got on Bernard's nerves as much as crying did.

Maud quietened and a moment later sat up. They regarded one another in the curtained gloom.

"How is Aiyaz?" she asked.

"Stitched up," Bernard said. "Had the ringworm treated, too. He'll be all right."

Maud nodded. Bernard decided to take the plunge.

"Bit of bad news," he said. "The Coolie Inspector couldn't get on to Savusavu — high seas on the Strait. He's coming here first."

"Here?" Maud drew the sheets up over her breasts and clasped her hands. "But we're supposed to be given warning, a few days' grace."

Bernard said nothing for a moment. He looked at his wife's hands. The one with the wedding ring was uppermost. The gold shivered in the moonlight.

"Shall I wake Ah Jack and get him to bring you some tea?"

"No. You mustn't wake poor Ah Jack." She turned her tearful face towards her husband. "Why weren't we given warning, Bernie?"

She hadn't called him Bernie since Levuka days, before he'd inherited the plantation and the care of his sister. He shrugged his shoulders.

"Can't tell you lies, Maud. The coolies'll tell him, and Ogilvy'll file a report and the way things are at the moment, you'll have to go to court."

"Not if you talk to him first. The same as you did with that other business, when that Australian overseer — you know . . ." Maud had forgotten his name. His tanned face and even, white teeth she remembered. At the time she had dreamt of them, longed for him.

"Jim Ryan," said Bernard. "That was different. That was just a coolie with a filthy mind imagining he'd paid her attention. And there were no witnesses, no Agnes Perkins-Whatsit."

Silence again. Bernard went to the window, drew aside a curtain and looked out towards the bures.

"Will Mr Ogilvy talk to her — to Miss Perkins-Green?" Maud's voice trembled. Bernard sighed.

"Oh, Bernie!" Maud's voice was full of anguish. And need, thought Bernard.

"Bernie?" She had her arms out to him.

"It's all right," he said, bending to remove his boots. "I'll take care of it," he said, unbuttoning his white duck trousers and shirt. He slipped into bed beside his wife. "Don't worry."

And there was Maudie slipping into his arms, kissing him with an open, wet mouth and lifting her nightgown herself. He took hold of himself and pushed his way in. It was a long time since they'd dispensed with the finer attentions. A year or so ago, Bernard had reached the conclusion that Maud had done with intimacy altogether, but here she was, with a little moan in her throat. He took a handful of her flesh. She had so much more of it than the coolie women.

Maud opened her eyes and looked at him when she sensed he was nearly finished. Always the same picture filled her mind — a great mustard dog, ears back, yellow teeth bared, the multi-coloured eyes rolling back, lost in his skull. She had perfected the loveless skill of dropping to sleep the moment she felt him lurch and fade.

Her breath in small o-shaped snores, Maud slept on now. Bernard got dressed and went downstairs, passing Ah Jack and tea-tray on the way. His own breakfast, Bernard supposed, would be cold by now. He had overslept by an hour.

In the dining-room the table was unlaid. The chiffonier was preposterous: it bore still some of last night's dinner, now fly-coated.

"Vishnu!" His enormous voice echoed down the hall. "Kalessar!"

The door from the kitchen opened and a tall figure came out into the hall. It was Winterson, Ryan's replacement, a New Zealander. It was Bernard's opinion that the New Zealanders were inferior to the Australians as overseers — they weren't tough enough, they believed all the coolies' cock-and-bull stories about being tired, or hungry, or sick. Winterson had a lump of bread in one hand and looked worried.

"They won't budge, Sir."

"What do you mean, they won't budge?" A chilling thought occurred to Bernard. "Not the influenza?"

"No," Winterson said. "Your wife, Sir . . ." But Bernard had turned already and was striding, as fast as his thick legs would carry him, to the end of the hall. He flung the door open on to the verandah and made his way across the grass. Behind him, Winterson, his mouth full, tried to dissuade him.

"They say Ogilvy's on his way, Sir," he said through the crumbs. "They say he left Somosomo by boat early and is already inside the reef."

The older man gave Winterson no indication he'd heard him. The Lines, when they reached them, were deserted.

"What the devil . . .!" Bernard exploded. He lowered his head to enter the second of the long sheds. After a last look around, Winterson followed unwillingly. At the end, in one of the dark, tiny rooms, a small figure lay on a pallet. Beside him sat one of the coolie women, one whom Bernard recognised as the mother of Aiyaz. As the men entered, she pulled a portion of her sari over her face. The child in the bed, Winterson saw when Bernard lifted the sheet, was Aiyaz himself. The woman brushed a fly from the scar on his cheek. The visitors may have been flies themselves, for all the attention she paid them. Before Winterson realised the older man's intentions, Bernard had thrown out a hand and knocked the woman sideways.

"Where are the men?" he thundered.

The woman folded her hands in a gesture of supplication and bowed her head.

"Answer me!" Bernard bent over her. But the woman had no English. Aiyaz's eyes, wide open in terror, pleaded past his mother's assailant to Winterson.

The sirdar took his employer's elbow and hauled him back

from the rank rooms, down the narrow passage with its flimsy attempt at partition — rigged lengths of cotton, ragged blankets — to the light outside. He lifted his face to the grey, tumultuous sky. Bernard pulled away. For a moment, his clenched fist and the angle of the arm led the overseer to expect a blow, but the moment passed. There were massed voices, drawing closer, approaching from the beach.

"Been having a pow-wow, eh?" said Bernard. "We'll see about that."

"Ogilvy will be with them," Winterson was whispering. "We should go, Sir, before there's trouble."

"Why the devil'd they move the boy? Maud wanted him cared for at the house," Bernard muttered. In fact, Maud had expressed no such desire but he didn't want to appear soft, or afraid.

"Come on, Sir," Winterson was almost pleading. Bernard shrugged.

"I'll see Ogilvy as soon as he's finished here," he said, and he followed the overseer back to the house. Had he not kept his eyes on the toes of his squeaking boots, he may have noticed his nephew slip like a shadow past him into the banana trees. The boy waited until he'd passed, then went on to find his playmate.

*A*s the boy approaches and the men depart, the coolies fill the Lines like ghosts.

*Y*esterday, when he visited, Ralph was greeted by Anil's mother with a broad smile. She remembered him from a visit three years ago when he was only four years old. Such pale eyes as had caused her to marvel. Hair that gleamed like mother-of-pearl. Today as Ralph approaches the door of Anil's family's room, Anil's mother gets up and goes inside, leaving behind the pot she was scouring with earth.

Ralph stops short of the door and calls, "Anil! Anil!"

In the silence afterwards, he realises what's different about today. The men are there, down on the beach, they haven't gone out to work.

"Go away."

There is Anil, standing where his mother was. Ralph feels wounded, hurt by his friend. Suddenly, he remembers that he is white and Anil is black and he has no right to speak to him like that. He flings out a rapid fist, which Anil perceives dimly as something soft and fluid, before it strikes him on the chin. He responds in kind and the two boys roll in the dust, knocking against a cooking pot, scattering chickens and two tottering, pot-bellied babies.

Ralph, heavier, better fed, has the advantage. On top, a knee on each of Anil's shoulders, he deliberates about what to do next. Once he saw his brothers Bill and Harry fighting, this is what Harry did to Bill. He takes a handful of Anil's hair and pulls.

"You fight like a girl," scoffs Anil.

"I'm not a girl!" screams Ralph. He lifts his fist to strike again, like a boy, when a sharp voice sounds behind him. Several pairs of hands lift him clear of Anil, who scrambles up and away towards his mother at the door.

Ralph can't understand what Anil's rescuers are saying. Fear rises in his throat. One of the men keeps digging his long fingers into Ralph's neck, pushing him around. Another man speaks quickly to him, reasoning with him in English. The man stops. It's a stranger's voice. Ralph looks up to see a small, tubby, white man in a solar topi and high collar.

"Let him walk," the white man says. But the men ignore him. Ralph is hoisted between the two men and carried away, a throng of men following, through the banana trees towards the sahib.

From his office at the back of the house, Bernard has a clear view of the garden. Along the verandah, his wife sits with her doctored tea and fruit bat. The grass stretches towards the banana grove. The men draw closer. In the lead is the small, dark-suited and sweating sphere that is Ogilvy. Two of the coolies are carrying something. Bernard's weak eyes strain to see — a sack? No — a boy — it's Ralph.

Maud lets out a strangled cry, "Bernard!"

Her husband takes his time. He checks the gleaming toes of his boots. He wishes he had his riding crop with him to conjure images of the sirdar's whip in the coolies' minds. He waits until they release the boy of their own accord and steps heavily on to the verandah. One of the coolies, one he recognises as Aiyaz's father, takes hold of Ralph's collar. The boy is covered in dirt and his shirt is torn. Bernard resolves to remain calm. When Ogilvy has gone he will find the culprit and he will have him whipped.

Maud gets up, unsteadily, and leans against the verandah rail. She holds out her arms to Ralph. He glares at her. Aiyaz's father maintains his grip.

"Let him go," says Bernard.

Ralph breaks free, stumbles up to the verandah and disappears inside the house. Maud closes her eyes and lifts her smooth white face to the cloud-cloaked sun. Bernard has opened his mouth and is about to speak when Maud's voice comes trembling to his ears and to those of the coolies.

"You need not worry about Aiyaz," she announces, looking past the gathered men to Gerald's stone angel. "He has been attended to by the doctor at Somosomo and is resting in the servants' quarters."

The coolies don't move. They stare at the white lady, the strange memsahib with the blurred words. An old man puts a hand behind one of his protruding ears to hear her better. Bernard wonders how much they've understood.

"That will be all," says Maud, happily believing her untruth. "Thank you."

She gropes her way back to her chair and pours out more tea. Bernard can see Ah Jack had a heavy hand this morning: Maud is not herself.

The coolies shift their eyes back to him.

"You heard Memsahib," he says. "Away you go. How do you do, Mr Ogilvy."

Ogilvy, sensing the time is right, comes away from the Indians and up the steps. He shakes hands with Bernard and together they go into the house.

Suddenly, anger leaves them. The old, dry powerlessness comes back. It will be like the other times. Ogilvy will remove his solar topi and cholera belt, the white men will drink together, the sahib will convince the inspector the outrage was just punishment, or an accident. On the slow, defeated walk back to the Lines, Aiyaz's father resolves to hear Manilal speak, next time he comes to Taveuni. Listening to Manilal there is hope for an end to this. Manilal says Gandhi also hopes for their liberation. He says Gandhi knows what it is like for them: not enough food, too few women, the red-faced Australian overseers with squeaking boots, abusive mouths and cracking, overactive whip.

The men are greeted on return by the sound of the women singing. They have gathered under the guava trees with the children.

"If I had known," they sing, "that coming to Fiji would bring suffering, I would have beaten a drum to announce that nobody should ever go to Fiji."

The Hindustani words and music slither to the ears of the men and deepen their misery. Soon, thinks Aiyaz's father, Fiji will be all we know. He thinks of Aiyaz, Vishnu, Anil — they have never known India. Fiji will become little India.

From his wife's arms he takes his youngest child and settles with him on his sweat-streaked pallet. Because Memsahib cut Aiyaz they are having a day of rest. Tomorrow they will work again, or not.

After the coolies have gone, Maud decides to check on Olive. On the dark staircase her feet ascend like fish, the white slippers giving no sensation of friction. It's odd, this feeling, the laughter just round the corner, the blurring of eye and tongue. It seems to happen more and more despite Ah Jack bringing her tea through the day, hot and strong, to steady her nerves. Here's Ah Jack now on the landing, with a broom.

"Where are you going, Mrs Gow?" he asks, extending a helping hand, smiling. Maud's heart goes out to him — could he be her most beloved in the whole world? She casts her eye down his trousers and wonders if he has desires like other men. He is old now, bent double over the mats as he rolls them up. The broom leans against the banister.

"Sweeping, Ah Jack?" asks Maud, giddy from the climb. The words spill untidily from her mouth — even to her own ears it sounds more like "weeping". She looks definitively at the broom.

"Oh — sweeping — yes!" says Ah Jack, "I am making dust, Mrs Gow — lots of dust!"

"Good, Ah Jack, good." She feels lost. "Why did I come upstairs?"

Ah Jack decides to answer the question, even though he suspects she addressed herself. "To sleep?" he asks.

"Sweep?" asks Maud. "No. You are doing the sweeping."

Ah Jack tries again, his tongue doing battle with the devilish "l". "Sreep — seep —" He mimes her doing so, his eyes shut and head sideways.

"Ah!" "Now I remember — Olive!"

"She is not there," says Ah Jack. "I just swept her room."

He tells the truth. Olive has gone. From the door, Maud notes woozily that her trunk is still unpacked. It stands open on the floor. The poor child must believe she's here for only a short stay, thinks Maud.

Sitiveni had brought Olive back that morning while Maud was dressing. She'd recognised his voice, heard the ayah's loud whispers of instruction from the end of the hall and had hurried from her room to help put her to bed. They had told her to stay there, but the child couldn't be trusted.

Ralph's voice comes from the open nursery door across the landing, arguing with Margaret, the ayah. She must be happy — a real child to look after at last, a child with knobbly knees and skinny chest, not the child with the body of a woman that is Bernard's sister Elvira. Maud watches as she holds up Ralph's ruined shirt and scolds him in Fijian. While her back is turned to the tallboy, rummaging for a clean one, Ralph looks up and sees Maud.

"Hullo, dear," she says softly.

Ralph's eyes flicker. He is pale, his hair still slicked with the sweat of fear. His lower lip trembles.

"I want my mother, I want to go home."

"Not yet," says Maud. How she would love to hold him in her arms. He's only seven, still a baby. But he is moving away from her, standing close to Margaret, leaning into her hip. Maud flares with the rejection.

"Do you know where Olive is?" she asks. "She's not in her room."

The ayah shakes her head. "Sorry, Marama."

Ralph's skinny arms slip with a soft rasp into the sleeves of the clean shirt. Maud stands still. Everything is so quiet. Just the whisk of Ah Jack's broom on the floor behind her, Margaret and Ralph's breathing. Silence from behind the closed door of her mother's room. She pictures Bernard downstairs in his office, pouring whisky for Ogilvy, both men working up a sweat while they bemoan the end of indenture. Soon they would need to call Vishnu to operate the punkah.

Maud goes to her room and lies on her bed. Within minutes she is fast asleep.

$\mathcal{O}$live, proceeding along the beach road towards the point, stops and spits. Swallowing is murderous and she feels a bit sick. No one will miss her, now she's escaped. A small part of her wishes they would. She couldn't have borne it a moment longer in that hot room. She'd lain there since morning, when Sitiveni had been prevailed upon by Ralph's ayah to carry her up the stairs. Olive had insisted she could walk, but nobody listened.

Then, after they'd all trooped downstairs, she'd started to hear the crying again. It was crying that went on and on and on, thin and wailing, like a kitten. But it wasn't a kitten, Olive was sure. It was too loud, and lower, more like a baby's cry. Or more like something that was not quite a baby. Olive had never heard anything like it before, not even after Rosie was born and she and her brothers were summoned from their long wait in the mosquito room to her mother's bedroom door. This crying was weak, bubbling from a tiny mouth. After the most plaintive, unsettling pule, Olive had got up with her throat pulsing and crossed the landing to the nursery.

There was no one there. Across the room from Ralph's narrow, neatly made bed and at the foot of Eric's stood an empty cradle. Olive stepped quietly up to the cradle and rocked it. A spider scuttled to safety under the mattress. The muslin trimmings were streaked with mildew, dust hung like old hair from the blue lace hood.

"Shshsh," said Olive, although the crying had stopped.

From the nursery window she watched Margaret the ayah crossing the grass from the servants' bures, smiling and greeting Miss Perkins-Green on the way. Miss Perkins-Green was only just now returning to her bure. Her Gibson Girl blouse bore evidence of comforting embraces for Aiyaz. Ever since the return of the Packard at three o'clock this morning, Agnes had kept a vigil at his bedside. Mohan and Vishnu, in neighbouring beds, were not pleased by her proximity to them, but Miss Perkins-Green was not a memsahib to be budged. She had been, she informed them, a nurse both in the Crimea and at Jericho after the fall. Mohan and Vishnu spent an uncomfortable night in their clothes. To her shame and consternation, Agnes found herself awaking, which could only mean one thing: she had been sleeping. As she lifted her head from where it had fallen on Aiyaz's pillow, she had noted with horror that her patient had disappeared. He had been stolen away from her care. Half asleep, she had cried out to the empty room, "Has he died?" Then rushing sleep-grimed to the kitchen, she'd found Mohan and repeated her question. The man had given her a steely look.

"He has gone to his mother," he'd said.

Olive noted how the brown-booted step was not as high as it had been yesterday, how her arms hung lifeless at her sides. Poor Miss Perkins-Green could hardly manage a return smile in Margaret's direction. Olive's eyes drifted across the hazy lawn. Something was raising a lot of dust in the narrow strip of dirt that ran between the two Lines. Two dogs fighting. Or two boys.

Olive went back to her room and got into bed. The agony in her throat caused her to wonder if she'd ever be able to eat again. Her stomach rumbled. At the breech of sleep the crying began again, despairing, innocent. Whatever it was, Olive knew, was not there now, but had been once although not for long and was not to be comforted now. She got up, pulled off her nightie and found a clean cotton print frock in her trunk. From a secret compartment she took her Lucky Lunaria, procured by mail order from an Indian Brahmin in Australia. Olive dropped the stone into her pocket. Nobody saw her slip down the stairs and out of the front door, just as, she hopes, nobody sees her now as she spits an egg of blood on to the dusty road.

She's come to the native school, which she remembers from her visit to Taveuni when she was eight years old. It looks out over a low stone wall to a pebbly beach and the sea. The school's clapboard sides shed paint, all is quiet. Perhaps the children are inside praying. She steps through the long grass to the door.

There's a sign, in Fijian and English: "Closed Due to Influenza

Epidemic, by order: C.M.O." It's exactly the same as the sign that had been hung on the gates of Suva Girls' Grammar.

Olive sits on the stone wall, takes her stone from her pocket and stares out to sea. The coast of Vanua Levu shimmers across the strait. The tide is out. Lifting out of the wet sand are a set of black stone steps leading nowhere. There had been a hotel there, once. It was washed away in a hurricane so severe it had changed the coastline forever. Behind Olive stands a small stone house, abandoned. Once, it was the storehouse for the hotel. Olive closes her eyes. How does she know these things? Had someone told her? Or is it just a steady silting up of awareness until she knew, like this afternoon, when she heard Aunt Maud's baby?

The Lunaria is ice in her hot hand and there, suddenly, shimmering in the salt air, is the hotel, the men drinking on its verandahs. There is a young man, European, with a shining blonde head, progressing drunkenly down the steps and along the beach. He carries a slim volume in one hand and a battered hat in the other. With a sharp stick picked from the debris of the beach he inscribes in the sand. He mutters and chews on his full lower lip. He engraves the beach with runnelled words.

A poet, thinks Olive. Like Aunt Maud's babies, he wasn't long for this world. A sense of terror grips her suddenly, despite the peaceful warmth of the stone wall. The Lunaria burning in her hand, Olive has images of fire, frozen mud, the faces of dying men, the same war Harry died in.

She wishes the poet gone. Her fingers close around the Lucky Lunaria, and she drops its milky lustre into her pocket. The hotel disappears, the dead poet and clods of frozen mud dissolve against the sparkles of the sea. Olive slips from the wall to the beach and makes her way down the sand to where the poet stood.

So lightly I played with those dark memories
Just as a child, beneath the summer skies,
Plays hour by hour with a strange shining stone,

For which (he knows not) towns were fire of old,
And love has been betrayed, and murder done,
And great kings turned to a little bitter mould.

From behind Olive, way out on Somosomo Strait, over the reef comes the seventh wave of a set. It courses about her feet like the water-jug crystal, erasing the poet's words. Olive turns and heads for Aunt Maud's, along the beach.

CHAPTER TEN

Towards Lake Tagimaucia

~ Agnes Perkins-Green ~

*C*onstance has agreed to share my bure with me, despite the cramped arrangement of our boxes and chattels. It was of no small relief for me to discover she is as light a traveller as I am, accompanied in fact by exactly corresponding articles of necessity to the female voyager. I confess I learnt my inventory of luggage from her books, never before having travelled the Pacific myself.

Constance is marvellous. Despite her long journey by canoe from the Kingdom of Tonga she shows no sign of weariness, unlike myself. After my sleepless vigil last night I droop. We sit on opposing sides of the campfire on our corresponding stools. There is no need for haste in our companionship — we have all the time in the world. While the light falls about us, Constance sits with my sketchbook.

"Truly, you are an artist," she remarks. "A natural. Untutored. I myself am more a comrade of the pen than the brush."

My heart swells at this, and I like her immensely. I shall describe her now, physically of course, as I do not yet know her well enough to describe her any other way.

She is tall for a woman, although not as tall as I. What she misses in height she more than makes up for in stature. Broad shouldered and wide-hipped, she is as strong as any man in his fourth decade. One does, in fact, think often of the masculine when looking upon Constance Prime-Belcher. Her hands, particularly, bring "him" to mind: strong, square, large knuckled and brown, fearless of fire.

Having earlier dismissed my native boy to find guides for tomorrow, it is Constance herself who prepares our tea, those nimble digits among the flames. Her famous pendant — the magnifying glass she wears at all times — flashes and spins below her pocket-padded breast. Over the kettle her bowed head shows streaks of grey among the dark curls and in the smudge of hair below her generous nose. A lesser woman would visit the cosmetician for its removal, but Constance wears it as a badge of courage. Her moustache curls around her mouth at the rise of her lips.

One of her endearing mannerisms is to flick errant whiskers away as she talks. Despite her advancing years, Constance has good, white teeth that gleam in this soft, approaching dark almost as brightly as her almond-shaped, brown eyes. The set of her face gives one the idea that Constance is quick both to laugh and to frown. There — she laughs now at one of my native sketches. If it is not too fanciful to suggest that laughter has colour, then Constance's laugh is like the earth: tawny, rich, pregnant with promise.

"My sketch amuses you?" I ask.

"Only as much as excellence always does," she replies. We exchange a smile, and I know myself to be blushing.

"Now, my dear," she says, putting aside my sketches and taking up her cup, "what plans do you have for our month together?"

No sooner do I draw breath to answer her than she goes on, "I, of course, have my own agenda." Constance Prime-Belcher's smile has the unaffected freshness of a young girl's. In it one can perceive her love of adventure. Over the top of her teacup her eyes are warm but instructive.

"You are most welcome to join me in my journey, as we arranged in our letters. And I shall join you in yours."

"Thank you," I murmur, my heart aflutter.

"I presume you have a plan?" prompts Constance.

"Of course. It is to venture further to another island, Kadavu, where we may live cheek by jowl with the natives, the experience undiluted by intercourse with our own kind. I have already corresponded with a Mr Agnew to convey us from Suva to the island by oil launch."

Constance nods. "I should be delighted. As you are aware, my dear, I have travelled much in Fiji, beginning in the last century, but never before have I visited Kadavu and never before my own choice of destination."

"Which is?" It is my turn to prompt. Constance's eyes at this moment are fixed upon a suicidal insect drawn to our fire. She sighs with anticipation.

"Ah. Lake Tagimaucia. You have heard of it, I presume?"

"Of course. I have read of it in the *Cyclopedia of Fiji*."

"Which makes no mention of its exotic encircling jungle," rejoins my companion, "nor of the floating islands that adorn its breast."

"It sounds magnificent," I murmur. What pleasure this is: to observe Constance Prime-Belcher in full flight. Her strong arms cut the air with her expressive speech.

"We must climb the Galau Mountain to a height of four thousand feet. I presume you are in top condition."

"Absolutely."

"Then, depending on our friend's success in recruiting guides, we will leave tomorrow morning at dawn."

Our conversation is timely interrupted at this point by the rapid approach of Atunaisa, my boy. Constance converses with him in flawless Fijian, then gives me to understand guides and bearers have been hired. We resolve to retire early in order to be well rested for our assault on the mountain, the tallest on Taveuni.

*C*onstance surveys our luggage. The sun not yet fully risen, she holds aloft a lamp. My friends in the kitchen have supplied us with food: bread, cold meats, condiments and tea. Fruit and water we will gather as we require, but still one of the three bearers will be needed solely for the food.

"We will take only our tartan rugs, a change of costume, one of our kettles, two cups, our curtains, my camp table, our stools and sun hats," Constance decrees, nominating each of the aforesaid with the point of her shooting-stick. This way only a further two bearers are desired, but, alas, none of them have arrived by the appointed time.

At first we are not so concerned. It gives us time to visit the Vale Levu, or Big House, as the natives call it, and make our goodbyes. Mr Gow is sitting alone at his breakfast in the dining-room, the doors open to catch the breeze, as Constance and I make our way across the lawn.

"Good morning!" Constance hails him, as we approach.

I do believe that due to her great, deep voice, Mr Gow assumes he is greeted by a man. He jumps up from his chair, his hand extended in order to shake hands with the visitor.

"Up already, Mr Ogilvy," he says, to whoever Mr Ogilvy may be. When his eyes, of opposing hues and possibly myopic, alight on Constance, his mouth drops open for a moment. Then he remembers his mouthful of egg and toast, chews and swallows. Constance shakes hands with him anyway.

"Mr Gow, this is Miss Constance Prime-Belcher," I announce.

Mr Gow's voice booms, as I have observed it does when he is excited. "Miss Constance Prime . . . well, well — what a dashed honour this . . . sit down . . . sit — Ah Jack! Ah Jack!" Mr Gow is flustered. "Will you have a cup of tea? Coffee?"

Constance is so used to this type of response to her presence that she merely smiles at him and draws up a chair. I can see the writer in her is aroused by Mr Gow.

"Coffee please, Mr Gow." Constance pats the chair beside her for me to sit down.

"Ah Jack!" With this last vibrating bellow through the door, the houseboy, an elderly Chinese, comes running.

"Coffee for three, Ah Jack," says Mr Gow, then returning to his seat goes on, "I must say how lovely it is to have company at this hour. My wife has read all your books. Shame she never rises before nine. Toast?"

"Please," says Constance, taking some as he offers the rack. Evidently, she believes our bearers and guide will not be with us for some time yet. "We are trekking to Lake Tagimaucia today," she tells Mr Gow, "and will be taking only a small portion of our luggage. Do you think the balance may be brought into the house for safe keeping?"

"Of course," he replies, "Ah Jack will do it. Ah Jack!"

"No, not Ah Jack," I say, without thinking. "He is too —"

But there is Ah Jack, entering on his silent, slippered feet with a large pot of coffee.

"Too what? Too old?" Mr Gow throws back his head and laughs. Ah Jack smiles, cautiously. "Are you too old, Ah Jack?"

The Chinaman is bewildered.

"Not at all," says Mr Gow. "Go out to the bure and fetch these ladies' belongings into the house."

It is on Ah Jack's third, shuffling, burdened return to the house that I can endure it no longer and spring to my feet.

"How can you be so cruel!"

The blue eye glints while the brown eye is almost apologetic. "Ah Jack is younger than he appears."

Constance's eye roves over my shaking hands to my face, which I suspect is flushed. She stands.

"We must go to meet our bearers," she says, shaking Mr Gow's hand again. Mr Gow grins, a small mouth in his too-large head displaying yellow, uneven teeth, rather like those of a rat.

"You could be waiting a long time. I'd offer you a few of my Indians, but due to the ah . . . trouble the other day they're not likely to be compliant."

"Trouble?" asks Constance, the writer further aroused. I have not had an opportunity to tell her about it. Truthfully, the whole episode was so unpleasant I had banished it from my mind. Not to dwell on disturbing events is a discipline I have perfected since Johnny's death.

"Miss Prime-Belcher," says our host, standing also, "I am not providing you with any copy."

Constance, bless her, takes his rudeness in stride. "As you like, Mr Gow. Good day Sir."

It is while we wait idly in the carriageway, fanning ourselves for the flies and heat, that Olive rounds the side of the house in her awkward, knock-kneed way.

"How is your throat?" I ask her, having heard of her unfortunate mishap from the cook, who seemed to take some perverse enjoyment in the telling of the tale.

"I'm not supposed to talk," whispers Olive, gazing steadily at Constance.

"And who is this young lady?" asks that lady, blowing smoke from her first cigarette of the day.

"Olive McNab," whispers Olive McNab. "Where are you going?"

"The famous lake in the centre of the island," replies Constance. "Should you like to accompany us?"

My heart swoops as Constance utters that invitation. Then, before I realise it, my lips have parted to pronounce her name.

"Yes, dear?" and Constance turns to me. But I blush to my roots and remain silent.

"Run and ask," Constance says to the child.

"Who?" asks Olive.

"There must be someone."

Olive shakes her head.

"Your uncle?"

Olive nods, then races up the stairs into the house.

"What an enchanting child," says Constance, watching her swallowed up by the dark hall. Myself, I rather hope she will never re-emerge.

"One for the collection, I think." Constance gives me such a look that it is not my heart that swoops now, but an organ that convulses lower down. She takes my hand and I almost faint at the frankness of our exchange.

"Don't be jealous of my company, my dear. Young women such as Olive McNab bring a curious energy to a pilgrimage such as ours."

She draws me down beside her to the garden seat and does not take her hand from mine until ten o'clock when the bearers arrive, leading three horses. Hard on their heels comes Olive, who has tied on her dusty boots, washed her face and made an effort to tame her unruly hair. Beneath the tan her face is pale, her throat must pain her still.

"Did your uncle give his permission?" enquires Constance, barely able to conceal her delight in the child.

"Aunt Maud did," says the child, croakily, her eyes on me, watchful for any response. Does she perceive my impatience, or has she not asked her aunt at all?

"There will be three of us, then!" Constance laughs, pats Olive's shoulder. "Follow me, bearers!" and she leads the way back to the bure to pick up our equipment.

Olive skips beside her while I follow slowly. How I would love to slip away and prevail upon the aunt to prohibit the girl from our journey. The prospect of raising Constance's ire is all that deters me from that course of action. She appears to believe our excursion will be all the sweeter for Olive's company, while I find myself unnerved by her. Olive is one of those children who watch the world for all its mists and ghosts, every detail.

One of the horses is to carry our heavier boxes, the other two to convey Constance and myself. Olive climbs up behind my friend, and the bearers, weighed down, follow on foot. Thus it is, by the time we are ready, that we depart in the heat of the day.

As I sit astride my half-wild mount I am grateful for Constance's early morning instruction to don my divided skirt. She insisted we ride bare-back. As she promised, it is a thrilling experience when one is unhindered by an acre of gabardine. Away in the distance, Bernard's cotton fields, the last in cultivation on the point, host the bent, fluttering bodies of coolie women. A sirdar lounges nearby, talking to a curious, spherical little man in a topi.

The Gow plantation gives way to Torte's. The latter's wealth shows in the fat cattle grazing among the orderly nut trees and the ornately twisted wrought-iron lamp posts beginning to rust among the roadside's lantana. The division between Torte's plantation and the next is obvious, the land reclaimed by breadfruit trees old enough to bear, and doing so. They say there is an exodus of Europeans from this colony, so perhaps this is one of the abandoned plantations.

In one place the road has given way to a freshet and we must pick our way through the gleaming boulders and stones to the beach. The muscles of my mount shift beneath me, my clever horse debates each and every step. Ahead of me Olive's arms are clasped around Constance's waist. As we reach the sand, she looks back and smiles. She excels at least in the gift for light travelling, coming downstairs as she did with a duffel bag containing little.

We remain on the beach until we reach Somosomo. The bearers call a halt and flop down beneath a spreading casuarina. We are in front of a small white church, which is almost overcome by a creeper. Its lush green tendrils traverse the stone at its girth, grasp the wooden weatherboards beneath its roof and reach for the steeple. Bracts of brilliant red lift their heavy heads, the small, white, cosseted flower within winks out. In the only stained-glass window, Jonah rides the whale, tossed on a froth of gleaming leaves. A great crack rents the door of the church, plugged by a muscular vein. I wonder how far it extends into the church, if at all.

To one side of the church a Chinese merchant's shop with drooping verandah, and bridles and seedsacks crowding the door, stands clear of the climber. It is as if the vine has chosen God's house for itself and would like to draw it back into the earth. I should like to sketch this curious phenomenon.

As I slip down the steep flanks of my horse, a familiar voice hails me. I turn to the steaming, smiling face of the Reverend's wife as she comes down the path from the vestry. Constance dismounts and sits among the bearers in the shade. Going with her, Olive lies flat on the ground tracing a heavenly body in the sky with a grubby finger. In the shade of Mrs Jamieson's lawn-encased bulk, three little native girls stand hand in hand. Traversing the air is the same peculiar odour of rubber, or is it burnt toast, that assaulted my nostrils on board the steamer. I sigh and long for the isolation of Kadavu. Mrs Jamieson is enquiring after my health and that of my hosts.

"They seem in as good spirits as you do yourself, Mrs Jamieson," I reply. The full sun makes me dizzy. Constance catches my eye, winks and takes a swig from her silver hip flask before resuming conversation with Atunaisa. The three little girls smile at me, but so dark their complexion and so bright the sun I can scarce make out their features. This marked contrast in the radiance of their faces and that of the day would make such a group impossible to photograph. They would have to be guided to an improvised studio of trees and blankets. Oh, if Johnny were here with his beloved camera and tripod, how he would utilise the moment . . . but he has entered my mind, crept out from the locked manrobe of my heart's luggage.

Behind the little girls, on slightly raised mounds trimmed with shells, stand three little crosses. Children's graves: companions in the afterlife for the three at Gow's estate. It is true, I see now, that Mrs Jamieson has a little of the pale, deranged martyrdom of Mrs Gow. I tell her our party is proceeding to Lake Tagimaucia.

"I have never been there myself," she says. Her voice originates in her chest, but seems oddly muted as if issuing from the groove of a wax disc. "My husband has. You see that vine that surrounds our church? He brought a seedling home from there — it has the most beautiful red flowers but is impossible to control."

"What is its name?" I ask, the untutored naturalist in me aroused. "It is very lovely."

"It has both a Fijian name and a botanical, but I am afraid I can't recall either."

The vestry door opens again and her husband emerges, stepping over a sinuous extension of the creeper. He brushes a red bloom away from his face and sneezes. At the sight of him, Constance rises and begins urging the bearers to do likewise.

"My dear," says Mrs Jamieson to her husband, as he draws near, "what is the name of the vine?"

The Reverend does not appear delighted to resume my acquaintance. His narrow eyes, almost swallowed by flesh, draw closer together, swimming in the sweat of his face like tiny fish.

"The vine?" he echoes. He sneezes again. One of the little girls follows suit, and Mrs Jamieson busily attends to her with a square of calico. I daren't even debate whether the cause of this catarrh is the pollen of the vine or the particles of influenza.

"Yes. Shouldn't you like to know also, Constance?" I seek help from my companion, who draws alongside holding Olive's hand.

This sight of intimacy brings a light stab to my heart. It is an enjoyable pain, if that is possible, at least it is not the dragging agony that followed Johnny's death. Less pain, perhaps, than challenge.

"Know what?" asks Constance. "Good day, Reverend."

"Reverend Jamieson," says that man. "You are?"

"Constance Prime-Belcher," says that lady, "Traveller and Naturalist." She holds out her hand. The Reverend looks at it, startled, and looks away. He clears his throat.

"The vine," he says, turning to look at the church, and his shoulders slump. "The Fijians here call it after the lake — Tagimaucia. Elsewhere it's tekiteki vuina or moceawa. It is a *Medinilla waterhousei*, of the Melastoma family . . . I pray to God for delivery from it."

He falls silent, and we all gaze at church and vine, which suddenly brings to mind mongoose and snake. The Reverend sighs, hugely.

"I made history with it," he goes on. "It's the only one of its kind to have been raised below an altitude of two thousand feet. God help me."

Mrs Jamieson is looking at her husband with concern. "Come along, Reverend," she says, "we have our patients to attend. The influenza, you know," she adds. "It is coming to the villages."

The bearers hoist their burdens, we make our farewells and take our mounts.

"Men of the cloth are all very well in their place — high in the Presbyterian pulpit — but they should not be allowed to roam the streets, least of all in Paradise," says Constance, when we are out of earshot.

"Reverend Jamieson is a Wesleyan," croaks Olive.

"Yes, my dear, I am aware of that." Constance laughs fondly.

"Are you a Presbyterian then, Constance?" asks the child.

"I have no faith but abiding affection for Mother Nature."

"Amen," I rejoin, for it is my creed also. There is no religion more profound than the love of all Her forms, Her flora and fauna.

It is cooler under the trees as we make our ascent. We will be hard pressed to make our destination by nightfall. I tip back my head to scan the leaf-framed sky. It is flecked with gold, and the bush around us is alive with bird song.

CHAPTER ELEVEN

Vale Ni Cula Laca

~ Hughie McNab ~

"Four men are lost when the ship rolls the lee yard-arm under."

All over Europe there is a laying down of arms and rejoicing. It is midnight, the eleventh of November and the news has just reached Suva. For a moment, at least, we can throw off our fears for the victims of the influenza, including my dear Adela, and give thanks. One of Fiji's own heroes, my son Tom, walks on one side of me, while Eddie and Bill flank me on the other. From the surrounding villas neighbours come spilling, women and men, native, European and Indian. At the end of Waimanu Road, we form an impromptu procession. One of the natives has a battered trumpet that he blasts with much vigour and verve. Tom takes my arm, and I see a tear glistening at the corner of his eye. He is thinking of Harry, no doubt, and the others he saw fall. Since Tom returned three months ago, he has spoken barely the words to fill half a page of a pocket notebook. It was Eddie and Bill who dragged him protesting from the room he once shared with Harry when the news came through. We all trooped through to Adela and kissed her, though she seemed scarcely to notice, and our affectionate display was probably foolhardy.

Victoria Parade is a carnival. The church bells are ringing

from all over town, motorcars creep slowly through the crowds tooting the horns, and on the harbour boats whistle. Though the War was far away, we lost sons to it. It filled our thoughts and fuelled our nightmares. Among the larger crowd our little procession breaks up. Tom's back is patted and he is congratulated from all sides. A group of young men from his battalion approach him and he is spirited away to the Grand Pacific, but not before I have tucked a few pounds into his back pocket. Let him go and drink — there has been precious little to celebrate these past few months.

Word goes through the crowd that a full procession will be held on Wednesday, together with addresses at the Town Hall. With the promise that the celebrations are not yet over, the throng disperses. I dispatch young Bill and Edward in the direction of home and make my way to the sailroom. It is all, of course, in darkness. I closed the doors to all incoming trade a week ago, due to the epidemic. Fred, my Rotuman foreman, has lost his wife and two of his children already. Passing through the office, I climb the narrow, steep stairs to the loft. Here the moonlight shafts through the tall windows, turning the hanging sails to shrouds. The long, low room is illuminated enough for me to make my way to the cupboard at the far end of the room where we stack the boxes of grummets and eyelets. There I locate my hidden bottle of whisky and glass.

Malt in hand, I perch on the windowledge and look about the room. Last New Year's Eve we held a ball here, for the Caledonian Society. Boxes of heather arrived by steamer from Scotland. Olive, dressed carefully by her mother in kilt and shawl, handed out nosegays to the guests. The Suva String Band played and Champak supervised the supper. It was a gay and successful occasion. Nearly all of Suva society was here: Mr Eric Emberson the boat builder; Mr Henry Milne Scott the barrister; Mr Howard Birkenhead Riley the dentist; Mr Christopher Sunderland the butcher, and Mr William Bayley who presides over the livery and bait store and stables . . . They were all here. And their wives. Them and more. Where are they now? Oh, that they were here! Mr Sunderland and Adela sang a duet, "Ireland Must Be Heaven For My Mother Came From There". Perhaps, already, the whisky makes me maudlin . . .

A sailhook glints, the sailmaker's third hand. It still has the sail attached to it, a round seam half sewn. On the floor, where Fred would have been sitting, lies Fred's fid. I get up to hold it, to take its warm, worn wood in my hand. The sail is for one of the native cutters. Another sail lies spread, ready for patching, a mainsail for one of the sugar schooners, a square-rigged beauty, the *Laura*. She lies at anchor still, three of her crew hacking on their sickbeds. I had young Bill at her sails. A roping palm, one I made for him specially, lies under a corner of it. The palm's metal cup is what gives it away, the puckered bowl of it twinkling in the moonlight.

A sudden rush of anger sweeps me and I swig on the neck of the malt. Sailmaking may not be the trade that whisks us further into the twentieth century, but it's a trade at least, for some of us a way of life. And the steamers still carry sails. The world will always need steamers. We are not reduced solely to the native trade. All is not lost, despite what Bill says.

I take a stool and needle, sit at Fred's hook, pull the sail to my left and continue his seam. I was apprenticed at twelve and can seam in the dark, especially with a malt inside me. With every stitch a step towards the hook, three stitches to an inch, with every stitch a wish for Adela to convalesce. I must be drunk. For Adela, I sew the strongest seam, the round seam, then take up my rubber to rub the seam flat. I've made a good job.

The unfinished sails of the *Laura* make my bed for the night. Propped on bags I drain the bottle before I sleep, and my thoughts drift and swell on a current of whisky, to the distant past and recent past and up the hill to where Adela lies drifting, remembering. Sometimes when I go through to her, she is like a girl again, the girl I rescued from a life on the stage. I know then she has been remembering those days, storing them up. Our tenderness at these times is as it was when we were first married.

As I drop to sleep tonight, it is not Adela's face that comes to me, but Keizo's. I haven't thought of him for years.

I am eighteen, able-bodied seaman to a British merchant navy ship anchored in Tokyo Bay. Japan is still closed to foreigners. We are not allowed ashore, and the natives of that land come on board with goods to barter. One afternoon a fight breaks out between a monolithic Scotsman with temper to match and one of the Japanese. The Scotsman throws the man overboard. The man, as we observe, can't swim. Neither can most of our crew. It is better not to be able to.

"Four men are lost when the ship rolls the lee yard-arm under," goes the adage. In high seas it is well nigh impossible to turn a square rigger to pick up a fallen man. Sailors would rather drown quickly than put up a fight and come slowly to Death's arms.

We rush to the brink of the ship and watch Keizo drowning. Various of my mates try to halt my disrobing and plunge to the autumnal tide below, but without success. Brought dripping to the deck I meet with scowls from the older crewmen and bowing and scraping from the man whose saviour I am. Solemnly, he follows me for the rest of the day, subjecting me to much ribbing from my fellows. It eventuates that having saved him from a watery grave, I am now responsible for his fate, according to his custom. He sleeps the night beneath my hammock and I wake to find him attending me with a mug of tea. When some of his trader compatriots arrive at noon, I get shot of him by bribing them to force him into their boat.

When we sail a week later, having made repairs and scrubbed the decks, Keizo sits alone in a small craft on Tokyo Bay. Paddling in our wake almost to the open sea, he stops and allows his boat to drift. He was returning himself to his destiny, allowing the sea to pick up again where it had left off.

Musings, half-asleep, on the subject of duty towards our fellow men, of fate brought about, do not conjure sweet dreams. I wake in a briny sweat at dawn, sick to the stomach and stumble home to my dying wife.

CHAPTER TWELVE

Camp

~ *Agnes Perkins-Green* ~

*B*efore Atunaisa assists us by converting a banyan tree to a private apartment, Constance delivers a brief dissertation on the merits of sleeping wrapped in a tartan rug, with only the stars for a ceiling. Atunaisa is sure that the lake's damp surrounds will make the dense, leafy bowers of the banyan more comfortable as the night draws on. As he rigs my curtain and locates the teapot, I sit by a kindling fire on the shores of this magical, green-hued lake to write my journal.

Forced last night to make uncomfortable camp in the bush, persecuted by giant moths and insects from the swamps of Hades, we rose before dawn to be on our way. I was comforted for a time by the nearby roar of the river and prior knowledge that this cataract proceeds from Lake Tagimaucia, our destination. At midnight, waking to more firmly secure my mosquito net, the river's song seemed to mock me though — so near, yet so far — so near, yet so far — so near, yet so far — it bubbled. My aching thighs and spine bade me wish I was a spawning salmon, leaping the falls . . . but this fantasy was interrupted by the shadow of Olive, coughing pathetically, as she crept to Constance's side.

The next morning I do believe Constance found my sulkiness

amusing. We met at the river's side, both returning to the camp after an uncomfortable and not altogether successful toilette. Constance's pith helmet had fallen from her head, pirouetted downstream and come to rest on a river stone. It was only just retrieved with the aid of a long stick. During this effort I had slipped in the mud and grazed my knee. The injury only served to blacken my mood further. Her warm smile soothing me as she spoke, Constance explained that Olive arouses her maternal instincts, which she undoubtedly possesses.

"And is it maternal also, the regard you have for me?" I queried.

"Not at all," replied my friend. "You give flight to my sensations of sororal love. That and perhaps a little more. Or less."

"Less?"

"Depending on the feeling one has for one's sisters," replied Constance. She loosened a wad of hair that had plastered itself low on her forehead, and smiled.

It is not like Constance to speak so cryptically. I must have appeared baffled or wounded or both. She took me briefly in her arms and kissed me sweetly on the cheek.

"Come," she said, "we must take some nourishment and be on our way."

We breakfasted briefly on ships' biscuit and sardines before taking our mounts. I took the lead, my horse clomping in the footsteps of Atunaisa, Viliame and Joni. The terrain being uneven and overgrown, we made slow progress. Olive amused us by reciting in her husky voice.

"*So lightly I played with those dark memories,*" she began, her arms around Constance's waist. I glimpsed back over my shoulder, and Constance's face seemed suffused with love.

"*Just as a child, beneath the summer skies,*
Plays hour by hour with a strange, shining stone . . ." prattled on the child.

"Who wrote that?" asked Constance, when she'd finished.

"I don't know," from Olive, "I read it on the beach, in the sand."

"It's 'One Day', by Rupert Brooke," I informed them.

"Did he die in the war?" asked Olive.

"Yes. He did." I didn't mean to seem abrupt with the girl, but I fear I did. Too much of Constance's attention is squandered on her.

"I saw his ghost," said Olive, conversationally, to Constance.

"Did you, dear?" Constance chose to humour her, but a dark chill ran down my spine. I urged my horse on a few feet ahead of them, then resumed my previous pace. Of the two of us, Constance is more the scientist and I the poet. Of course she wouldn't believe the child's story, but I can, with ease. Olive has the most watchful pair of eyes I have ever seen. Wide, violet, absorbing, they take in far more than Nature intended them to.

A goshawk crossed in front of us, swooping from the trees, grey and sinister. The Fijians stopped and pointed.

"Reba," said Joni. "Did you see, Marama?"

I nodded and bowed my head for a moment, wishing to dispel this sense of doom that had suddenly overcome me.

"*Accipiter rufitorques*," said Constance, catching up. "See the swiftlet bones."

To the side of the track lay fragments of wings and bones, remains of the goshawk's past repasts. The predator squawked at us from his lofty nest, side by side with his mate.

"On!" Constance instructed, and the bearers resumed their climb.

We took the last half hour to the lake on foot, the way too steep and unstable to remain on horseback. Everywhere proliferated the red flowers of the tagimaucia. As we made our descent to the crater, the tree hibiscus deepened their hue from morning's bright yellow to noon's apricot. My horse brushed up against a datura, setting the trumpet blooms swaying, heralding our arrival. It was another, lusher, Paradise we were breaching, although Paradise hard gained. Exhaustion weighted my every step, only just remaining secondary to my delight at having finally reached our destination.

Olive rushed straight to the lake, kicked off her boots and twirled in the shallows. Constance followed more slowly, quite ignoring me as I set about organising the bearers and our midday meal. My requests to Atunaisa for fish from the lake went unfulfilled, even though I knew the Fijian word: ika. He shrugged and held out his hands to me — how could he, he was asking, he had no lines. If his English was better I would have given him a speech about necessity being the mother of invention. As it was, I had to let it go.

Olive made another curious statement during lunch. Nibbling on her cabin bread, she suddenly said, "My father is happy today. Something has happened. I think the War is over."

This time Constance was stern with her. "Perhaps you are indeed one of us, Olive, an adventurer and writer. But for now, my dear, you must keep your fictions in check. Either that, or write them down. Would you have a spare notebook you could give her, perhaps, Agnes, dear?"

"Back at the Gow's estate," I replied stiffly. "One of us" indeed! Both Constance and I have had classical educations, which is more than can be said for young Olive, past or future.

Wrapped in Constance's rug, Olive sleeps now as I write. She and Constance spent the afternoon collecting blooms. Constance sits companionably by me, fixing the flowers in her sample box. The petals flop between her strong fingers like the wings of weary birds. Stamens leave her strong hands streaked with pollen: red, orange, yellow and purple; the hot colours of paradise. A short way off, Joni, Atunaisa and Viliame have made camp where they talk in muted, abrupt whispers. Perhaps the lake affects them, as it affects me. Its surface weighs heavy with floating vegetation, the water itself more overwhelmed by green than blue. It is ghostly, unearthly, especially as the sun dips down behind the trees.

Constance sighs and sets down the box. "Shall we bathe?"

"That would be most refreshing," I agree, realising that one of my dreams is about to come true. So as not to arouse any curiosity on the part of the natives, we remove our boots at the fireside and make our way soundlessly to the gravelly shore.

"This way," directs Constance, taking my hand and leading me further from the camp. Wax flowers and ixoras tremble among the candlebushes. Their reflected glory in the setting sun lights our way to a protected, private curve in the lake's shore. From the west comes the roar of water slipping over the lip of the lake to the river.

I am filled with a desire to remove every speck of sweated dust and to this end I disrobe entirely and loosen my chignon. As I step into the warm shallows my only covering is my long, shining hair.

"You are beautiful," comes Constance's voice from behind me, thick as malt elixir. "A Venus."

I turn to her. She is as naked as myself, and though we are of the same sex, two more different bodies you could not hope to compare. Where I am tall, narrow shouldered and sapling hipped, my breasts small and firm, Constance is broad in all aspects of her anatomy. Such a vision of strength, health and happiness I have never before beheld, even during my nursing of the varied physiques of the King's soldiers. Arm in arm, we enter the water and float together. Constance's thick, wavy hair rides the ripplets as she draws me close. My lips search her face for hers, her tongue active and wet below her tantalising moustache, while our legs entwine beneath the lake's surface. Such animality and softness in our kisses, a paradox of yielding flesh and thrusting passion — I gasp with desire and wonder. Her hands slip from my nipple to naval, from naval to my dark hair, wet and flashing in the moonlit froth of the lake like a seal.

At length, we find ourselves washed ashore, two exhausted naiads, a sobbing, sighing plait of womanhood. Before we disentangle to dress, our final kiss is all tenderness, all exigency soothed. Then, linked arm to waist, we return to our banyan tree, lie side by side on my tartan rug and sleep like nuns until dawn.

It is Atunaisa who wakes us.

CHAPTER THIRTEEN

The Tussock Throne

Olive, waking and finding herself alone, had also followed the shore of the lake away from the camp, but in the opposite direction to that taken by the Misses Prime-Belcher and Perkins-Green. There was no wind, the night was warm and moonlit. From inside her boots, Olive's toes reached carefully for each step on the small slippery stones. Once, close into shore, the surface broke with a watersnake's luminous stripes, then stilled again. Night birds muttered from the surrounding jungle. The cool night air filled her lungs of its own accord and where her steps hollowed the shingle at the water's edge, the tiny waves stretched to touch the flanks of her boots. As she went, Olive picked up pebbles and skimmed them across the lake. She was better at this than her brothers — her hands dry and strong and warm, her eye sure. After a spectacular series of leaps, seven and a half before the stone disappeared, the moon went behind a cloud. Olive felt the world draw back and realised that this particular night, with the Lucky Lunaria rounding her pocket and a likely skimmer flat in her hand, would be a perfect time for making a deal with Providence.

The perfect times were times like this, when she felt separate from everything, so separate that if an artist, Miss Perkins-Green for instance, was to draw her then she would be compelled to take up her widest nib and surround her with a thick outline in the blackest ink. Thus the world stood apart from her as Olive intoned:

"However many skips the stone makes will be the years Mother lives from tonight." She held the Lunaria in her right hand for the charm to work and hooked the forefinger of her strong left hand round the flat stone. There was no one here to see her using her left hand, no one to upbraid her for that deviant behaviour as they did at Suva Girls' Grammar. The stone flew out and skipped once — twice — three times, with a curious half twist at the end.

"Three years and a bit," thought Olive. "That's all right. I'll be sixteen. I'll be grown up."

The next stone she threw went twice as far, although with the same number of jumps. On its final landing there was a small rustling thud. Olive, peering into the gloom, saw the stone had landed on a floating wedge of grasses. The watersnake forgotten, she undid her boots, tied them round her neck and waded out. The water was at her waist by the time she reached the little island. It tipped alarmingly as she clambered aboard, but once up it was wonderful. It was like a damp, springy sort of raft. Moisture bubbled up between her toes. In the centre was a clump of tussocks. A kind of throne, thought Olive, for the Queen of the Lake. For me.

A light breeze sprang up and combined with the currents of the lake to blow and eddy Olive away from the shore. Rocking in her tussock throne, the island sometimes spinning round, some-times bobbing in what seemed like one spot, Olive grinned from ear to ear. She imagined the watersnakes and fish below her, the forests of lakeweed. Every now and then her raft bumped up against another, most of them too small to bear any weight at all.

Even a skinny Minnie like me, thought Olive. What a stroke of luck I found this one.

But then it occurred to her as she drifted close into shore again, not far from the camp, that her bottom was getting wet in

100

the tussock chair and that the island may not last for much longer. It was while she was considering the swim in and whether she should save her boots by hurling them ashore that a flash of white caught her eye. There was a leap of laughter, of women's laughter to be precise and more precisely Miss Perkins-Green's. Miss Prime-Belcher's sounded alto below it.

The two figures, naked, floated not twenty feet away. Olive flushed. They were playing some kind of game, something intimate and exciting, a game that by its splashings and guttural intonings excluded Olive. She hunkered further down in the tussock and shivered. The island seemed curious itself and drifted closer. From her hiding place, Olive made out the women's entwined arms and floating hair and saw the gasping connection of their mouths. As the grass wedge passed them by, they rolled ashore like cast-up fish. There was something melancholic in the sight, something that brought unheeded tears to Olive's eyes. The tears overflowed, dripped down her cheeks and into her mouth. While her gaze was fixed on the two white bodies, turned murmuring to one another on the sand, Olive extended a tongue and hooked up a tear as a frog does an insect. It surprised her. Why was she crying?

The partially submerged raft drifted on until it bumped up against a rock on the other side of the lake. Dawn saw Olive hugging her knees, wet and trembling, underneath a spreading tree. The night's voyage had left her sense of direction confused. Which way lay the camp? Olive was not even sure that she wanted to return.

Atunaisa would have preferred it if the two maramas had stayed beside their banyan but they insisted on helping. He dispatched one with Viliame and one with Joni and took the eastern shore himself. A scuffed, flat patch in the fine stones at the water's edge worried him. It was as if a struggle had taken place there, and no one knew what horrors this lake kept hidden. He called out the vavalagi girl's name. There was no answer. He proceeded on.

Too far away to hear Atunaisa's voice, Olive curled up in the sun. A vine she recognised as the same type as the one that enveloped the church at Somosomo graced a copse of nearby trees. While she slept, a red flower brushed her cheek.

*M*iss Perkins-Green, climbing a steep hill behind Joni, could not help but curse the girl. She had never known ecstasy such as the night before had held. It would have been pleasant to sit today and sketch. The subject of Constance herself would have been grand, now that she would have no trouble in capturing her loved one's true essence.

Joni was turning and descending.

"No good," he was saying, "no good."

"You mean, if she'd come this way we would have had evidence of that by now?" said Agnes.

Joni nodded, uncertainly. The lady spoke loudly, but that didn't help him to understand, necessarily. On the long walk back to camp, he wondered when he was going to be paid. As soon as he had the money he would go straight to Doctor Rickett's in Somosomo and get a cure for his son. He would pay him to ward off the influenza.

Viliame and Atunaisa not returned, Joni lay down under a tree to get some sleep. His night had been disturbed, owing to the eeriness of the lake and then by the maramas' return from a night swim. But this one, the pale one, here she was ordering him to stand up. She was above him, holding out her kettle. Joni pretended he was asleep and rolled over. Let her make her tea herself, if that's what she wanted.

Finding, with Viliame, Olive's footprints leading into the water, Constance feared the worst. Had she been a superstitious woman, more like Agnes, she thought, she might've suspected before that Olive was of morbid character. All that talk about a dead poet, ghosts and wordless long-distance communication with her father. Now it appeared as though the child had walked down to the lake and allowed it to take her away. Constance stared at the horizon with her hands on her hips. The sensation of Agnes's white neck beneath her mouth came unbidden to her mind. She dismissed it with an angry snort. It wasn't that Constance was given to guilt but more that the Irish woman in Oxford, England, whom the world knew as her housekeeper/secretary/companion was given to wild fits of jealousy. Also, Constance knew from experience that women like Agnes, recently bereaved and new to Sapphic love, did not gracefully fade away. She did not regret the night's sport in the least and admonished herself only for the sharp pang in her heart. It was the vision of Agnes's sweet brow that brought it on, also unbidden.

"Ridiculous," she said, aloud.

"Na cava?" asked Viliame.

"Nothing," muttered Constance.

Viliame shrugged. Constance felt the need for a nip, but she'd left the hip flask under the banyan tree.

"Shall we go on?" she asked.

"Sega." Viliame shook his head. "She went in here." He pointed again at the footprints.

"No point, I suppose," said Constance.

"No point," agreed Viliame.

At their approach to the camp, Constance's knees ached from the uneven ground, and Agnes ran gaily down to meet them. She kissed Constance's cheek.

"Have you found her then?" asked Constance, misinterpreting Agnes's smiling demeanour.

"What? Oh, no," said Agnes, taking her hand. "But Atunaisa will, I'm sure. Come and have some tea."

"Tea is not what I have in mind," grumbled Constance, but suffered Agnes pouring one for her anyway. At the generous dollop added to the cup from the hip flask, Agnes's perfect eyebrows rose almost to her hair, but she said nothing.

But perhaps, thought Constance, drinking deeply, perhaps those delicious lips are pressed just a little thinner. She sighed at her friend's wifeliness, if that's what it was, Agnes's immediate proprietorial instincts towards her lover. It is the most tiresome aspect about the love of females, thought Constance, squinting at the lake, the way they made their lovers responsible for every detail of their happiness or otherwise. Here I am disappointing her by having my morning tipple, God help me!

Before returning to their camp for a sleep, Viliame and Joni marvelled at the ability of English ladies to have a tea party under any circumstances.

*A*lthough at first she didn't recognise the sound, it was the hacking of a bush knife into wood that woke Olive. She seemed to have tumbled further into the bush. The sun, now high, was muted by the canopy of the trees. The lake glinted distantly through green leaves and red flowers. A soft breeze shifted the bloom above her head and dusted her brow with pollen. It appeared that during her sleep her feet, encased in damp boots, had become tangled in a vine. She tried to kick herself free. The boots slipped off but her legs were held fast. She attempted to sit up but found she couldn't. It was as if the arm of an affectionate friend held her ribs. It was the tagimaucia. It had crossed her upper arm, slipped its leafy point between the buttons of her dress, across her breast and through the fabric of her dress before plunging into the soil below her. Olive cried out. The vine tightened itself around her ankle like a restraining hand. At her ribs it gave a sudden squeeze, like a pulse, and forced the breath from her. Gasping to fill her lungs, her nostrils filled with the scent of the forest floor, that gentle decay.

The hacking again. A heavy metal blade ricocheted off a sinewed extension of the vine circling Olive's shoulder. She whimpered and twisted in the trap like a wounded bird.

There was Atunaisa, his reddened eyes peering down at her,

his face wet with fear. Throwing his knife down, he hauled at the vine. Great clumps of roots tore from the earth, scattering Olive's frock with rich, brown powder. Atunaisa threw her over his shoulder, slipped his knife into his belt and backing out of the jungle, as if he faced a mortal enemy, made his way back to the shore. On the other side of the lake, the fires of the camp smoked and mingled with the fleecy mist of the waters. He fixed his eye on them, and with the child heavy, ran. Upside-down on his back, Olive remembered her boots but kept quiet about them. She didn't like this place and neither, obviously, did the Fijians.

"Put me down now," she said to Atunaisa when he slowed, "I can walk now." Atunaisa put his hand on her shoulder.

"What happened back there," he said urgently, "you don't tell the maramas. Nobody."

"Why not?" asked Olive. She swallowed and remembered her throat still hurt. On return to Aunt Maud's she would stay in her room and read books. Uncle Bernard had all of Henry Rider Haggard.

"Kalou," said Atunaisa. He bowed his head.

Gods, or spirits, thought Olive, powerful enough to tangle me in vines, shorten my breath and put Providence in the shade.

"Did they want me to die there?" she asked.

Atunaisa nodded, and Olive imagined how Aunt Maud would deal with this situation. "Nonsense," she would say, and stride ahead.

"Nonsense," said Olive, and strode on. Atunaisa followed, but his stride was longer. That, and the fuel of his slow anger with the arrogant child meant he overtook her easily.

Half an hour later, Constance shifted from her held pose at the sight of Atunaisa rounding the curve of the shore. A smaller, bedraggled figure in a tattered dress followed.

"Constance!" snapped Agnes, then pleaded, "Just a moment longer."

Constance glanced back at Agnes and noted fondly a bruise of India ink on her chin.

"As you wish," she said, "but you must hurry. Here comes Atunaisa with the errant Olive."

Agnes's brush flew. She made the finishing strokes just as Constance left her shooting stick to wrap the grubby girl in her arms. Olive struggled free and glared at her.

"I want to go home," she said. "To Aunt Maud's."

"Yes," agreed Atunaisa, "home."

"Nobody asked your opinion," Agnes said, coldly, taking her brushes down to rinse in the edge of the lake.

Olive suffered Constance's warm arm around her damp shoulders as the Fijians began to break camp. Constance knew better than to argue with them, even though it meant another uncomfortable night's camp on the trek to Gow's estate.

Returning with her gleaming sables and a wet hem, Agnes had her lips pressed together once more. In high dudgeon, she adjourned to the banyan and resolved, while folding her mosquito net, to make for the intimate solitude of Kadavu as soon as possible.

"Are you all right?" Constance asked Olive. "What happened, dear?"

There was such concern in her deep voice that Olive's eyes filled with tears. "Nothing," she said, "I just got lost."

Her curiosity not satisfied, Constance bent her ear to the muttered Fijian of the bearers.

"I-talanoa?" she asked. "What story? Viliame? Talanoa cava?"

But Viliame turned his back and went to fetch the horses. Olive gathered up her duffel bag and its contents and waited by the sputtering fire for departure.

CHAPTER FOURTEEN

This Patriotic Little Colony

~ Hughie McNab ~

*H*aving ensured that Adela will be as comfortable as possible and that Elena will attend to her throughout the day, I go to fetch Tom from his room. He's lying on his bed, in full uniform, holding Harry's photograph.

"Take it with you, son," I say gently. "Put it in your pocket. Then he'll be there, too. In a manner of speaking."

He's looking so much older, my son Tom. His tall frame is a little bent and there's grey hair at his temples now. He was always a serious boy but the War has aged him, accelerated him past his twenty-four years. Adela is thirty-five and they seem as peers. Tom and I smile at each other, remembering Harry, remembering the life of him. Once, at fifteen years of age, he went to Bua to measure up a cutter for new sails. It belonged to some natives there. They wouldn't let him go. By the time I arrived, enraged at his tardiness, they'd built him a bure and found him a native wife. Harry was as good as the Fijians at "keeping the wide grin", which is probably why they loved him so. But he was a lazy sod with too much of the beachcomber in him. That came from my mother Minnie's father — a useless cove if there ever was. There. I won't be one for turning either the youthful or elderly dead into saints.

Thunder booms above the house. Tom twitches, his hands grasp at the blanket. Then the rain falls, heavily on the tin roof, and he relaxes.

"Come on, Tom." I keep my voice soft. "Let's go. Eddie and Bill are waiting on the verandah."

Sitting on Eddie's knee in the wicker chair, and not wishing to be left, is little Rosie. I am against taking her, especially in such weather, but Tom will not deny her anything.

"Of course," he says. He runs to the back of the house, to the kitchen, and is back in no time with the oilcloth from the table. We tuck her up in the pram with it. All the way down Waimanu Road she peers out at us, hugging her knees, as dry as a chick in a nest. Women would never be as inventive.

A bustling, noisy crowd pushes through the Town Hall doors. Many of the wives, observing that I have sole charge of five-year-old Rosie, shake their heads in sympathy. One of Adela's fellow members of the Ladies Hygienic Mission tries to relieve me of her, but the child gives such a screech I ask the lady to replace her in her pram.

"You're making a rod for your back," whispers Mrs McWhannell in my ear, "letting a wee bit of a lass like that tell you what's what."

Tom takes leave of us and joins the other returned servicemen at the stage door. In the end we leave Rosie's pram under the overhang of the grand verandah, and Eddie carries her as we force our way through to the European section. The Indians, Chinese and Fijians are seated at the back with a distant view of the Governor. Already they have surrounded themselves with orange peel, sweet wrappers and gobbets of spittle. It is precisely this sort of spectacle that has upset Adela since her arrival.

Suddenly, a trumpet blasts and all eyes turn to a native in full livery from waist up, and sulu from waist down. He gives his instrument vent once more, then the crowd rises and cheers the Governor, his wife Mrs Rodwell and a spotty young man from the Colonial Office. After them come the famous Ratu Sukuna, magnificent in his French Foreign Legion uniform, Captain McFaddy, several riflemen from the King's Royal Rifle Corps, uniformed officers from the Navy and some of the Fiji boys who fought with the Australians and New Zealanders. Some of the poor sods are still bandaged. One of the members of the New Zealand Imperial Force is accompanied by a nurse. He sits in a bathchair and stares vacantly around like a simpleton. I don't recognise him, the war has changed him so much. Just as I draw breath to ask Eddie who the boy is, or was, Mrs Austin-Roy, becomingly draped in a Union Jack, takes her seat at the piano. We all stand for the national anthem, sung with gusto by the Europeans and Fijians.

"*Santa Victorious, Happy and Glorious!*" we sing. Looking about at all the shining, merry faces, I feel such a surge of joy, the first since Adela took to her bed. To my shame tears prickle at the back of my eyes. While I wipe my face, pretending the mopping is for perspiration, the Governor, who is a squat man, steps up to the lectern. The upright has been shortened, I notice, by a good foot, to accommodate his limited stature. He clears his throat and begins.

"We are assembled today to celebrate the conclusion of the Armistice with Germany. It is a little unfortunate the day is not a finer one, but I think it would take a good deal more than the rain to dampen our enthusiasm."

The terms of the Armistice follow, read by the younger member of the Colonial Office who does not suffer from the Governor's asthmatic wheezing. Each of the terms are greeted with loud cheering. As the younger man draws to the end, the older draws a deep breath, mops his brow for the humidity and loosens his starched collar.

"I think you will all agree with me," continues his Excellency, "that the terms are pretty good. I think it means the end of Germany as we have known her."

Further cheers.

"It means that all these years of weary struggle have ended in an overwhelming victory for our arms."

Further cheers, at which little Rosie extends the victory fist. Those around us chuckle.

"They have ended in the colossal ruin of a system which was based on greed and ambition, which was built up with blood and tears and which was designed for the terrorisation and enslavement of mankind. It still remains to be seen what punishment is in store for those responsible for the outrages and brutalities which the enemy has continued up to the last moment. The ex-Kaiser —"

At the mention of this deluded fiend the crowd erupts. Hats are thrown into the air. A hail of green-skinned oranges descend from the native section. The Governor seems glad of the pause and mops his face again. Among the other war-heroes on the podium, Tom allows himself a small smile. The crowd subsides and the Governor continues.

"The ex-Kaiser and his gang of accomplices are reported to have fled just as rats flee from a sinking ship. Their pride has been humbled to the dust, and a lesson unexampled in the world's history has been meted out to those misguided masses who have been drilled and driven to their doom."

This brings on such a cacophony of joy in the hall that poor Rosie begins to howl. Eddie jiggles her in his arms.

"Let us therefore celebrate this Armistice, which appears to all intents and purposes to be the end of the war, with pride in our soldiers and sailors and with thanksgiving to Almighty God. In our rejoicing, let us remember those who have suffered *"Lest we forget."*

At this the men on stage bow their heads. Ratu Sukuna folds his hands in his lap. Physically he is not a big man, although he somehow dwarfs his white brothers on the stage. He has the bearing and presence of a noble warrior. His very name must've terrified poor Fitz out of his wits.

"Nothing is too grand for those fellows who fought for us, and when the time comes to celebrate their return, this patriotic little colony will not be backward in showing its appreciation and gladness. The Kaiser was the greatest autocrat the world has ever seen, he caused the war, and now he has gone, and gone for ever more."

The Europeans shout "Hooray", the Indians "Jai", the Fijians "Vinaka" and the Chinese indulge their talent for the ear-splitting whistle. The officials and heroes stand amidst the racket and file out to take their places at the head of the procession. Still cheering, the crowd begin to take their leave too. From out on the Parade, the Suva Brass Band is already in the beginning strains of "Rule Britannia".

CHAPTER FIFTEEN

Boxes Upstairs

The return of the Tagimaucia travellers was scarcely noticed in the rush to get to Tortes at Vuna Point by six o'clock, in time for the celebrations. The travellers had made slow progress. Soon after setting out on the journey's second morning, one of the horses had torn a tendon on the downward incline. When Joni's rhythmic encouragements with the stick grew harsher and drew blood, Constance had felt it necessary to put herself between man and lame beast, but the horse, accustomed as he was to more persuasive methods, did not respond to her gentle words. He stopped every few steps and hung his head. Joni, walking ahead of the rest, also gazed surlily at the ground they passed over. Well before the track reached the flat, he stopped at the side to await the horse bearing the maramas Perkins-Green and McNab. He stepped out before them.

"I want my pay," he said. "Vinaka."

Agnes shot Constance an agonised look. Had they not agreed, before departing, on two shillings apiece for the bearers, but only on condition they completed the journey?

"I go that way," Joni pointed through the trees. From high on the uninjured horse, Olive could see sunlight breaking through and a clearing. It was the village Sitiveni had taken her to.

"Very well," said Constance. In the drawstring purse that hung from her belt, she dug for the two shiny silver coins that were Joni's. He took them in one smooth palm, closed over his fingers and then made off.

"He moves so quietly through the bush," mused Miss Perkins-Green, her head to one side, listening. For a moment it was his retreating footsteps she heard, then silence, then the beginning rain.

$\mathcal{A}$fter drenching the procession that followed the Governor's Address in Suva, the very same cloud had flown north to the Windward Islands. When it struck the mountain that cradled the lake, the cloud broke. Within minutes the narrow forest path became a shallow, turbulent stream of mud, leaves, bones and twigs. Huddled under the brim of Agnes Perkins-Green's hat, Olive avoided the worst of it. Miss Perkins-Green, her weather-side rain-lashed, listened to the cacophony of rain on leaves and suffered a tightening of Olive's arms. Constance, now leading the injured horse and still at the rear of the party, took advantage of the jangle of the storm to uncap her flask and take a secret, warming swig.

At four-thirty they passed through the gates of the Gow Estate and paid off Viliame and Atunaisa. The rain had not lessened in the intervening hours, and the two lady travellers did not need much persuasion from Maud to make use of the bath. Maud herself had just bathed and was feeling still moist and vaguely uncomfortable in her mauve artificial silk. She was determined to wear it to the festivities, however. After this business with the coolie boy, she had to put on her best face. A letter had arrived that morning setting a date that was frighteningly close for her court appearance.

"Forgive me, Mrs Gow," said Agnes, as they made their way along the verandah. "Is that a new dress?"

"It is," said Maud. "The latest cut. It came on the last ship from New Zealand."

Agnes privately considered that the effect of the outfit was rather ruined by the smeary lawn shawl Maud had draped around her shoulders, quite concealing the empire neckline. Perhaps she'd made the addition to protect the dress from possible ravages inflicted by the fruit bat. Its little bright eyes regarded Agnes and Constance with a curious, all-knowing expression, as their hostess held the bathroom door open.

The bathroom was not so much a room as part of the verandah closed in, across the yard from the washhouse. Ah Jack and one of the Indian house servants were refilling the clawfoot tub, bucket by bucket.

"You will not want to sleep in the bure in this weather, surely?" Maud enquired of her guests, as the rain thundered on the iron above their heads.

"I would appreciate a dry night, certainly." Agnes had a sudden longing to hold Constance close in linen sheets, to kiss those full lips among feather pillows. She blushed. Constance noted her sudden colouring and gave her such a knowing, masculine smile that Agnes was filled with urgency, a sensation that bordered on panic.

"Whatever you would like my dear," Constance murmured at the one who loved her. The lilt of her housekeeper's voice chimed a warning in her mind's ear, as it did when her indiscretions threatened to take on meaning. Constance ignored her but suspected sadly that love such as she and Agnes had thrilled to in the gleaming waters of the lake would not be repeated.

"I had your trunks and boxes taken upstairs," Maud told them. "Come. I'll show you."

As their hostess turned away, Agnes took her lover's hand and squeezed it, once, twice and would have thrice had not Constance pulled it away and given her a warning glance. Such stern vigour only served to inflame the fires in the younger woman's belly. Quiet and pale, she followed Constance and Maud up the stairs, holding her wet skirts away from her legs. The room was next to Olive's, but thankfully the child was nowhere to be seen. Maud sensed the travellers were keen to gather dry garments to don after their baths. She began her farewells.

"Oh," she said, at the door, "please — if you would like to accompany Mr Gow and myself to the Armistice celebrations at Vuna Point, you are most welcome. We're leaving in an hour."

"My God!" said Constance, as soon as the door was shut. "The child was right. The War has ended." Agnes sunk to the bed, her eyes filling. The War was over, the world was full of promise and light and warmth. She held her arms up to Constance, who came and kissed her.

"Help me off with my damp things," she said, undoing the mother-of-pearl button at her neck.

"*I'll* get in, shall I, Ah Jack?" asked Olive, appearing in the steam like a spectre and giving him such a fright he almost dropped the twin pails that bent him double. Olive leaned over the edge of the bath. She was shivering and her throat had resumed its throbbing in earnest.

Ah Jack peered at the child. He remembered her from her previous visits, robust and at least as mischievous as her brothers. Since the incident with the bone she'd been a funny colour. Perhaps a bath would do her good. He nodded and the girl immediately began to disrobe. He emptied his buckets and left, Olive's white back and buttocks flashing like a fish at the corner of his eye. Usually white girls were full of shame about their bodies. It was curious, something the women taught the girls. He wondered who would teach Olive. It wouldn't be Mrs Gow. When he'd heard of the children's impending visit, Ah Jack had thought it wise to increase his employer's dose. It was the lady's wont to visit the babies' gravesides, usually at night, and howl at the sky like a dog. Ah Jack, or sometimes Mr Gow himself, would go and lead her back to the house. That was frightening enough, even when there was no company in the house. As he guided her through the cane toads squatting on the lawn, Ah Jack's heart would thud against his ribs in fear of what the lady may have roused from the dead. He had wanted to save the children from such a sight, and an extra two or three grains of laudanum seemed to have done the trick.

After her cold night on the lake and damp sleep in the bush, Olive's bath was blissful. She hoped the Misses Perkins-Green and Prime-Belcher would find something to distract them. The steam rose to the iron roof, curling through the cobwebs and licking at a lizard, who scuttled away behind a beam. Olive held her breath and slid beneath the surface. Her ears filled with water, her dark curls floated above her eyes, all was warm and muffled and the opening door escaped her notice.

"However long I stay underwater is the number of days I have to stay at Aunt Maud's. One, two, three, four . . ." Olive bargained with Providence.

A banging on the iron wall of the bath sounded strangely far away, and yet inside her bones at the same time. Bursting out of the water, she was confronted with the fierce visage of Grandmother McNab. The old woman lifted her cane from where it had been leant against the bath and made as if to strike Olive on the head.

Olive yelled "No!" so loudly that the iron above their heads rang and rumbled. Grandmother's yellow eyes rolled upwards and seemed to vibrate in time with the roof. Olive watched her carefully.

"Now," said Minnie McNab, when all that could be heard were the squeezeboxes of the cane toads. "What do you think you were doing gallivanting off up the mountain with a mob of hussies and savages? And where are your boots?"

Olive, meditating on how best to answer without enraging, reached for the soap in its wire basket. The cane reared, a black blurr. Olive's hand plunged safely to the water. Grandmother leaned over the bath, and the steam curling round Olive's nostrils took on that familiar cargo of peppermint and yeast and gin.

"You take off like that again, Missie, and I'll have Bernard take the coolie whip to you."

"He wouldn't," Olive momentarily forgot her vulnerability in the bath, "even if you asked him."

"Ralph's in the parlour with him now." Grandmother was smug. "He's been causing trouble as well, down at the Lines."

At Olive's wide-eyed horror, the old woman laughed. "I expect Bernard will punish him soundly. You McNabs've never had a firm hand."

Olive removed her eyes from Grandmother's bleary ones and wondered if she was hearing the truth. The truth was something Grandmother never let get in the way of a good story. She closed her eyes and leant back.

"Open your eyes," said Grandmother.

"I'm tired." She was also, Olive realised, ravenously hungry. Grandmother was turning, carefully on the wet floor. Olive knew this from the pop and smack of the cane's rubber sucker.

"I'd like a sandwich in bed," Olive said to Grandmother's retreating back.

The lady gave out a short, scoffing exhalation and went out, slamming the door after her.

"If Mother was here she would get me a sandwich from the kitchen and bring it up to me herself and sit beside me while I ate," said Olive to herself.

Actually, this was not a kindness that Adela had extended to her fourth child and first daughter, but there had been other moments of tenderness Olive was sure, if only she could remember them. After little Rosie was born, ever since then, for a long time, Mother had been pale and sad and hot.

There was the sound of Uncle Bernard's Packard being brought round to the front of the house. Olive put her eye to a knot-hole in the thin walls. The rain had stopped, but the leaves and shrubs surrounding the carriage-way gleamed and dripped. Arm in arm on the steps stood Grandmother and Aunt Maud.

Both were smiling at Uncle Bernard who was full of whisky and acting the goat, opening the rear door of the motorcar and bowing low. The driver, who had got out of his seat to perform that part of his duties, got back in again. He watched the two memsahibs in the wing mirror, leaning together like banana trees after a hurricane. Mother and daughter made their way laughing to the comfort of the red horse-hair seat.

Eric appeared in the light of the door. A smaller figure cowered behind him, and Olive saw that it was Ralph. Both brothers were scrubbed and starched, hair slicked back with pomade. The little one's arms were crossed in front of his jacket and his gaze fastened on the back of his brother's knees. When he moved again, this time in response to Grandmother's waving arm from the Packard's open door, it was slowly, as if in pain. Grandmother had been telling the truth after all. Ralph crept to the car and climbed in to perch on the dicky seat. With another low bow, Uncle Bernard closed the door.

Olive sank back into the cooling water, feeling sick. Through wood and tin, Uncle Bernard's voice boomed: "The gentlemen will walk. What ho, eh, Eric?"

There was the thump of fleshy hand on slender back and a silent acquiescence. The motor pulled away, then stopped.

"Bernard!" Grandmother's voice. "Make sure Ah Jack remembers he is to bring Olive when he brings the fire-crackers."

"Rightio," from Bernard, then in tones of recrimination and surprise, "The guests! Maud, you forgot the two ladies —"

Maud's voice now, soft, more slurred than usual, "I knocked at their door three times to no reply, my dear, so I can only assume they are sleeping."

For a second time, the door was closed and the engine died away on the road.

The bath was almost cold. Olive got out and realised as her feet hit the clammy floor that she had no towel. Fijian children, she had observed, ran around in the air to dry themselves after a swim. She would do the same. She would run from here to her room, through the kitchen, across the hall and up the stairs. To ensure she would encounter no one on her flight, she fished her filthy dress from a puddle and took the Lucky Lunaria from the pocket. Having first checked the verandah, she ran full tilt, stone in hand, and burst through the fly-screen into the kitchen. It was empty, the staff having been given the night off to celebrate the Armistice. The hall, though still lit, was uninhabited. Her long legs took the stairs two at a time, carried her across the landing and into her room in seconds, breathless, excited and almost dry.

$\mathcal{V}$ishnu held the door and stood aside while young Sahib and the two memsahibs, the daughter drugged and the mother drunk, made their way out of the motorcar. The boy spied a group of children playing beyond the gathered Fijians on the lawn and ran off without a backward glance. Gazing up at the splendour and transformation of the Torte mansion, the memsahibs slumped back against the Packard's bonnet. Red, white and blue electric lights gleamed from both upstairs and downstairs balconies. From the flagpole flew not only the Union Jack as she always did, but also, below it, the flags of France and Belgium. A table offering scones, club sandwiches, pots of tea and an enormous bowl of mint julep was set beneath a bower of palm leaves. The European guests milled around it, both the women and the men in starched festive white. Gathered on the lawn in neat rows and two divided masses were the coolies and natives. Sitiveni and one of the Torte boys walked the gap, keeping the waiting throng quiet.

"Well!" said Minnie McNab. "Old Hortense always was a show-off."

"Come along, Mother." Maud took her mother's arm and led her away from the line of motorcars towards the refreshments. The crowd at the table — the Reverend and Mrs Jamieson, Father Terrien and Father Lejeune from the church on Waiyevo, Mrs

Stone with her knitting bag, planters, overseers, a tradesman or two, their wives and daughters — all fell quiet at their arrival. The young Mrs Moffatt, recently married in Sydney to the constable, hid her nervous smile but failed to conceal a nervous giggle. Minnie pulled up short and met every stare, one by one.

It was many years since she'd experienced this kind of public derision. There was a moment when she was at a loss as to what had brought it on. True enough, there were a few old Fiji families who remembered her youthful profession, but many of these assembled faces belonged to new chums. Then she remembered, just as Maudie's eyes filled with tears: Maudie's little accident with the shard of crystal. Minnie's mind raced.

"The planters among you treat your coolies worse than dogs," she said. "It was just my girl's bad luck that the coolie inspector visited the day after it happened." She looked up into all their mocking eyes and continued, "Go and boil your ugly heads." Mouths dropped and the crisp backs retreated.

"Those that mock invite shock," Minnie noted with pleasure to her daughter. She lifted a ladle of julep to her nose and took a sniff. Gin, and lots of it. The pale-green liquid filled one cup, and another for Maud. Minnie regained Maud's arm and led her firmly past the rabble on the chairs, up the steps to the verandah. Seated there, in her bathchair, was old Horte: the thinnest, most discomforting spectacle Minnie considered she'd ever beheld.

"Dysentery for a decade, that one," she hissed at Maud.

"Shshsh!" said Maud, but her mother had pulled away and was greeting Hortense Torte like an old friend. The hand empty of julep grasped a bony claw.

"Hortense, my dear," she was saying, "we're all so glad you're still with us to see the end of the War."

The diamond tiara atop the greying curls trembled with orange and yellow lights in the setting sun and the pale lips parted. Minnie bent her head but no words issued forth. From two seats away, Alphonse Torte leaned across and removed the old whore's hand from his mother's. Minnie glanced at him. He was too much like his father was as a young man — raven haired, strong chinned, arrogant of eye — not to be a whore-monger himself. His snooty wife — nose so far up in the air it'd make a two-roomed nest for a honeyeater — well, she couldn't hold a man's attentions. Unperturbed, Minnie examined her old rival. All was not well. A ball of spittle rolled down her chin and her head slumped forward. The tiara slipped, its diamonds shivered.

"Mother!" Maud broke her concentration. "Here!"

There were several empty chairs at the end of the verandah, placed there for the European children who were, at this moment, nowhere to be seen. As Alphonse glared and stood to prop his mother up with cushions, Minnie stepped over unfriendly legs to her daughter, shaken to her soul. The fiendish beast beneath her skirts took its cue and nipped and burned worse than ever. She took Maud's hand.

"If ever I am like that," she said, "no more sense in my head than a cocoa-nut — I want you to stick me in a dinghy and push me out past the reef."

"Oh, Mother!" Maud's nose dripped. "Don't speak of such things."

And neither could she, just at that moment, for Doctor Ricketts had stood to begin the speeches. There was an instant hush as Constable Moffatt stepped up, clicked his heels and handed the doctor a loud hailer. He projected it towards the Fijians.

"Sara qaqa na mataivalu ni Peretania," he told them. "Sara vakadrukai na kai Jamani." Turning then to the Indians, he addressed them in Hindustani. No sooner had he finished than the residents stood behind him, and accompanied by a mammoth Fijian with a battered tuba and his small son with a trumpet, most of the assembled sang the National Anthem. Some of the coolies knew the words but most didn't. They formed lines and danced.

CHAPTER SIXTEEN

Alabaster Queen

$\mathcal{C}$oming downstairs in her white church frock, which had been washed and pressed by the laundry-wallah, Olive pulled up short. There, on the carved hall seat with a wooden crate on the floor between them, sat two Ah Jacks. Their faces were identical in every way, even to the length and density of the wispy beard clinging to each identical chin. She frowned and stood before them.

"Miss Olive," said Ah Jack before she could start with her questions, "this is my brother, Ah Sam."

The two men stood. Ah Jack's brother wore a silk jacket and had a plait. He smiled broadly.

"And what have you got there?" asked Olive.

"In here," said Ah Jack, tapping the box lightly, "are the crackers Ah Sam made in his Suva Emporium. We must take them up to the Torte's. Come along."

The box slung between them on its rope handles, the brothers beckoned for Olive to follow them. With Ah Jack's bandy legs and poor swollen feet, progress was slow. As they neared the end of the Gow's carriage-way, Olive's stomach rumbled and she said, "Will there be food, Ah Jack?"

Both brothers nodded in reply, too weighed down to find words.

Among the roadside lantana grew little furry-mouthed

flowers. Olive touched one of the green petals and the flower slammed shut. It gave her a lovely feeling on her fingertip. She poked another, and another, and another. When she looked up, Ah Jack and his brother had drawn a little further along the road. As they stumbled through mud and knee-deep puddles, they seemed to have forgotten her. Olive debated the strength of her hunger and poked at another furry lip. It curled closed over her nail like a kiss. She pulled it free and ran to catch up.

"When are we having the fire-crackers?" she asked.

"After the pudding," sighed Ah Jack, his old chest bent level with the road.

"I'm very strong you know, Ah Jack," said Olive. "Let me have a try."

The brothers put the crate down, and Olive immediately grasped the handle.

"No, no," Ah Jack was panting, "we are just making a whistle-stop." His arms hung at his sides.

Olive made an attempt to lift the box. Every muscle strained and stretched, her eyeballs grew dry in their sockets. The corner of the box lifted infinitesimally and Olive farted. Red with shame, she stared at the toes of her scuffed Mary-Janes, but neither of the old men made any response. It was then, when she felt brave enough to lift her eyes, that the woman among the lantana allowed herself to be seen.

She was European, in a long white nightgown streaked with mud. Her hair, rough as a horse's tail, curled unkempt to her waist. She looked strong and squat, like a pony. A broad mouth spread into a grin, dividing a face so large it seemed to have been attached to the wrong body. Olive smiled back. With a ferocious jerk, the woman brought her finger to her mouth and shook her head.

Was Providence having a joke, Olive wondered? More spectacles were sent at sunset than at any other time. She closed her fingers around her Lucky Lunaria, but the woman remained among the bushes. Giving Olive a wicked grin, she bent down and put all ten of her fingers into the open furry mouths of ten flowers, all at once.

Ah Jack nodded to his brother. Once again they took up their burden and stumbled on. The box, Olive could see, was bumping up against their thin, black-trousered legs, barking their shins. She looked back to where the woman had been and startled. Silent as a cat, the woman had come down on to the road and was standing just behind her, breathing softly. She giggled, and it seemed to Olive that the giggle was as out of place with the rest of her as her head was. It was a baby's giggle, the giggle of a baby younger than Rosie. Olive's eyes travelled up the woman's nightgown, from her large breasts to her thick neck, to the massive face, level with hers. One of Uncle Bernard's eyes looked down at her: the blue one. In place of his brown eye, the lady's other eye was green. When she spoke, her voice was like his too, loud and deep.

"You're Olive," she said, "and you've got my ayah." A frown creased her fleshy brow and she grasped Olive's arm in a gesture as rapid as the one that had pleaded for silence. "You've got my Margaret."

"No — not me," Olive's arm was hurting, "my brother Ralph."

"Your brother?" The hand loosened. "You tell my Margaret to come back to her Elvira."

Olive nodded, and Elvira let her hand thud back to her thigh.

"Come on." Elvira suddenly ran off, crashing back through the lantana and hibiscus towards the cocoa-nut plantation of Torte's estate. If I let her run on, perhaps she'll forget me, thought Olive. But Elvira turned and called, "Hurry up, slowcoach!" and, waiting for her, swirled around a young cocoa-nut palm, holding on to the trunk with one hand. Olive ran after her then, her legs splattering with mud. When she drew level with Elvira, Elvira ran too, but not so fast as to outstrip her. There was such a revelling in her heart with every strong-footed step, every swish of her thigh beneath the gown.

When Olive cast her eyes sideways, she realised she'd never before seen a woman's body move in this way: breasts swinging unrestrained, buttocks jiggling. Elvira's whole squat skeleton lifted with each step. The wind lifted her thick hair and the force of her breath sounded like surf on the reef.

At the brink of the Torte's lawn, they stopped short. A group of Fijian children playing by the fence looked up. They seemed to know Elvira, or at least she held no curiosity for them, and they went back to their game. Olive sniffed at the aroma of baked meat on the warm breeze and gazed at the Torte's mansion, lit up with coloured lights.

"Let's go and spy," whispered Elvira with one of her strange giggles.

"No." Olive, tired and hungry, was puffing. Dinner would be served by now. There would probably be a special children's table, weighed down with good things and attended by chokras, just like the grown-ups. She began making her way to a gap in the fence not far away, but the vice of Elvira's large hand was back on her upper arm. Along the rim of the homestead they ran, behind the outhouses. At the steps to the verandah, Elvira once again gave her signal for silence, before they crept along the verandah. The French door at the very end had a gap in the heavy curtains that allowed them a glimpse of the dining-room.

Olive had expected something quite grand, at least as grand as the dining-room at Gow's and she wasn't disappointed. The electric lights had been switched on because, although it was not nearly dark outside, the velvet drapes blocked out all the light. The matchlined walls of dakua gleamed around an immense, crowded table. Luckily, Grandmother McNab, Aunt Maud, Uncle Bernard and Eric sat away from the window, with their backs to them. There was no food yet, but at either end of the table, in large trays on the damask, were Union Jacks, perfectly executed, in flowers.

"Them orchids are white," said Elvira, loudly. "How'd they get them red and blue?"

"They sit them in bowls of ink," Olive told her, having seen similar efforts in the Red Cross Exhibition on Suva Grand Gala Day. She pointed to the ceiling. "Look!"

A punkah of French flags swung there, setting the feathers on the ladies' hats waving.

"Look what?" asked Elvira, peering.

"That's the flag of France," Olive told her.

A chokra by the door sounded the gong, and all seventy sweating diners looked up. In navy blue cummerbunds and white gloves, four Torte servants came through from the cookhouse bearing outsize platters of meat. First came a cluster of beef roasts, then a grove of mutton legs, then a litter of suckling pigs, followed by a brace of ducks. Other chokras followed, some in the maroon cummerbunds of the Gows, some in yellow or green. They bore loads of vegetables and salads. Olive's stomach groaned painfully. She experimented with a tiny step away, but the mad woman's instincts for desertion were finely tuned. Quick as a startle, she took Olive's arm before turning and galloping away. As they flew past the windows, surprised diners parted the curtains by a chink — it was as if a horse were running the length of the verandah. Such was Elvira's speed that the most any of them caught was the hem of a grey nightie and the heel of a horned foot.

Between the cookhouse and the pump, a trestle table had been set up, bowed with food and surrounded by hoards of hungry children, Indian, Fijian and European. Elvira didn't pause. From among the children, Ralph raised a chicken leg to his mouth and munched on it as his sister flew past.

"Please, Elvira," panted Olive, "I'm so hungry."

"I'll feed you in my bure," Elvira told her as they reached the lawn. Then, before Olive knew what was happening, Elvira had picked her up, swung her on to her back and they were racing through the plantation, across the road and back into the Gow's estate.

*H*idden at the end of the beach in a grove of guava and paw-paw trees, beyond the house, the Lines and the three little graves, atop a low cliff, stood a tattered bure. Great holes were rent in the thatch of its roof, and through them, white smoke lifted like mist. It was here that Olive's peculiar pony, gasping harshly, set her down. Margaret came through the low door. At the sight of Olive, bedraggled and bewildered, she threw up her hands.

"You mustn't stay here," she said, "Go!"

The instant Olive turned to do her bidding, Elvira's grasp once again restrained her.

"No — she's hungry. Please, ayah." Elvira wrapped her guardian's waist with one arm and squeezed affectionately. "After we feed her she go."

Margaret rested a hand on Elvira's cheek for a moment. She had the scars to prove that once Elvira had set her heart on something there was no point in denying it. There had only been one other time, the time of the poet, and Margaret suspected Elvira's violence then would not have been so extreme had she kept quiet and lied to Saka Gow that night. Then he may not have discovered them. She nodded, and Elvira immediately let go of Olive, gathered Margaret in her arms, pulled her head down and kissed her full on the lips.

"Ah Mata-ni-waitui," the Fijian woman laughed, patting her charge, her over-sized child, on the back. Over Elvira's shoulder she said to Olive, "Curu yani."

Inside the bure an attempt had been made at a European ideal of comfort. An iron four-poster, draped with a smoke-grimed mosquito net, rested unevenly on the layers of the springy mats. It had no mattress, but was spread with sulus and a sheet. On a table, similarly uneven, sat a tin mug and plate awaiting Elvira's supper. The fire at the end of the room burned with acrid fumes. Olive's eyes stung as she gazed with longing at the egg and chunks of dalo sizzling in a pan over the grate. Water boiled in a black billy, rigged on a bar over the flames. Elvira was hungry too — she smacked her lips and giggled.

"When you come back, Margaret?" she asked, squatting at the fire beside her friend.

"Just tonight," Margaret answered carefully. "While Ralph is at the dinner."

Elvira took this in, then her big lips trembled, her eyes hid their contrasting colours and she upended on the mats, kicking her heels and moaning. Margaret's eye, steady and compassionate, held Olive's. After a while, when Elvira had quietened, Margaret said, "Why don't you show Olive your book?"

Elvira sat up then, her cheek patterned by the weave, and smiled. She crawled under the bed and scuffled among the mats.

"Look," she said, giving Olive a book, wrapped in a scrap of sheet. The cover of the book was a dull red and heavily mildewed.

Olive sat gingerly on the edge of the bed, which was wet from the day's heavy rain.

"I knew him, you know," whispered Elvira, snuggling up close. "We did this."

Olive looked up from the book, which was a collection of Rupert Brooke's verse, to Elvira's hands. The forefinger of one hand darted in and out of a circle formed by the thumb and forefinger of the other. Olive wondered why two adults would play with their hands in that childish way while Margaret, from the hearth, made a shushing noise through her teeth and shook her head.

"It was lovely," Elvira went on. "In here we did it, when he stayed with us." A dreamy look came over her face. "He had a bure of his own but he liked to visit me. He didn't know they said I was mad. He thought I was noble. He said my breasts were like ripe mangoes, my thighs strong as a man's. We were like this — " she flung herself back, jiggling on the wet bed, her legs flung up, her arms embracing an invisible body, "— when Bernard came. My brother came in and wrecked it. He took Rupert away."

Elvira brought her hands to her chest and clasped them there. Tears rolled first from her green eye, then from her blue. "He was so beautiful and now he is dead and no one believes he was mine."

"I do," said Olive. She reached out and patted one of the huge hands. "I believe you."

"He wrote a poem and it's in this book," Elvira whispered. "Adela sent it to me from Suva."

"Adela? My mother?" Olive was shocked. What would her mother feel for a person such as Elvira? Compassion, as she had for the influenza victims before her relapse? Or perhaps, just perhaps, she understood this kind of love, Elvira's love for the famous poet, which was surely illicit. Olive shivered. For the past year or so, since she had started at the Grammar School, she had begun to notice the differences between her mother and other women of Suva society. She felt them more keenly than anyone else. There was powder and lipstick for instance. Her mother wore more of both than any respectable lady, and perfume so strong that it often stung Olive's nostrils, like the smoke from this fire. In her smile there was sometimes the ghosts of the laughter of audiences, in her gaze faint reflections of full houses of adoring eyes . . .

"Yes, your mother," said Elvira. "She was here then, after Rupert. And you. Remember? You was just a nipper."

"I didn't know about you then."

"Course you didn't," Elvira sneered. "Bernard won't let no one near me."

Margaret stood up from the fire and scraped the egg and dalo on to the tin plate. "You," she pointed at Olive, "eat then you must go."

The food was delicious, the dalo fried crisp on the outside but crumbling and soft on the inside. Olive devoured it, watching Margaret fish another piece of dalo from the boiling water, cut it into pieces and cast it into the pan. Elvira brought the book from the bed.

"Read me the poem," she said.

"You read it to me while I'm eating," Olive said. She was keenly interested in this impulsive, muscled creature. There was something unpredictable about her, with her wild swings of mood. She could be dangerous even, like a fire lit in a dry place. She imagined what Miss Perkins-Green would make of her. A quick sketch captioned "Mad Woman, Taveuni" and she'd be done with her. Elvira was shaking her head.

"I can't read," she said. "If I could, I'd read his poems all the day."

"How do you know it's about you, the poem?" asked Olive, her mouth full.

"Couldn't be no one else," said Elvira, inching the book across the table towards Olive, "that's what Adela said."

Olive bolted her last chunk of dalo and began reading, squinting, holding the pages to the gleam of the fire:

Eden Lost
Child, remember how, outside the bure door
Cocoa-nuts rained down their fatal spoor
And sparing us — our iron bed 'neath fragile roof —
Sent both Life and Heaven's Proof.

Still sometimes now your Heart's Wild Surf
Beats 'gainst my Reef of Reason and I curse

Those who would immure you — Strange
Creature of fulsome breast and leonine mane.

Embrace me, my Savage Alabaster Queen,
What see you now, with that eye of green
Or blue? I see you weeping, sweet, benign,
Immortal on the sands of the Sea of Time.
                              The Pacific, 1913.

"It is me, isn't it?" asked Elvira, when she'd finished.

"Yes, I do believe it is," said Olive.

Elvira gave a great, contented sigh and lay down on the wet bed.

"I must give her her supper before she goes to sleep," said Margaret. "Will you be all right?"

Olive nodded. "Vinaka, Margaret. Moce."

There were no stars to light Olive's way as she wandered back towards Aunt Maud's house, but after a few moments, her eye was caught by a plume of light above the Torte's. It shot into the dark, clouded sky and exploded into a shower of coloured sparks. She stopped and watched. Ah Jack and his brother were working their magic. Giant chrysanthemums of pink and yellow, enfolded in fiery green foliage, leapt and dissolved. A patriotic flare of red, blue and white hung for a moment in an oblong before dying away.

Olive changed direction for the Torte's. Apart from the intermittent tosses of light, the night was, as Grandmother McNab would say, like the inside of a cow. Once Olive's foot met with a soft croaking resistance before the toe of her shoe sank slowly to the ground. A toad. She shivered and felt sick.

When the sky flowered in pink and lilac, Olive saw she had strayed off course to the wrong side of the banana palms, near the Lines. A tiny, shadowy group of women were gathered outside, gazing at the sky. Olive waved to them, but the light had died. In the dark she was a stranger, a ghost. The women didn't wave back.

On the road to Torte's, Olive passed no one, her ears filled with the bang and whizz of the fireworks and the underlying hum of insects and toads. Suddenly, the dark formed out of itself two darker shapes that, as she approached, became Miss Perkins-Green and Miss Prime-Belcher arm in arm.

"Hullo!" called Olive gaily. "You've missed the dinner, you know."

"We do," came Constance's voice from the larger shape. "But we don't mind."

Olive thought there was something in Miss Prime-Belcher's voice that suggested she did mind, very much. At Lake Tagimaucia she had always eaten heartily, beside the campfire. They walked on in silence.

"There might be some pudding, still," Olive said, after a moment, comfortingly.

"That would be nice," said Constance, with appetite.

Miss Perkins-Green said nothing. Olive wondered if she'd been crying. The atmosphere around her was damp and she leaned into Miss Prime-Belcher's side. Her height bid her to wilt a little over Constance's head and to rest her cheek on her friend's hair. Olive wondered what they'd quarrelled about. Miss Perkins-Green was definitely sad.

"That's our Ah Jack doing the fireworks," offered Olive, to cheer her up.

"Really?" said Constance. Her mouth was lifted to Miss Perkins-Green's ear and she was whispering something. Immediately Miss Perkins-Green broke contact and strode on ahead.

"Where have you been?" asked Constance. "Didn't you go to the dinner?"

Miss Prime-Belcher had the tone that adults use when there is something they would prefer children not to notice. But Olive had noticed. Miss Perkins-Green was in a huff.

"Olive?" Constance prompted.

"No," said Olive. "I've been with my new auntie. I didn't know I had her."

"A new auntie?"

"Yes. She's mad and she lives in a bure past the beach."

"Olive," Miss Prime-Belcher was stern, "are you telling me the truth?"

Olive nodded and saw, as another flare lit the sky, that Miss Perkins-Green had missed the turn into Torte's private road.

"Miss Perkins-Green! You're going the wrong way!" called Olive, stopping at the gate. From a few steps ahead Miss Perkins-Green spun, gave a faint cry and sank, clasping her foot.

"Oh, Agnes!" Miss Prime-Belcher sounded annoyed.

"Don't! I couldn't bear it! It was an accident — a rock — I wouldn't intentionally . . ." Miss Perkins-Green was trying to stand but the pain was too great. She sat down in the mud, her legs out in front of her like a doll. "You will have to run and get help, Olive."

Olive took off up the drive picturing, as she went, Agnes on the same litter they'd used to convey the prize ram from Vuna Point. A huge ball of silver bloomed and drifted above her, and by the light of it she looked back towards the women. They were two hobbling black silhouettes in the road. Miss Prime-Belcher had got Miss Perkins-Green to her feet and was helping her slowly through the gate. Every time her injured foot met the gravel, Miss Perkins-Green gave a little gasp. Olive felt disappointed. The spectacle of a litter-borne lady traveller was now unlikely.

The residents were gathered once again on the lawn. As Olive passed through the gathered cigar-smoking, coolie-bemoaning Cocoa-nut Planters Association she noticed a fair bit of surreptitious unbuttoning of trouser tops to ease dyspeptic stomachs.

Whisky fumes mingled with the aroma of bay rum and Macassar. Lamps had been set up near a cluster of chairs where the women were seated. Grandmother lounged uncomfortably in one, head back and snoring. She was, Olive could see, as full as a boot. Many of the ladies fanned themselves weakly, hot and faint and wreathed in gunpowder smoke. Ah Jack and his brother laboured over a near-empty box.

Opposite the chairs, beyond Ah Jack, Olive spied Eric lying on the ground with his legs sprawling. She ran to him.

"Where've you been, Sis?" Eric asked, amazed at the sight of her. "Look at the state of your dress!"

Olive shrugged and flopped down. Probably she shouldn't tell Eric about Elvira. Most of her adventures ended with trouble, usually with Grandmother. Sometimes Eric tittle-tattled and made it worse. Head and shoulders above her, he stood in judgement.

"Is there any pudding left?" she asked.

"Haven't a clue," said Eric. "Up to the Plimsoll line myself. Stay here for a while and watch the fireworks. They're nearly finished."

There were three more: an immense blue waterfall; a snow-covered mountain, and flock of darting, yellow, song birds.

"It's just as well the night is cloudy," Eric told Olive. "Otherwise the fireworks would get muddled up with the stars."

Ah Jack lit the fuse of the last squat canister of magic, bowed and stepped back. Fire spurted forth in two diagonal flames, a victory "V", red and strong. Olive saw the faces of the Taveuni lords and ladies bloom and their white hands clap as luminous as moths. Pushed to the front row, old Hortense Torte looked much the worse for wear, head on her bony chest. Behind her bathchair stood her son Alphonse, eyes glinting, keeping a grip on her shoulder to hold her upright. Then with a start Olive saw, at the edge of the cluster of chairs, Aunt Maud with Ralph asleep in her arms. In the brief moment the light caught her, she wasn't clapping, but looking down at the sleeping child with all her bereaved love and tenderness. Ralph's mouth was smeared with food, his knees nicked and scabbed. Gathering him in close, Aunt Maud kissed the top of his head and Olive remembered how he smelt of mice.

As the light died, a small commotion began at the steps up to the house. Doctor Rickett's silver head, gleaming like water, was bent over a prone body. Olive stood up and ran over. It was poor Miss Perkins-Green, her grey eyes standing out like lamps in her white face. A chokra ran inside to fetch bandages, and Olive realised, with a sinking feeling, that she should've called for help after all.

CHAPTER SEVENTEEN

Departure

~ *Adela McNab* ~

Such a curious dream, I wonder if it was Ming Lo sent it me. There was a smiling Asian face, afloat in a vast ocean. His tiny boat was laden with vegetables and crocks of water, but it was a pretty, japanned box he offered me. I could not tell if I, too, was on a boat. It seemed more that I was somehow drifting beside him, above the grey sea. As his smiling face was the only sun, my arms and legs felt chill. I reached for the box, sensing that there was somehow a gift of warmth concealed within it. Dreams have no logic — I did not ask how this yellow man could have come by such a thing, or how warmth could be so transported. In reality, a glowing coal would lift the lacquer. I woke as my hands clasped the smooth surface and his hands formed the oriental gesture of gratitude.

Waking now surprises me, first that I have slept at all and second, that I come back to myself. They say the dying often wait to bid farewell. Perhaps I wait to see my children back from Taveuni. After her breakfast, little Rosie is brought to the door for me to smile and wave at, but she buries her face in Elena's warm shoulder. While they stand there, the front door bangs open and closed and Hughie's feet scuff on the grass mats. In the dim hall his dark shape passes behind Rosie and Elena, without so much as a turn of the head in my direction.

"Where has he gone?" I ask.

"To the dining-room for breakfast," says Elena.

"Surely he has already eaten." Elena must be mistaken. Hughie has always been an early riser.

"No, Marama. He has been to see Fred the Rotuman."

"Why? At this hour?"

Elena shakes her head in that secretive way the natives have and I fear for the worst. Fred's wife, perhaps. I had heard she was taken ill.

"Rosie, my dear." The child lifts her face to me, finally. "Go and see Ming Lo. Ming Lo will give you a sweet."

"Moce, Tinana," says Rosie, wriggling free of Elena and waving a dimpled hand. The wave was for me. The Fijian for "Mother" is for Elena. The child disappears.

I bid Elena come in, which she does, rolling her eyes with fear. From the top bureau drawer I ask her to take a hand mirror, hidden at the back amongst scarves and gloves. She hands it to me, then retreats back to the doorway as I begin a coughing attack.

"Don't go yet," my voice cracks, the voice of a pantomime crone.

Elena's image booms and fades with each wracking cough, but I can tell from her breathing she stands there still. When the attack subsides, I lift the mirror to hold my reflection.

My hair is lank and sad, lines deepen around my mouth and eyes, my complexion is yellow and my throat sports the dewlaps of a turkey.

Mrs Pollard told me once that I would always be beautiful. She told me after we turned away thousands in Sydney at the State Theatre. They had all come to see me — "Adela Knight: Fiery Star of the Female Constellation" — according to the *Sydney Morning Herald* of the day before.

"Bring me the hatbox, Elena."

Elena had just begun to slink away and is halted just in time. But the girl is shaking her head.

"Take some eucalyptus from the hall table, shake it on to the hem of your dress, hold it to your nose and bring me the red hatbox."

The long speech has left me breathless. I fall back among the pillows as Elena does as she is bid. Whereas Ming Lo dashes and pants inside this room, our ayah walks on tiptoes, as if it is contact with the floor will make her sick, not ingestion of my exhalations. She lays the box on the bed beside me and hastens out. I must wait for the strength to open it.

The house is quiet. My mind's eye takes me to the diningroom, where Champak would have had Hughie's breakfast congealing under the pewter covers this past half-hour, or more. I see it as clearly as if I'd prepared it myself, the same morning meal Hughie has eaten on land and sea, in the tropics or arctics: a porridge of oats, with salt, soured cream if cream can be got at all and a small tot of whisky. This breakfast never fails to set the partaker sweating and Hughie is a great believer in starting as one means to go on. By the time the sun is high in the sky, Hughie has been awash for hours.

I lift the lid of the red box and survey the contents. When Bill first joined the Suva Entertainment Society, he begged me for this. I couldn't give it up, it was my last link with the theatre. I was invited to join the Society, of course. I imagine they couldn't believe their luck — a real actress arriving in Suva. I contemplated it, but decided against it. The amateurism of their productions such as Niobe — All Smiles is crushing.

The first grease-stick I lift out has mildewed and mouldered in the damp. The next, one I need more than any other, is still in its paper wrapper. I pull it free: No. 5. I kept all my stage makeup so proudly and well. Here lie the orange sticks firmly clasped with a rubber band. After loading one with the pale grease, I bravely face my ravaged coin in the handmirror. I've worked magic before and so I shall again. My canvas perhaps is not so well stretched or primed, but I am an artist and I am determined.

Before, before the children, before Fiji, I had only one defect that needed concealing: a pock where one of my brothers' slingshots had caught me. Now it is difficult to know where to start. Every actor highlights the shadows of the nose and the awnings of the eye, so I begin there. But as I chase away the shadows they multiply before me, under my eyes, in my brow, in vertical glooms parallel on either side of my mouth.

Finished with the No. 5, I replace it and marvel at how I haven't coughed once since I began the transformation. Even the spectre of well-being must frighten away the daemon. A jar of foundation leaps almost of its own accord to my hand, but its shade is too dark now, I need one lighter by far for my influenza-darkened complexion. In the saucer of my breakfast cup I mix some of the No. 5 and the old foundation and spread it on with a rubber sponge. Already the illusion of health is master of my face. Gone are the dark patches — all is a monochrome pale beige, a complexion the envy of any young woman. I wonder how far Hughie is with his breakfast. It would be a tragedy if he hurried and witnessed the nuts and bolts of my sleight-of-hand.

Now, powder to set. My puff, a present from Alfred Pollard, is veiled with scents of the past. Foolishly, on impulse, heart swollen with nostalgia, I lift the pink, yielding bloom to my nose and breathe deeply. Particles of powder from long-ago sessions before mirrors from Darwin to Invercargill invade my sinuses and I cough until my ribs would break. But it seems malady enriches memory. My heart beats vivid blood all the faster with each spasm. There is the scent of Alfred's cheek as I kissed him for my gift, his heavy, blushing, yellow head, his answering mouth seeking mine, his brutal but welcome tongue. In this perfume is the loss of my innocence on a pile of velvet blacks in Wanganui, our rocking love-making on the train on the Kaikoura Coast line, all our nights in crumpled hotel sheets in one-horse towns between Perth and Adelaide and Darwin, secret, melting moments of desire backstage in innumerable flea-ridden theatres in any town who'd have us anywhere in the Australasias.

There — in my affliction I have left a smudge of brown grease on the pillow. The puff dips into the pearly powder and I school myself not to breathe in. Now I am so pale and smooth I could be *La Dame aux Camélias*, the tragedienne Alfred foretold, at last.

Tucked away in the corner of the hatbox is a tiny pot of brilliant peacock blue. Spread thickly on my eyelids, it makes me exotic. I first wore it in *Aladdin*, in Invercargill, when I was promoted from chorus to genie:

> *The curtain will rise at a quarter to eight precisely*
> *on the Grand Topical, Comical, Historical,*
> *Mystical, Sophisticated, Laughable, Chaffable,*
> *Too-awfully-jolly-by-halfable*
> *Burlesque in three acts*
> *ALADDIN*
> *UP TO DATE*
> *BEING A NEW VERSION OF AN OLD LAMP*

Isobel took the title role, in her inimitably charmless but shapely legged way. It was my beloved, however, who delighted audiences in his role as Widow Twankey. At the dress rehearsal he entertained the chorus by splitting his seams. They tittered at his pale stomach spilling like lemon jelly from the sides of his black, fitting gown. In the months since the fire, while the costumes were being re-created, since we'd last performed the burlesque, Alfred had augmented. After the dress rehearsal, he enthusiastically took to callisthenics and weight training as a cure. I, too, was in need of a cure. A puzzling nausea had begun to take hold of me at dawn and sunset. My stomach made me ill, if not yet larger. By the time we took *Aladdin* to Auckland, Alfred had lost half a stone and I'd gained by the same.

"Ta ra ra boom de ay," he sang, wildly dancing in the hot

lights, exposing voluminous combinations and reducing audiences to helpless laughter.

The blue makes me exotic once more. Perhaps Hughie will be transported by it, as if by magic carpet, back to our first meeting, our first affection. It wasn't until we were here, after our marriage, that my passion began to bloom for you, Hughie. But you must never know that. You were my cure. You were a father for William.

My eyebrows have faded to ghosts beneath the paste of beige and powder, so I darken them with a pencil and give them a flirtatious arch. It was Isobel who noticed I'd not needed the rags for eight weeks and then troubled herself to explain to me why. It was Isobel who delivered me up to Alfred as a criminal, and Isobel who later told Mrs Pollard. Alfred, it was hoped by both his mother and father, would marry J.C. Williamson's dreary daughter and thus re-combine the two theatrical empires. He never did marry her, he never married anyone. I don't think he ever considered it a state suitable for him. Myself, born Ada Knight, daughter of a Grafton drudge and a drunkard schooner-rigger whose tipple and employment combined to make his life precarious and then attenuated, had nothing to offer the Pollards beyond my profession. I was beautiful yes, and lively, very, but there were others in Alfred's eyes who were livelier and more beautiful. Isobel, for instance.

Under my lower lashes I draw a thick black line, lifting at the outer corner of my eye. I am Cleopatra now. Not a serious one, but a music-hall Cleopatra. I wink at myself and myself winks back.

"You little fool," said Alfred, after Isobel told him. "I thought you would've taken care of all that."

His informer smiled wickedly. How well I remember his words and her smile. Isobel ushered me out then, out of the dressing room at His Majesty's, out and away from Alfred. I turned back once to see his look of regret, an expression Isobel also caught. Immediately, she attempted to remedy his solitary remorse by falling into his arms. She didn't have even the decency to wait until I was in the dark corridor.

That night we opened with *La Poupée*, with Alfred and myself in the lead. There was sleet in the wind outside and sleet in my heart. Sitting in the auditorium, though I did not know it yet, was in one slight body, my dearest friend, sweetest lover and life's companion.

The fever's bright spots are looming even beneath the grease, and I consider for a moment discarding the brush loaded with rouge. I apply it anyway, even if it is to save the mortician the trouble. During the interval Mrs Pollard came to see me, her gaze avoiding mine and her mouth grim. Isobel had borne my news to her, too.

"We will have to arrange something, Adela," she said. "There is a woman in Newton."

Carmine in hand, I turned bravely from the mirror to say to her, "There is no need for an arrangement."

It was as if I'd sworn. Mrs Pollard blanched and said, as kindly as she could, "Here is her address. Don't think you're the first. Isobel will accompany you, tomorrow."

The rouge has lifted my looks, and the tiny stub of carmine, held carefully between my thumb and forefinger, reddens my mouth. Then I remember an old trick: a dab of No. 5 in the middle of the lower lip. In youth, my lips were full but Isobel's were narrow and this was a trick of hers. Now my dry, fever-chapped mouth is moist, magically sparkling and plump.

I don't think I have ever felt so tired. It's as if my very bones are emptying of their marrow, as if my body mimics an ebbing tide. The mirror tells me all is complete, but for the damned dewlaps and my dank hair.

Once, in Melbourne, we were part of a charity concert for a children's home. There was an old trooper shared our dressing rooms. His act was to sing, with an eerily youthful voice, "The

Wild Colonial Boy" accompanied by no instrument but his yodelling fox terrier. From the stalls he was as youthful in appearance as in voice. As I had watched him prepare, I knew why. In the trade, we call them "lifts"; narrow strips of silk glued to the temples and tied by means of hooks and threads over the top of the head. Last time I opened my hatbox I was seventeen and had no need for lifts, so nothing can help me here, unless . . .

I ring the bell and Elena comes running. Fear of my miasma must be what stops her at the door, her eyes staring, protuberant.

"Marama?" she says, as if she's not sure it is me.

"Come here, Elena," I say, "I want you to plait my hair."

"But your hair was cut short, Marama. Don't you remember? For the fever."

"Never mind. Come here."

"But Rosie —"

"Rosie will be all right."

"Ming Lo is giving her too many sweets."

"Hush! Come here."

Once again on tiptoe she comes to my bed like a giant, pear-shaped wading bird.

"Two thin plaits. One here, one there."

With hasty, fumbling fingers, Elena braids the hair at my temples, fastening the plaits with narrow ribbons I pull from my bed-jacket. Together, we pull the plaits tight to the back of my head and fasten them there with pins.

"But Marama, we will hurt you."

"A small price," I tell her.

At my bidding, Elena fetches a lace shawl from the tallboy and we drape it over my head to hide the improvised lift.

"Shall I wash your face, Adela?" she asks, gently, in the same sweet voice she has for Rosie. She doesn't realise she's used my name and my heart turns over. I shake my head.

"Could you, Elena, before you go, could you hold the mirror?" My eyelids droop with exhaustion but I catch my image

143

before they close. All is perfection. Perhaps I will sleep a little before Hughie comes in.

The front door bangs and Bill slouches past. He is eighteen now and pink, huge, uncomfortable, just as Alfred would be if somehow he'd landed in the tropics. All of your boys, Hughie, are thin and easily browned by the sun, all of you are nimble and light. I've told you many times how heavy my father was, how Bill is so like his grandfather. Hughie, if you came to me now, while I am beautiful again, I would find the strength to tell you the truth. You would understand then why the sailroom is anathema to poor William. To sailmaking he is, as the Fijians say, an mBuan drinking nut. No quick brine runs in his veins, but slow, slovenly greasepaint.

Ah! Raised voices from the dining-room. Alfred's voice. Your voice. Alfred's voice. Your voice. The richness of your voice. The history in it. All these years together, my dear heart.

And now, and now, and now . . . will I drift at peace? I will. Here is the heavy approaching sleep, the dark tide. From the dining-room again — how uncanny — Alfred's voice, your voice, Alfred's voice, you.

I'm going, I go, I'm gone . . .

CHAPTER EIGHTEEN

$\mathcal{G}ifts$

$\mathcal{W}$aiting downstairs on the carved hall seat, Olive was once again in her broderie-anglaise-trimmed church frock, which once again had been miraculously revived by the laundry chokra. Beyond the open front door, a low grey sky threatened more rain. Olive half hoped it would, then perhaps Uncle Bernard would reconsider the journey to Somosomo to church.

It had rained all day Saturday. After the party on Friday night, everyone had been inactive. Olive had spent most of the morning lying on her bed reading *Eric Brighteyes* and wishing she was Gudruda the Fair, although the cold of Iceland would be something to deal with and Ospakar was surely even worse than a Hun. Waiting on her bedside table was a tale of Allan Quartermain in Africa, *The Ivory Child*, another Henry Rider Haggard. Just as Olive was wondering if Constance had ever written anything so wonderful and feeling sure she'd written better, there was a commotion of voices from downstairs.

It was Miss Perkins-Green and Miss Prime-Belcher directing the loading of both the Packard and a horse-drawn carriage from the protection of the verandah.

"Are you going?" asked Olive, hearing her voice ringing around her on the quiet landing. "Miss Prime-Belcher? Are you leaving us?"

So intent was Constance on her packing that she didn't hear

Olive until the child arrived fleet, barefoot, down the stairs to stand beside her.

"Yes, my dear." She laid a heavy hand for a moment on Olive's head. "The copra boat is calling for us on its way back to Suva."

"But why?"

"Why?" Miss Prime-Belcher's tone was gently instructive. "Because the influenza has worsened considerably on the main islands and the steamers have been cancelled."

"No," Olive's voice rose to a wail, "I mean why are you going?"

From her seat on a bench, her foot bandaged and face pale, Miss Perkins-Green shot her a withering look.

"Don't you like it here?" persisted Olive.

"Yes, of course. But we have further travelling ahead." Constance took Olive's hand.

"Are you going back to England?" Olive was suddenly full of curiosity. England, after all, was where Henry Rider Haggard lived. "Do you know Henry Rider Haggard?"

But Constance's attention was elsewhere. "Careful with that box, Atunaisa! It contains my samples and microscope."

Atunaisa laid the wooden box in the carriage as carefully as if it were a baby and went back to the slowly diminishing mound of cases, bags and boxes for another load.

"Everything will be wet through and full of mildew if this keeps up," groaned Agnes. "Just look at it! Not a breath of wind, just endless bloody bloody rain!"

"It'll be better when you get back to England," Olive comforted. "It might be bloody snowing instead."

"We're not going to England, you ninny," spat Agnes, "we're going to the island of Kadavu by oil launch."

"We might dear. It depends on your poor ankle and whether or not there is a wire waiting for me in Suva." Constance hoped there was, one from her dear, comfortable Brigid. The intensity that was Agnes was beginning to grate on her very bones and she found herself longing for the sanity and day-to-day affection that was her lover at Home. Brigid had loved her for thirty years and seemed in some ways inured to Constance's philandering.

Mind you, Constance reminded herself, there hasn't been any philandering for nearly a decade and if Agnes starts making a nuisance of herself . . . it didn't bear thinking about.

From Agnes's seat on the verandah there was a rapid drumming and Olive half expected her to do what Elvira had done — fling herself to the floor and kick her heels.

"But you promised! You have to honour your part of our bargain. We've been to the lake, now we go to Kadavu." There was a blue vein standing out in Agnes's neck and a strand of shining hair had worked itself over her eyes. She flicked it away, irritably.

Constance sighed, and Olive saw she was tired.

"Answer me, Constance!" Agnes shouted. The Fijians, working in the rain, looked up in surprise, and the chauffeur, standing to attention while he waited to drive them to the point, flashed the whites of his eyes in alarm.

"My dear," said Constance with great patience, "you are overwrought and suffering considerable discomfort. We will rest up at the Grand Pacific for at least three days. The saltwater baths will do you good."

"I am not an invalid." Agnes spoke through gritted teeth. "I have merely sprained my ankle!"

"That's all, Marama," said Atunaisa, gesturing at the now-empty ground. "All finished."

Vishnu saluted and made his way down to the Packard, turning the crank on the way.

"Besides," continued Agnes, "in case you don't remember, there is an epidemic in Suva."

"I have been amongst epidemics before; we will take two grains of quinine sulphate and two of quinine hydrochlorate every morning before breakfast. The influenza won't touch us."

"Oh, really? And is this preventative of yours medically proven? I say we go straight to Kadavu."

A muscle in Constance's cheek twitched violently, and she rapped her shooting stick hard on the verandah floor. Agnes grew a shade paler and bit her lip.

"Should you like Atunaisa to convey you to the car?" Constance asked, levelly.

"Very well," said Agnes, graciously, as if it were a favour to her friend. Atunaisa came up to her bench and lifted Agnes in his arms as if she were a string of fish or cocoa-nuts.

"Where are Uncle Bernard and Aunt Maud?" asked Olive.

"Making themselves ready for church, I expect," said Constance. "Don't worry. We made our farewells last night."

Atunaisa settled Agnes into the car while Vishnu stood by with a rug for her knees.

"Goodbye." Constance bent to kiss Olive, but the child wrapped her fiercely in her arms.

"Goodbye," Olive whispered. "Have a good life. I'll never forget you." Laughing, Miss Prime-Belcher drew back and Olive saw she had tears in her eyes.

"I should like to give you something, Olive. A gift. What would you like?"

"A gift?" Olive's eyes were wide. They lit upon Miss Prime-Belcher's magnifying glass. "Could I have . . . do you think I could . . . would you . . .?" Olive pointed.

Without a word Constance removed the pendant and lifted it over Olive's head. "You will have to shorten the cord," she said.

"Thank you!" Olive's head was bent, gazing with delight upon the magnifying glass. The steel-rimmed disc of light flashed blue in her hands and the handle of ebony had a small silver oblong set into it. "C.P.B." was engraved there. Even the cord of soft, worn leather was wonderful. It was the best present she had ever had.

"Goodbye, dear." Constance kissed the bent head and went down the steps to the motorcar. Through the window, Olive saw her take Miss Perkins-Green's hand to comfort her. The chokra started the engine.

148

"Wait a moment!" Olive's hand flew to her pocket and she leapt down all three steps at once. "Wait!" She leaned in the window, across Miss Perkins-Green, who gave her a watery, reluctant smile, and dropped into the lap of the other lady the Lucky Lunaria. One of Constance's square hands picked up the stone, the other ruffled Olive's hair.

"Thank you, my dear. I'll write to you. Goodbye."

Olive pulled back and stood upright. The car moved away.

"It's a Lunaria! It'll bring you luck from Providence!" she called, but Constance couldn't hear her. Her firm brown hand closed over Agnes's paler one, her eyes set on the road ahead and her heart already ached, just slightly, for the simplicity and passion of their night at Lake Tagimaucia.

$\mathcal{P}$assage to church in Somosomo by Packard was impossible because in places the road had been washed away by the heavy rain. They would go by sea; Uncle Bernard had his own, new oil launch, kept in a boat shed at Vuna Point. It was operated by an Indian and a Fijian. Before they set out on a voyage, the Indian scrubbed the decks and polished the bold brass lettering *Island Princess* high on the hull. As they travelled, he tended the engine while the Europeans and the Fijian navigated.

The Indian did not eat enough, he did not look after himself, thought Maud, looking past him as he assisted her aboard. He looked like a wrung-out black rag. Maud herself felt a little wrung-out. Despite the heat from the sun and engine, she had cloaked herself in a hooded duster to keep the flecks and soot from her muslin dress. She sat in the stern of the boat, a damp, brown mushroom.

"Where's Grandmother?" Olive demanded, sitting beside her as the boat pulled away from the jetty.

A figure in white raced down from the palms at the end of the beach. It lifted its garment to its waist and turned around, winking a broad, bisected pink stern at the little steamer. Aunt Maud gave out a little choke. As she and Olive watched, Margaret also came down to the beach, at a more leisurely pace. Elvira had seen her coming though, and straightened. Keeping her gown high, she raced along the beach away from her, a black triangle of hair appearing and disappearing with the pumping of her broad, white thighs. Margaret quickened her pace.

"She'll cut her feet on the stones," said Olive. Aunt Maud stared at her.

"Who will, dear?" she said.

"Elvira, of course," said Olive, patiently. Aunt Maud pressed her lips together and prised open the mouth of her reticule for her handkerchief.

"You know — Uncle Bernard's sister. I suppose she's a kind of aunty," continued Olive, since this aunt didn't seem to know who she was talking about.

"That's enough," said Maud, flashing a panicked gaze at her husband. He sat bolt upright in a white duck suit, his back to the beach, a pearly panama jammed on his ragged head and an ivory-handled cane clenched between his knees.

"Where's Grandmother?" repeated Olive. Grandmother would be interested in Elvira, perhaps. She sucked on the leather thong of the magnifying glass. It tasted wonderfully of Miss Prime-Belcher.

"You know very well Mother is an Anglican," replied Aunt Maud from inside her hood. She had turned her head and was looking up at the house. The hedge of ixora she had planted around the small cemetery was getting out of control. From the sea, the little graves were hardly detectable. Maud made a mental note to get the vegetation cleared.

"But I am an Anglican too," protested Olive. Perhaps the steamer could put her ashore and she could make her way back to her book.

"Not until you're confirmed, you're not." Aunt Maud's speech seemed to cost her hugely and to come from further back in her hood than her head was. "Besides, Reverend Jamieson's sermons are always terribly interesting."

From the starboard stern, Ralph crossed his eyes at his sister, and Olive giggled. Perched beside Uncle Bernard, Ralph was lifting his buttocks from one side to the other, still sore from his whipping.

"Sit still," hissed Uncle Bernard. "You're more trouble than you're worth, boy."

Tears pricked at the corners of Ralph's eyes and Olive held her arms out to him. Her bony thighs were only marginally more comfortable than the wooden slats, but he sat in her lap anyway. Aunt Maud extended a soft hand and laid it comfortingly on his knee, and in this way they chugged up the coast, inside the reef.

From a distance, alone in the bow and brooding in his dark school clothes, Eric could have been a spindly smoke stack. As they'd come aboard, he'd noticed Olive's new acquisition, a splendid, strong magnifying glass. It was, she'd said, a gift from one of the Lady Travellers. A girl wouldn't even know what it was for, he thought, forgetting for a moment the gender of the bestower and setting his mind to bribing it off his sister. The only object she would value more would be that silly stone, her "Lucky Lunaria". If that somehow could fall into his hands . . . For a moment he pulled himself up short. What a thing to be thinking of on the way to church, even if it was Methodist. But there did seem to be a kind of fairness to Eric having the glass. So far he'd missed out on all the adventures; it was Sis who'd swallowed the bone and Sis who'd trekked to the lake.

There was a sudden squeal from Ralph. Eric heard it faintly and turned. There was Aunt Maud hauling the little boy on to her lap and reprimanding Olive. She didn't appear to be listening, holding the magnifying glass up to the sky and gazing at it with reverence. Eric guessed that Olive had been examining the bumps and scrapes on Ralph's legs with it, not realising that the sun could find its mark in the glass and burn. Being a girl, she wouldn't have realised that it could inflict pain. Eric sighed and hoiked manfully into the bow-wave.

The boat came to rest at a little jetty below the church. The Tortes, in their identical gleaming launch with its twelve-horse-power motor engine, had arrived before them. Alphonse, Sitiveni and a number of Fijians were in the act of lifting old Hortense from the deck to the pier, bath-chair and all.

It really is a shame Grandmother isn't here, thought Olive, as the old lady lolled alarmingly to one side and would've tipped head-first into the tide had not Alphonse's wife reached for her glittering, slippered feet. Grandmother would enjoy this.

*B*ut Grandmother, sitting at this moment in Maud's place on the verandah, with undoctored tea and fending off the fruit bat, would not have appreciated the sight. Her night after the revelry had been sleepless, the chill, long-departed beauty of Hortense looming at her in the dark. The spectre wore the shell-pink gown Hortense had worn all those years ago in Levuka, in 1867, at the crowning of King Cakebau. It was the social occasion of the year and Minnie had attended in a huge picture hat. As Hughie was to come into the world less than a week later, her gown was tight over her belly and Minnie felt shamed, even though she was now married and not a moment too soon. When she laid eyes on Hortense, she knew that despite the glow of her own cheeks and gloss of her hair, she'd lost. From the arm of Young Torte, as he was then, Hortense drew all eyes, even the bloodshot orbs of King Cakebau. With Captain McNab once again away at sea, Minnie was compelled to stand alone, at the back of the European section. Her own chagrin helped her to see Cakebau's as he struggled to keep the cheap crown of painted wood and paste jewels from slipping off his springy hair. The crowd tittered. At last the crown fell over the King's eyes and the spectators exploded into laughter. Cakebau tore the crown away, looked at it with distaste, dropped it beside the chair and stood. The crowd now trembled beneath his most fierce, most cannibal gaze and waited in silence as he stalked away. Minnie considered running after him and flinging herself at his feet.

Young Torte, as he was then, visited her that night, having left his new wife safe in her virtue at the Royal Hotel. Minnie admitted him to her new abode above the chandlery, but because of her condition deemed it unseemly to revive her old trade. Eventually, with the aid of some cocoa-nut oil she'd relieved him with her hand. Afterwards they'd quarrelled about payment and he'd left. From below her windows he'd yelled abuse, calling her by name. The town was full of people come for the coronation. Fifty-one years later, the old lady felt a glimmering of shame at what they may have heard. Not normally given to meditation, Minnie McNab saw now with horrible clarity how beauty goes to ruin and proud savagery to ridicule. She called for Ah Jack to dispense with the tea and bring the gin bottle.

CHAPTER NINETEEN

Backsliders

With Hortense in her bathchair, the group of whites, Tortes and Gows, made their way up the dirt road beside the stream, towards Saint James and the Wesleyan Mission. Olive walked at the front flanked by Ralph and Eric, leaving the grown-ups to the rattle and bang of Hortense's iron wheels on stone.

"Can I borrow your magnifying glass, Sis?" asked Eric.

"What for?" Olive took the pendant in one hand from where it knocked against her stomach. A Fijian lady emerged from the low door of her roadside bure, clutching Bible and prayer book, and fell into step beside them.

"Bula," she said.

"Bula," said Ralph and Olive together.

"To look at things," said Eric. "Bugs and beetles. That's what it's for. To examine small things."

"Really?" said Olive, kicking a stone. "Miss Prime-Belcher used it for flowers, big ones and small ones."

Eric rolled his eyes at Ralph in exasperation, but Ralph was holding tight to his sister's hand and trying not to think about how his tight shorts rubbed on his stinging welts as he walked. Another Fijian lady came from a cluster of bures on the other side of the stream. She was carrying a little girl about the same age as Rosie. The child's nose and eyes ran. Behind her came her husband and three other children. The father sneezed and paused to clean his nose in the stream.

"Bula," said the lady with the little girl.

"Bula," replied the first lady, Eric, Olive and Ralph together. The church bell began to ring. Immediately the ladies stopped and looked at one another.

"Sa malumalumu talega na i rogo ni lali," said one lady.

"The bell?" asked Olive. "What do you mean, Marama?"

"Listen."

It was true, the bell was lop-sided, as if it were being held on one side and struck with a stick. The women and children quickened their step, leaving the bathchair and its attendants further behind.

Rounding the corner by the Chinese store, they saw the whole congregation gathered in the cemetery. The church itself was hidden, screened by all the tall Fijians. Something was preventing them from going inside. Keeping hold of Ralph's hot hand, Olive pushed her way through the legs.

The cemetery showed evidence of many recent burials, even since she'd passed this way with the Lady Travellers. There were mounds of freshly turned earth, bright, white crosses. Most of the new graves were little ones, for children. For a moment, she thought it was this, the deaths from the epidemic arrived on Taveuni, that was causing all the long faces, but it wasn't just that. The Fijians' eyes were fixed on a point on the other side of the fence, where the church had been. Now, there was only a steeple.

Olive ran forward, dragging Ralph with her. The uprights of the cemetery fence, slung together with wire, danced mid-air above a gaping hole. Except for the flowers, it was like the snake pit in the Suva Museum, the one behind glass and full of dead, stuffed snakes. Thick, static tendrils of green and brown passed over one another, the roof of the church buckled three feet below. The walls and beautiful stained-glass windows were invisible. Luscious red bracts of the vine, cosseting the tiny white flowers, curled around the steeple and frothed over the submerged roof. One flower seemed to reach out for a dark trousered leg standing on the other side of the gap. The leg belonged to the Reverend Jamieson, who was redder in the face than usual and emitting angry puffs of rubber odour. This close to the dangling fence, the ground was uncertain. A faint tremor reached her legs, and Olive took a step backwards, dragging Ralph with her.

"There is no explanation for this," the Reverend was muttering from the other side. "Nothing the rational mind could equate with such a calamity." He cleared his throat and spoke loudly. "This morning I was going to preach from Leviticus, but I have changed my mind. Instead we will hear from our founder John Wesley, from his sermon on "The Imperfection of Human Knowledge".

Here the Reverend paused while his congregation made themselves comfortable. Olive sat on the grass with her arm around Ralph. The Reverend leafed through his worn copy of *Sermons on Several Occasions*, thanking the Lord for the gift of vocal magnitude and reassuring himself with the thought that Wesley himself often preached in the open air:

" 'It is by their very nature that the wisest of men know in part. How amazingly small a part do they know, either of the Creator or of His Works. This is a very necessary but unpleasant theme, for a vain man wants to be wise. Let us reflect upon this. May the God of wisdom and love open our eyes to discern our own ignorance.' "

The Reverend paused again. At the back of the crowd, Mrs Jamieson had been organising chairs for the white ladies and thus causing a distraction. A procession of Fijian boys bearing furniture came from the door of the mission station. The Reverend silently thanked the Lord again, this time for the miracle that he had not planted a *Medinilla waterhousei* against that wall, frail as it was from a battering received during the last hurricane season. If he had done, then not only God's house but his own would've been swallowed up by the earth. No matter what he preached today, he would be praying alone, long and hard, to dissuade himself from searching for a reason, an unforeseen measure of subsidence in the earth, a botanical explanation for such a voracious root system, a place in God's plan for such an unholy vine. Backsliders, he saw now, were just as prevalent in the plant kingdom as they were in the animal.

The white ladies were all seated in a row and the Reverend wound up to top volume again. "'Now consider the earth on which we tread and which God has given peculiarly to us. Do we understand this? Suppose our planet is properly measured. How much more of this do we know? Who can inform us what lies beneath its crust, the region of stones, metals, minerals, and other fossils? This is only a thin layer, which is a very small proportion of the whole. Who can teach us the inner parts of the globe? Is there a central fire, a grand reservoir, which not only supplies the volcanoes, but also ministers to the ripening of gems and metals and perhaps to the production of vegetables and the well-being of animals too? Or is it a great, deep, central abyss of waters still contained in the bowels of the earth? Who has seen and who can tell? Who can give any solid satisfaction to a rational enquirer?'"

Eric, who had been listening attentively, grew irritated with the idea that the pursuit of wisdom is vanity and that God would prefer him ignorant. The Anglican God, the one he'd left behind in Suva, wanted him to have that magnifying glass and use it to examine minutely as many things as he could in His world. It was after eleven and the sun, hidden behind a grey helmet of clouds, had begun to pound on his unprotected head. He wandered off to the overhang of the Chinese seed store while the Reverend closed his book of sermons.

"It is one of the first principles of religion that God's Kingdom rules over all. Let us sing, with confidence, Psalm 8."

All assembled stood. The whites, as usual, pretended to fumble for the place in their Bibles. They were really waiting for the Fijians to find the note for them.

"Oh, Lord our Lord," they sang, *"how excellent is thy name in all*

the earth! Who hast set thy glory above the heavens." Olive stood and joined in. *"Out of the mouth of babes and sucklings . . ."*

There was a thud on the other side of the dangling fence. Fallen to his knees in the soil, the Reverend's arms were above his head, his face contorted in prayer. At first his voice came in chokes and starts, and then in strange, half-formed words.

"What is man, that thou art mindful of him?" sang the congregation while their shepherd, beside the grave of his church, raved in tongues, wept and tore his hair.

Above the singing throng, the sky suddenly darkened. Faces tipped upwards and received the first drops.

"The fowl of the air and the fish of the sea, and whatsoever passes through the paths of the seas . . ."

"Quickly!" The Reverend had leapt to his feet, panicked, his trance broken and mind full of a disturbing vision of his church, not only buried, but swimming, drowning, in a rain-filled chasm. "Mats!" he shouted. "Fetch mats!"

The Fijians ran for nearby bures and the mission station. Some of the pavavalagi men ran too, but most of the Europeans clustered on the verandah of the Chinese store and watched as first the steeple was wrapped, then the crippled bell tower. Then the torrent was too thick to see the Fijians bending and working over the hole, they became dark, gleaming shapes passing to and fro, heaving heavy, rolled-up mats from their houses.

"I wonder," mused Mrs Jamieson, "if any of us would be so quick to give up our beds. Those are their beds, you know, that they are laying over our church."

Those assembled under the roof pretended they hadn't heard her. Olive and Ralph genuinely hadn't. They were sitting on the step, allowing the cool water to course down their knees and pool in their shoes. The rattle in the guttering above their heads was too loud for them to hear even one another, but Maud, standing close beside the Reverend's wife, felt further accused.

"My dear Emily," she said, "wouldn't you say that the less one has, the less one notices it gone? Surely, the degree of comfort one has while sleeping on those mats is only marginally greater than sleeping on the bare earth."

"You are wrong on both counts I believe, my dear," replied Mrs Jamieson. "But don't let us quarrel."

"No, let's not," agreed Maud. Emily was one of her oldest friends on Taveuni. The same year she and the Reverend arrived to take up the mission, Bernard brought Maud to the island as his bride.

From a few steps behind Maud came the grumble of male voices and, once, Bernard's laugh, which made her jump. Ridiculous, to spend your entire married life startling at your husband's mirth. Already the men were ignoring the Reverend's sermon. They wanted to know why the earth had opened to swallow their church.

"The island is volcanic," said one.

"So is Waiyevo," retorted another. "The Papists are still standing there."

"It's that vine. The natives have a legend about that vine, you know. They're frightened of it." That was Bernard.

"Bosh!" said the other man. "They're frightened of everything."

The screen door into the shop opened and the storekeeper emerged. He smiled and bowed at the Europeans, among them some of his most valued clientele.

"Hullicane," he said.

Bernard guffawed. "Don't be a donkey, Charlie. Where's the wind?"

"Wind come up," said Charlie. "You come inside?"

"No, thank you," said one of the planters. "We'll get along home soon."

Charlie, impassive, nodded and retreated back into the dim, sack-filled room.

"Hurricane," murmured the Reverend's wife. "That's all we need. After this."

"We have been lucky, so far, haven't we?" said Maud.

"If you mean with regard to the weather, yes we have." Emily Jamieson cast her eye sadly at the blurred figure of her husband, shouting and leaping at the edge of the hole, directing the laying of mats. He might fall in. This was such a likely possibility that Mrs Jamieson immediately transferred her concern for him to the more needy and propinquitous soul of Mrs Gow.

"I see Mr Ogilvy has returned to the island with the Honourable Baxendale," she prompted. But Mrs Gow's face was uncommunicative.

"They are staying at the Guest House," she went on. At this the corners of Mrs Gow's mouth depressed, which Mrs Jamieson took as incentive.

"And when is your court appearance, my dear?" she asked, although she knew very well.

The wives and daughters around them fell silent at the words "court appearance" and waited with interest for Mrs Gow's reply. She had blushed an unbecoming cerise.

"Tomorrow morning," she said, praying no one but her companion would hear her.

"Indeed? What time?"

"Nine o'clock," whispered Maud.

"Beg yours?" said Mrs Jamieson, loudly.

"Nine o'clock," repeated Maud, louder. She wondered if the Reverend's wife had developed a vindictive side to her nature, or whether middle age was sending her deaf.

"I think it would be wise to stay the night with us, if this rain keeps up. There's no sense in making the journey back to Vuna Point this afternoon in any case, is there?"

"Oh," said Maud, paling at the thought of the mould-streaked and sticky mission station and its traveller-smeared sheets, at the prospect of having to face the row of brown-faced and catarrh-nosed orphans over porridge and prayers. "We came by *Island Princess*, you know, our new oil-engine launch and —"

"Launch or not, it would be madness, dear."

Above their heads, although it hardly seemed possible, the rain grew heavier.

"Bernard will want to —" began Maud.

"Yes. I'd heard you'd had a spot of that." Her friend's tone was reassuring now.

"Spot of what?" Maud had only been about to say that Bernard would want to get home.

"Coolie trouble. Since your . . . whatever. Let him go back then. You stay here, then you can return tomorrow with your head held high."

Previously, Maud had suspected Emily was on the coolies' side. You never could tell with people of the church. She wondered now why her friend had fallen quiet with the rest of them that dreadful time with her mother, at the julep table at the Torte's.

"I don't know the full story, of course," the Reverend's wife continued, looking out at the rain and trying not to glance in her husband's direction. "I'm sure you had a perfectly good reason for striking the boy. I know only too well how aggravating household chokras can be." She lowered her voice. "We make no secret of the fact that we've had very bad luck converting them. I can't have them in the Mission as servants, not around the children, with all their silly Hindi carry-on. Incurable idolaters, the lot of them."

"Yes," agreed Maud, in a small voice. Perhaps Mrs Jamieson didn't know she'd cut Aiyaz.

"Yes? So you will stay. Very sensible. David! David!" At the edge of the verandah Mrs Jamieson clapped her hands. Olive looked up from beneath her and saw how work-sore they were, the rashes and cracks. She'd only seen hands like that once before, on the Samoan laundress in Suva. One of the Fijians, on his way back to the mission station for more mats, halted.

"Run and get the Reverend's black umbrella and bring it back to me."

The Fijian ignored the first part of her command, walking in a careful and leisurely way across the grass now churned to mud.

"Oh, good heavens! I almost forgot!" said Maud. "The children!"

"What children, dear?" said Emily. She'd heard of how poor Maud tended her children's graves. Perhaps she held to some daily ritual.

"My brother's — my niece and nephews. I'll have to take them back to our place." Maud was turning and looking for them.

"Oh, of course. The McNabs. Keep the little one here and send the older two back. Ah Jack will surely keep an eye on them," advised Mrs Jamieson. The girl was too watchful for her liking and the older boy too gloomy. Observing their aunt in court would not do them any good and the aunt even less.

"I want to stay here." Olive was suddenly at her aunt's elbow. "With Ralph."

Mrs Jamieson noticed the immediate tension in her friend and saw that the watchful child had too. Ralph, still holding his sister's hand, leaned his head into his sister's hip.

"He's my little brother," Olive went on. "He's not your baby."

How Olive's black hair needed a good scrub, thought Maud, how her skin and budding breasts and gangly height all spoke of uncomfortable emergence from childhood. Maud reminded herself that she was the adult of the piece and that Olive was, in fact, still a child, and besides that, Adela was dying. She steeled herself to put an arm around her niece's shoulders. They were almost of a height. Beneath the soft weight of her forearm, Olive's muscles tensed.

"Can she stay, Emily?"

"Of course," the Reverend's wife smiled. The McNab side of the Gow family was, if she remembered correctly, Anglican. At least they were Protestant.

A smile flashed briefly across Olive's face and fell. A conniving child, thought Emily Jamieson. When Daviti finally arrived with the umbrella, she found herself sharing it with Olive. Behind her, Maud Gow spread her duster above Ralph's head and hurried through the mud like a wing-stretched ostrich sheltering its young. Mrs Jamieson thought of her sister's children in Scotland and conceived immediately of a plan to invite them to Fiji for a lengthy and educational holiday. Surely her own sister, although not given to magnanimity, would see the fairness of that. Fijian children were endearing, of course, and the three orphans she had now were quick and full of charm, but how lovely it would be to care for some children of her own kind, especially since the ones God had sent, he'd seen fit to snatch away again.

Eric saw the magnifying glass fall from his sister's neck as she was hustled into the mission station, but he waited until she was well out of sight. Then, casually, as if he hadn't a care in the world, he picked his way through the mud to where it lay. The leather thong, he saw, was frayed and torn from all Olive's chewing. He picked it up, wiped the glass with his handkerchief and put it in his pocket.

Having located his wife in the mission station and promised to return in time for the hearing, Bernard and Eric returned to the *Island Princess* and set sail on the evening tide. During the voyage the wind came up, just as the Chinaman had predicted. Enormous waves began to break over the reef and the little ship was tossed around, which Bernard didn't enjoy. He watched his Fijian's face for signs of fear, but there were none. Eric, too, seemed calm, almost unnaturally so. Glittering at his neck, tied on a piece of sennit, hung a magnifying glass that Bernard hadn't noticed before. Boys always have a liking for such things, he thought.

At day's last light as the launch berthed at his pier, Bernard looked up to his house and saw, through the heavy rain, that someone had left a large black parcel in Maud's place on the verandah. Or perhaps it was an effigy. Those blasted coolies.

They'd stop at nothing. He climbed out on to the pier, gave instructions for the crew not to waste any time in getting the *Island Princess* into her boathouse and strode off. The black shape was sinister and must be heavy, otherwise surely Ah Jack would have removed it. It wasn't until he and Eric were past the Lines and crossing the lawn that Bernard saw what it was. His mother-in-law. Dead, or possibly just dead drunk. From the smell of her, discernible from the lawn despite the wind, it was the latter. Bernard climbed the steps and blinked. The fruit bat, in the absence of his wife, had made do with Minnie. It clung to her breasts, rising and falling with each shuddering bombazine breath. The old lady's black lace cap had slipped over one eye. If Minnie was an old man, Bernard thought, he would deem it medicinally necessary to throw a bucket of water over her. But she was an elderly woman and the fruit bat was his wife's. They might catch cold.

"We'd best get her inside," he said to his nephew. "Grab her legs."

Appalled, Eric had backed up against the verandah rail. At home, if Grandmother got like this, the servants and his father conspired to keep her a secret from the children. It was horrible, horrible, and he wasn't about to grab her by the legs.

"Ah Jack!" yelled Bernard. Minnie grunted sharply, but didn't wake.

"Ah Jack!" yelled Bernard again, this time through the dining-room door.

From far away, from the other end of the corridor, a door closed softly and Ah Jack's limping tread came closer.

"Take her inside, will you?" said Bernard, just before Ah Jack appeared.

"Sorry, Mr Gow — too heavy." Ah Jack's legs and back still ached from the heavy load he and his brother had lugged to Torte's.

"Give us a hand then. Shift yourself, Eric." Bernard threw his hat and cane down. "We're in for a storm. Can't leave her out here, for Pete's sake."

It took much longer than he'd expected to get the old lady inside and up the stairs to her bed. He took her legs, Ah Jack and Eric a shoulder each. Ah Jack, who seemed to be in some kind of pain, kept stopping on the stairs and wincing. Eric would go no further than the old lady's door and abandoned them there, muttering goodnight and disappearing into his room. When they laid her down, Minnie hardly stirred, and the fruit bat, when Ah Jack tried to remove it, just dug its claws in deeper.

"Leave it," said Bernard. "Open the window and it'll fly out when it needs to."

He hoped for the bat's sake that his mother-in-law didn't roll over.

Downstairs the door on to the verandah was flapping back and forth. It banged shut. There was a quiet moaning from the Strait, which grew louder, rolling towards the house and whistling around the eaves. On his way to open the window, Ah Jack paused and looked at his master.

"No, you're right, don't. Come and help me to do the shutters."

When Old Man Torte had added another storey on to his bungalow, so had Bernard's father. Two storeys were impressive but impractical in the hurricane season. As Bernard struggled up and down the ladder to the many windows, he cursed the chokras. As further sugar to sweeten them, he'd given them all of Sunday off, rather than the usual half of it. Surely they must see the hurricane coming and want to help. But none of them had come, not Vishnu, not Kalessar, not Aiyaz, whose wound must be nearly healed.

Eventually, necks aching with keeping their heads up in the gale, Ah Jack and Bernard finished letting the shutters down and latching them, and staggered inside. Ah Jack went straight to his quarters and lay on his narrow bed, heart thudding and a sharp pain in his arm. Bernard went to his den and drank whisky, waiting for the hurricane to do its worst.

Settled in the wing chair under the framed photograph of the last governor — the Hon. Everard im Thurn in feathered helmet surrounded by a group of Taveuni planters including himself — Bernard's head had wedged itself comfortably into an upholstered corner. The remaining whisky in his glass was slopping at the rim and trickling across his red, square fingers when a sudden flapping at the window, behind the shutters, propelled him to his feet. His short legs had carried him across the floor to peer through the slats before his eyes were properly open.

It was something white and round, pushing up at the shutter then rushing away. Bernard clutched his whisky more firmly and his scalp prickled. It was Elvira's face, looming close through the squall, darting back and blowing in, and there — that cackle — that was surely her demented laughter. There was nothing for it but to struggle on to the verandah and send her back to her bure.

The door, unlocked, straightaway blew in. Bernard needed all his weight, leant into the blast, to push his way out. Just past the step, the white thing blew in at him and struck him on the face. It wasn't Elvira at all, but his panama hat, which he'd left on the verandah with his stick. He flung out a hand just as an upward draught caught the hat, and it flew up and away, spiralling through the bruising, buffeting dark towards the Somosomo Strait.

Tui Cakau

~ Agnes Perkins-Green ~

As happens all too frequently in these otherwise paradisiacal islands, the wrong information had been imparted. The copra boat did not arrive at noon, as promised, but sailed in at dusk. Both lunch shelter and lunch were graciously provided by the Customs Officer's Swedish wife. It was her only child, an overly indulged boy, who saw the mast of the cutter first.

"Here she comes!" he yelled, darting out of the low-roofed, stone cottage into the rain.

Constance and I exchanged a low, conspiratorial sigh of relief. Had it been Saint Brendan himself in his flimsy coracle, we would have hastened to board, at least I would have. There was so much nagging at me, so many questions I needed to ask my dear one. Mostly they spring from fear for our future together, and in part they concern her companion in Oxford. Once or twice during the damp and stifling morning, she had wondered aloud if there would be a wire. The longing in her voice brought the truth to me with wrenching clarity: we are returning to Suva not to convalesce my ankle, but to hear from Home.

The Customs Officer's wife, a fay little bird in strange, old-fashioned clothes, looked up from her needlework to the thrashing cocoa-nut palms on the shore and white horses beyond the reef.

167

"Might be wise to bide a while," she said, mildly. "Do you not think so, Madam?"

It was Constance she addressed in this way, not myself. She did not see us as two independent beings.

"I could make up a bed for you and your daughter in Sven's room, if you so desire."

"My daughter?" said Constance, startled, while it was as much as I could do to keep from laughing out loud.

"If she is not so by blood then she is by love. I sense a deep affection between you."

The little woman looked directly at me, and I realised she knew the truth, but she said nothing more and bent to her work. It was then, with the candle guttering in the draught from the poorly fitted sill and the native mats lifting and billowing on the floor, that I had the odd sensation of being blessed. More than that. It was as though she'd married us together, that brown, tired little priest, the Customs Officer's wife. My heart softened and gladdened and I thought, at that moment, "We shall never be apart."

The boy, Sven, was gesturing wildly to us from the water's edge where we had left the dinghy, loaded with our boxes and covered with tarpaulin. Constance and I made our farewells and scrunched our way across the pebbled sands. As we went, I glanced at her, to see if she, too, felt that our love was solemnised, but her rich hazel eyes were fixed on the cutter, the sailors aboard racing to pull down the sails and fling out the anchor. Now that it was closer, just beyond the reef, we could see the state of the ship, the flaking paint, the dents, and every now and then, on a particularly vibrant gust, we had a whiff of the overpowering copra. Although impervious to my earlier tender thoughts, Constance immediately sensed my present quailing.

"Come along. I've sailed in worse," she said.

We climbed into the dinghy and sat atop our things. The

Customs Officer and his boy dragged it out to knee-height in the snapping waves and took an oar each.

What happened next should have been an omen, if the little woman's blessing was not one already. Constance's precious box, the polished mahogany box containing her microscope and samples, slid from the mound of luggage. The Customs Officer, his beard glistening with spray, leant from the dinghy, oar extended, and scooped it towards him. The box bobbed and splashed, the man heaved and grunted, but sadly his efforts failed and it was swallowed up by the grey and spiteful sea.

A larger wave heaved through the opening in the reef and would have caught us broadside had not the Customs Officer quickly regained his seat and turned the bow back towards the *Tui Cakau*, for that was the copra boat's name, rearing now and again above the swell. I could scarcely bear to look at Constance's face, expecting to find it stricken. But she was thoughtful, riding the chop as if it were a pesky horse and the loss of her box no more distressing than the loss of a treed hat. I wondered then, not for the last time, if my Constance, on her many journeys through the East, has not picked up some strains of their fatalistic religion. Had I witnessed the loss of my "tent" and all it contains, I would have stood in the stern, howled at the sky and beaten my breast.

How I wished I had donned my divided skirt in anticipation of the freakish climb to the boat. The ladder of rusted iron and frayed rope did not inspire my confidence. Despite the best efforts of Officer and boy, our dinghy banged and scraped at the copra cutter's side and sometimes swerved away altogether. The captain, a European, instructed two of his Fijian crewmen to form a human chain and pull me aboard, almost as soon as my foot found the first rung. I sustained bruises from that rough elevation I am sure, but I was to sustain so many more, so shortly after, that these first blue marblings of my flesh are insignificant in memory. As I was deposited on the greasy, foul deck, my wrenched ankle gave out a tremendous shot of pain and I sank to the boards. Thus I was spared the enviable spectacle of Constance, my senior by many years, bounding up the ladder like a goat.

"I say," she said, on landing, "what an appalling tub." She gave me a broad smile, which took in my trembling hands clasped around my pulsing foot. "Up you get, and we'll go below decks. I should think those bindings need tightening."

The hideous stench of copra, which even now seems lodged in my head, combined with her concern for me so soon after no small loss to the domain of science, to bring me to the verge of tears.

"But, Constance," I managed, "your box . . ."

"No sense in mourning that. What the sea takes for her own, she takes for ever."

Such a chill ran down my spine then, even as the very core of my being cried out that that was not so, that Constance was wrong, but she was helping me to my feet and we were struggling against the wind towards the cabin door. Our boxes and chattels were being thrown on to the deck with little care, so we paused to make sure all were present. I collected my "tent", which I had sensibly stitched shut.

"My friend and I are going below," Constance shouted at the Captain. "Could you cover our baggage, please?"

The Captain nodded, although I doubt he understood English, nor would he bother with anything as remotely genteel as a tarpaulin. He did not appear to speak Fijian either, but yelled loudly at the crew in French.

Constance opened the cabin door. The effluvia given off by the putrefying cargo flung up the steps at us like a hoof.

"Mary and Joseph!" Constance gasped.

"Let's ask to be put ashore," I begged her. "We could leave in the morning by another means. This is awful."

"There are no other means." Constance removed a large, white square of lawn from her pocket and held it to her nose.

"Besides — look!" She pointed back to the dinghy rowing hard against the offshore wind, already a number of yards away from the ship.

The handkerchief. Who, I wondered, had so neatly hemmed it, whose initial was "B", stitched in moss green in the corner?

"But . . ." I said and that was all, though the fearful word "hurricane" had formed in the back of my throat. I had never experienced one, but these rude gusts could be the precursor.

"But what?" Constance was growing impatient with me. "Quickly, it's beginning to rain."

What lay below was a nightmare to all five of the senses. Until Constance struck a match, we were quite blind. Spilling from their sacks, dried, stinking husks had overflowed from the hold and been packed in against the cabin's walls. A load of green bananas swung in a net above our already bowed heads. Bilge water sloshed around our feet and set up currents around the only stick of furniture, a rickety chair, which lay on its side. A groan escaped my lips and Constance fixed me with a fierce look.

"You will have to bear up better than that," she said, striking another match and glaring ferociously at the roof in search of a lamp. Dangling on a hook, we found a paraffin lantern, almost hidden by the bananas. Given the lurching of the boat, it was a struggle to light it, to hold up its cracked and smoky glass and aim the match at the wick. Once it was aglow, I wondered if we would not have been happier in the dark. As my dear one hung the lamp, insects scuttled among the bananas and copra. Glancing up into the nets, the only time I dared, the multitudinous eyes of a giant spider met mine.

"Oh, Connie!" I gasped, never before having used the diminutive. I flung myself forward, into her comforting arms. It was while we stood thus, swaying together, that the boat gave a violent shudder and threw us backwards, into the copra.

"The anchor coming up," murmured Constance, as we stood. "We are away."

The cabin doors forced open and a pair of feet thumped down the steps. The captain nodded and smiled, spreading his hands in an enquiring manner.

"Yes, thank you," said Constance, "we are content."

"Merci," I added, and the captain's face lit up.

"Parlez vous Français?" he asked.

"Un peu," I replied.

"Une fois que nous sommes au large, il ne sera pas aussi désagréable," he said. With a flourish and a courtly bow, he righted the only chair. "Et excusez-moi pour cet eau de cale," he added.

"Il est en bon etat, ce navire?" I dared to ask.

"Ce n'est qu'un coup de vent sud-est, rien a t'en faire du mauvais sang." With one grimy digit he dared to touch my cheek, and for a moment I entertained the idea of biting him. He must have seen the murderous intent in my eye for he continued immediately, "Je chercherai une autre chaise," before he left, never to return.

As soon as we were alone, Constance sat on the stool and drew me down to her lap.

"This is the meat of travelling. Tagimaucia was merely the bread," she told me, lifting a strand of hair away from my eyes. "I had thought, from your letters, that you had travelled like this before."

"Not at all," I managed, as the ship tipped alarmingly to one side and we braced our four legs on the slimy floor, "never."

"It's good for the soul," she murmured. "Character building."

"It has been my observation that people reserve that expression only for the most unpleasant experiences. I have never been able to accept that suffering of any kind is beneficial, for the soul, the character or anything else," I replied, as the stool beneath us raced to the opposite bank of copra.

"Tell me then," prompted Constance, "if you were twelve or thirteen years old, if you were, let's say, our friend Olive McNab —"

"But I am not," I protested, "and never should I want to be."

"Hush. If you were, wouldn't this be a jape?"

"A jape? Olive is not a fool."

"I am not suggesting that she is. I mean only that in childhood one's trust is complete."

"Trust in what? In God?" I shouted, leaping from her lap. "Surely you are not one of those pious pinheads who perceive childhood as kindred to sainthood?"

Constance shook her head at me, maddeningly calm. "No, my dear, I am not. But I do believe Olive would trust in this ship to convey her to safety."

"Then she would be a fool, indeed."

After that, we fell silent. While I clung to the upright poles supporting the cabin roof, the ship climbed waves and fell, its rigging and sails screaming in the wind. Then, another watery sound joined that of the cruel depths that surrounded us: heavy rain, thundering on the deck above like the plimsolls of an entire navy.

"Shall we smoke?" I asked. "It will pass the time."

My Capstan lay somewhere in my "tent", at that moment resembling a small, swollen, buff whale in a lake of bilge. One of Constance's many pockets, however, yielded up her cigarettes. We stood to inhale, and at that moment the lamp gave out, as if it sensed its pathetic light exceeded by our two glow-worm embers.

"Not to worry," came Constance, my sweet Buddha, from the dark. "Nothing much to look at anyway."

Suddenly, with my lungs full of sweet smoke, I was taken by a fit of giggling. It was as if that merry ghost of my girlhood mania had been called by Constance to join us. If she wanted pubescent bliss, then she would have it. Lord knows, nothing was amusing me. My foot ached abominably, we were sailing into the teeth of a hurricane, and the captain was a man who did not honour his word, at least with regard to furniture. At first Constance was quizzical, then her girlhood heart returned also, and our gales of laughter were equal in tumult to those of wind, wreaking the sails above to rags. When our sides ached, our noses and eyes ran, our mirth was shaking us still.

"Stop it," I said once, firmly. "We are hysterical."

Constance made gulping noises, and I took a pull on my cigarette. A match flared in the gloom.

"You —" began Constance, but she was off again. Oh, her deep, musical laughter is so dear to me.

"What?" I said, suddenly sober, suspecting I was the subject of her amusement now.

By the last light of the match, Constance, unable to speak for gasping, took up the pose of a flamingo, a terribly elegant and progressive bird, a flamingo that stands on one leg and smokes. She pointed at me, for it was I she mimicked, and we laughed again.

Then it happened. Perhaps it was a subterranean reef or simply a behemoth wave, but the side of the ship split open and a terrifying mass of seawater fell in upon us.

CHAPTER TWENTY-ONE

Five Pounds
and a Riot

The room Maud shared with Olive overlooked the ruins of the church, and beyond that, on the other side of the road, the district court-house. Built of the same grey stone as the mission station and the church, streaked with green fungus and squatting low to the ground, it was so disguised that a newcomer to the island may well miss it altogether. At the front, a small, raised portico offered protection from the rain and sun. Above the portico a façade puffed the little building up to a third more than its actual size. Entrance to this tattered, hurricane-battered seat of justice was gained by ascending three level steps, crossing the portico and going in by an arched double door. Then, if a person didn't know before, they would know then that the grand pitch of roof as seen from outside was a lie. The stud was low, and the long, narrow room dim and musty. At one end stood a high bench of polished kauri and, behind that, the pale and sombre face of King George.

Having lain awake most of the night with her ears full of roaring wind, slashing rain and every now and then the snuffling sleep of her niece, cursing herself for not returning to the refuge of the estate, Maud did not hear the court-house doors crank open at dawn. She was finally and deeply asleep.

Mr Geo. Austin, the Court Bailiff, was readying the premises for the day's appearances. The night before, Ogilvy the Coolie

Inspector had braved the weather to put him in the picture — a fine figure of a man, too, thought Austin, giving the judge's bench a quick dusting with his cuff — even if he was a little rotund, he at least dressed well. A man always looked smart in uniform. Had it up top, too, having passed with distinction all his exams to enter the Colonial Office. His Hindi and understanding of those excitable blacks was respected all over Fiji.

But for Mrs Gow to be brought to trial at all, thought Austin, she must have perpetrated a terrible cruelty. He gave the dust-misted face of King George a wipe with his handkerchief.

It was after Ogilvy had told him his long ago examination results, which Austin already knew, having heard the story at least a dozen times before, that he suggested the court-house be looking its best. They were expecting a big crowd, he said, and as well as that, all coolies on Taveuni who hoped they could get away with it were set to gather on the road outside during the trial.

Austin shook his head and edged his thin, grey body between the chairs, straightening the rows. The day would be long, sticky and hot. Already in the tiny gaol at the back of the court-house the three prisoners were restless, banging spoons on their tin plates. The gaoler's wife would be along shortly with their breakfasts. There was one Fijian, arrested for drinking liquor, and two coolies, one brought in for murdering his wife, which was common enough, and the other a bloodied mess from a sirdar's beating. Climbed in the overseer's bedroom window, apparently, a knife clenched between his teeth and murder in his wild eyes. No doubt Ogilvy would be along to get his story soon.

The scraping of the chairs on the floor had disturbed the fauna of the red runner, which traversed the length of the court-house. The myopic Austin could not see the fleas hopping above the scarlet in a faint black cloud, but as he paused there to debate the possibility of a floral decoration, they invaded his trouser legs.

"Damn stupid thing," muttered the Court Bailiff at the runner.

He'd had this trouble before. Frenzied and itching to a mid-point on his thighs, he rolled up the carpet and pushed it outside to the porch, where a small cupboard contained a stout stick kept for the purpose of beating. Mr Austin beat the rug as hard as he could.

It was the steady thump, thump, thump that woke Maud. For an instant, she forgot where she was and made to roll over and go back to sleep. It was merely the lali on a wet, steamy, muffled sort of morning, calling the plantation workers to muster. But her body knew that wasn't so, even if her mind was fooling itself, and fear gripped her stomach. Maud opened her eyes to Olive leaning out of the window.

"The court-house doors are open and it's an old man beating a red carpet," she announced. "The church hole is full of water, and some of the mats have floated away."

"Thank you, Olive," said Maud.

"The road is flooded, and Doctor Ricketts is under his umbrella waving at me. He's all dressed up, Aunt Maud. Why would that be?"

"Because he's . . ." Maud stopped. Why would that be, indeed?

"He's coming this way," reported Olive.

Maud got out of bed and pulled her dress on over her petticoat. Unless Emily aided her in some way with her toilette she would go to court looking like the Wild Woman of Borneo. There wasn't even a blessed comb in her purse. She pushed in beside her niece at the window.

"Doctor Ricketts —"

Her voice halted the doctor, who had been about to slosh his way up the muddy path. She beckoned to him, and Olive was right, he was resplendent, hair pomaded, his collar starched and pinned above a bottle-green waistcoat of shot silk.

"Mrs Gow," he said, staying where he was, "I was coming to see you."

"Don't come in. Talk to me here," said Maud, surprising herself. If he came in she would have to entertain him in the mission station parlour, attended by orphans who would report every word to Mrs Jamieson. She supposed he wanted to prescribe her something to keep her calm throughout the trial, but it wouldn't matter what he talked about, so long as he took her mind off the dread of the morning. And if only that greasy little Austin would leave off his doleful beating. He had the carpet spread out now, its ends in the rain, and was beating up and down it with one hand on the stick, the other shoved in at his waistband and ferociously scratching. Maud was reminded briefly of her mother.

"Well." The doctor eyed the puddle that spread wide beneath the lady's window and advanced no closer. "I came to make sure that Bernard had explained to you that in lieu of a lawyer, I will appear for you."

"No lawyer?" Panic reduced Maud's voice to a whisper.

"No. Well, we'd hoped one would arrive, but what with the hurricane —"

"What hurricane?" Maud found her voice and made it scathing. "We had a storm, that is all."

"A hurricane is expected. This is merely a curtain-raiser. The lawyer is delayed."

"Oh!" said Maud as Olive moved behind her and pointed out, loudly, that her aunt's dress was undone. Maud hoped the carpet basher's din and the doctor's good breeding would ensure his surdity.

"At any rate," he was saying, "I was to have pleaded mitigating circumstances."

"But you were not there," exclaimed Maud, suffering Olive's fumbling at her back. "I mean, at the time, when I —"

"Quite," interrupted Doctor Ricketts. "But in this case it should not matter. Now, if you will excuse me, I must attend to several of my native patients before we begin. The dratted flu, you know," he added, conversationally, before turning away.

Even before he reached the gleaming road, there was the loud approach of horse hooves. At first Maud thought it was the continued antics of old Austin, but no one could beat a rug that fast. She swatted Olive away from her back.

"Look," she said.

It was a Fijian, mounted on a sweat-flecked, rolling-eyed horse. Olive, pushing in at the window beside her aunt, recognised him as Joni, one of the bearers on the trek to Lake Tagimaucia. In his left arm he cradled a child, a baby, wrapped against the rain in a scrap of blanket. Just as Doctor Ricketts reached the road, he hauled the horse to a standstill and thrust the child at him. Water foamed at the horse's hocks. Then Doctor Ricketts was hurrying away, his umbrella angled over the limp infant, towards his own house.

Joni turned his horse and followed the doctor. The baby was his youngest child, his only son. The first signs of sickness had appeared a few mornings after Sitiveni brought the pavavalagi girl with the bone in her throat to his mother. When he'd got back from Tagimaucia, a journey that all his instincts had warned him against, he found Josefa sneezing more than he was before he left. The pavavalagi girl, everyone in the village agreed, had brought the disease with her. His mother lay dying even now. Once, Joni had approached the place where she lay, exposed to the rain and sun, but she had waved him away. She wanted to die in the old style, but she was taking a long time about it. If it wasn't for the lotu, Joni would help her. Sometimes, in the hill country of Viti Levu and Vanua Levu, widow-strangling still went on, he knew, and sometimes, it seemed, it was the kindest course to take.

Anyway, his mother was old and ready to die. The village was letting her get on with it, but Josefa was precious beyond all else. From where his mother lay, she'd whispered to him the cures: Tavala, puzzle nut; and dabi. He tried them, but none had worked. Now he waited on the white doctor's verandah, holding the silver coins so tightly they dented his palm, and gazed in wonder at the sunken church. It was all due, of course, to that vine. When it took a liking to something, it had to have it. Centuries ago it took the girl of the legend, running crying from her mother. It had made an attempt on the pavavalangi girl, and now, away from its misty mountain kingdom, it had destroyed the thing its transplanter valued the most. As Joni watched, the Reverend himself came out of a side door of the mission station and made his way to the dripping chasm, where he stood gazing down.

The doctor stepped softly behind him. He had Josefa in his arms, the child's face covered with a cloth and his own set in grieving lines. He stared at Joni.

"You should not have attempted the ride to Somosomo with him," began Doctor Ricketts. "His lungs were too delicate . . . " But there was no point in going on. Huge, quivering tears had formed in the father's eyes, and the strong, square hands that reached for the small bundle were trembling.

𝒜s Mrs Jamieson was busy with one of the flu-struck orphans who had suddenly taken a turn for the worse, it was Olive, observed closely by Ralph, who readied Maud for her trial. She fetched water from one of the cans brought each morning from the stream to the mission, and she carried it carefully down the dim corridor to her aunt. Both children sat on the edge of the bed and watched quietly as Aunt Maud washed her large white face, and smoothed her rough, brown hair in its round bun on top of her head. From beyond the curtained window came carriages pulling up and the clunk of the chocks against their wheels, the snorting of rain-soaked horses, the chug-chug of Cole 8s, Dodges and Maxwells. Voices hailed one another, and occasionally, when she recognised a shout or laugh, Aunt Maud would freeze and look towards the drawn curtain.

There was a gala outside, thought Olive, which was odd since her ears were tuned to news of that kind of festivity and she'd heard nothing. Or perhaps it was something more to celebrate the Armistice. Perhaps, like in the picture books from England, the circus had arrived in town.

"What's going on?" she asked her aunt, slipping from the bed and going towards the window.

"Come away!" snapped Maud. "Sit down."

Olive hung her head. "But what is it? Is there a fair today?"

Maud looked at her with disbelief. Perhaps it was just those wide, violet eyes that made the child appear watchful, nothing innate.

"Fool of a girl," she said. "They're here to watch the trial."

"What trial?"

Maud sighed. "You'll see. Now, help me, please."

Olive battled with the tiny mother-of-pearl buttons while Ralph yawned and shivered. The night before, with a firm-lipped kiss that was more a bite, Mrs Jamieson had dressed him in an over-sized nightshirt of the Reverend's and settled him into a makeshift bed at the closed end of the verandah. Every so often squalls of rain had found their way around the corner and flung themselves at him. Ralph had known without asking that he couldn't have shared with the orphans — besides being girls, they were Fijians — but all the same he wished he'd asked Mrs Jamieson if he could sleep inside. What if there really was a hurricane? He might be blown away to sea. He'd wished he'd gone home with Eric, until the rub of the sheets on his welts reminded him of Uncle Bernard and the frightening way he'd talked to him before he'd picked up the cane. He'd tell his Dad, who'd never taken the strap to him yet. His Dad would be angry with Uncle Bernard. When he eventually slept, he'd dreamed of his father and Uncle Bernard wrestling on the lawn. Holding his hand, Aunt Maud watched with him from the verandah and they cheered Hughie on. Triumphant, his father sat on Bernard's chest, just as Ralph had done with Anil.

Now he watched Olive struggling with Aunt Maud's dress and wondered why ladies wore clothes that were too small for them.

Olive was picking and brushing at the smears of mud on the white frock.

"Never mind," said Aunt Maud, impatient, "I'll hide the worst of it with my duster, hot as it is."

At ten-to-nine precisely, Maud and the children set out towards the court-house. The wind had returned, flinging water in their faces and wrapping Maud's skirts tightly around her legs. Behind her, the children were whispering.

"What is it?" asked Maud, sternly, without turning around.

"We're hungry," said Olive.

"I couldn't impose on Mrs Jamieson any more than we already have." Maud herself wished for Ah Jack and his tea, that lovely tea that softened the edges of the unforgiving world, the tea that numbed all anxiety. And where was Bernard? How could he let her go through this alone? Surely the seas were not so high he couldn't motor up in the *Island Princess*, or at least ride; the way would still be passable by horse-back. How could she possibly hold her head up after this? Perhaps she should go away to New Zealand or Australia immediately after the trial, as soon as passage could be arranged and Bernard could sell up and follow her. Fiji was simply not a colony for white people — the climate, the end of indenture, the uncooperative natives — it was impossible. A sudden gust leapt at her back and threatened to blow her over, face down. As she regained her balance, firmly planting her feet, Olive gave an exclamation of horror.

"Whatever is it?" Maud feared the child was suddenly taken by apoplexy: she was grasping at her neck.

"My magnifying glass! It's gone!" She searched the ground at her feet and began to whirl, the wind blowing out her dress like a balloon.

"Don't, Sis!" cried Ralph. "You'll fly away!"

As she spun, Olive was whooping and sobbing. Maud repressed an urge to slap her. She pulled the child close.

"Stop that. Right now!"

182

Olive's silence was immediate and her gaze over Maud's shoulder trembling. Maud turned.

Coming down the street towards them was a crowd of Indians, men, women and children, some armed with cane knives.

One of their number must also be on trial, thought Maud, they committed such heinous crimes among themselves. She ushered the children ahead of her, up the stone steps and in through the double doors.

The court-house was full. A few Fijians clustered around the door, but the rest were Europeans. The men among them wore their usual workaday clothes, trousers and jackets in shades of white topped with a dusty planter's hat, but the women had dressed for the occasion. Maud recognised gowns only last out of mothballs on Friday night, at the Torte's. Annie and Alphonse Torte themselves sat in aisle seats. They must've ridden all the way from Vuna; he was in jodhpurs, she was in a habit and they were both soaked to the skin. As Maud moved through the crowd, familiar hats above set faces turned and looked at her, then back towards the bench, which so far was unoccupied.

At the sudden attention, the children fled to the last remaining chairs. Old Austin came forward, hair slicked and sombre, and took Maud's arm, leading her down to the dock. A chair had been thoughtfully placed there and she sank into it. Ogilvy sat rigid in the front row, eyes ahead, his pith helmet on his knees, the buttons on his shoulder straining at the tight fabric of his shirt.

They say it's all the roti he eats makes him so fat, thought Maud. The traitor. He should have brought Aiyaz, so these ghouls could see for themselves the superficiality of his wound.

Aiyaz at that moment was astride Bernard's horse, clinging to its mane, as it scrambled up a fall of rocks. He closed his eyes for fear and the rain, but his nose filled so with the acrid sweat of

Sahib and the rotting wet of the great surrounding jungle that he'd felt sick and opened them again. They'd left before dawn, stopping only for Ah Jack, who'd followed them down the road, calling out, bearing a thermos flask of tea on a strap. When he handed it to Sahib he didn't look at him at all, as if the flask's content was distasteful to him, thought Aiyaz.

"For Memsahib," the old man had said. Aiyaz had watched over his shoulder as the horse cantered on and the old man hobbled off, through the dark sheeting rain, back to the house.

Hours later, the man and boy made their way through fallen trees and down a precipitous slope to find the road, where it emerged from its blanket of rocks.

"Not much further," said Bernard. "Another bend in the road and we're there." He supposed the boy understood him, although he gave no indication of having done so. Several times during the journey, with the movement of the horse, his little head knocked back against Bernard's chest. Once, Bernard looked down at the child's face, the thick lashes on the smooth flushed cheeks, his straight, rain-glistened nose and beside it, the dark pucker of the scar. The wound had closed, more or less, but infection still welled at the edges of the scabs. Now Bernard regretted not having it dressed before they set off. At the time he'd decided a bandage would worsen his wife's chances, but now, seeing how pale Aiyaz had become and how livid the wound, he wished he'd used some foresight. Of course, the child was exhausted — not only from the long ride through the storm, but also from the protracted terror of sitting so close to Sahib.

As they came into town, a silver-haired figure with a black umbrella and doctor's bag raced out of one of the bures opposite the Chinese store, unsuccessfully dodging puddles. Doctor Ricketts pushed his way through the waiting throng of coolies, up the stairs of the court-house and inside. At the sight of the coolies, some of whom looked familiar, Bernard slowed. No wonder no one had come to help with the shutters the night before, still less to shelter on the verandah when a great gale flattened one of the Lines. They were hiding out in the bush, already half-way to town.

One of them approached the horse, arms out-spread. It was Aiyaz's father. Bernard lifted the child down to him, and the father gathered him in his arms, glaring over the top of his head at the sahib. The child was shivering, feverish.

Damn, damn and blast it, thought Bernard. He followed the father to the top of the court-house stairs where they stood side by side, peering into the gloom.

"May it please you, Sir," came Doctor Rickett's voice, "my name is Doctor Arthur Ricketts and I am appearing for the accused."

There was a silence, while the Honourable Baxendale took in the doctor's besmirched appearance: soiled waistcoat, trousers wet to the knee; and jacket dripping enough to form a small lake a few inches behind him. A sheet of iron lifted and banged on the court-house roof.

"A doctor?" he said, finally, his nasal voice like him, thin and tired. "Where, pray, is the accused's lawyer?"

"Delayed by the storm, Sir."

Maud, lifting her eyes above the rim of the box, thought the doctor's voice had a begging quality to it.

"This is most irregular," said the Honourable Baxendale, "I wonder if we should not adjourn the case to a later date."

"That would not be advisable, Sir." This from Ogilvy, popping up and down again like a cribbage peg, gesturing towards the open doors. Baxendale looked down the flea-hopping runner, past the shaggy head of the haunted-looking planter on the porch, to the crowd of coolies outside. Some of them, he noted, were armed, after a fashion, and none of them looked happy. The young Constable Moffatt, sweating in his serge uniform, stood to attention just inside the door. Baxendale couldn't see that he'd be much use if the crowd took it into their heads to riot. He sighed.

"Very well." He flapped his hand at the Court Bailiff, who stood and read, "Maud Elspeth Gow, you are charged that on the —"

"Excuse me." Baxendale turned his yellow, feather-lined face towards her. "Would the Accused please stand while the charge is read?"

The same tingling of shame that Maud experienced the night it all happened filled her once again, and she stumbled to her feet, whispering, "I'm sorry, Your Honour." Old Austin, curse him, had a sardonic twist to his toothless mouth.

"Maud Elspeth Gow," he began again, "you are charged that on the eighth day of November, this year of our Lord 1918, you did wilfully assault Aiyaz Singh. How do you plead?"

Maud licked her dry lips. Hammering and leaping on the tin above her head, the rain had begun again in earnest. The wind was stronger, too, lifting the deluge away from the building, then dumping it against the walls and roof. The judge put his hand to his right ear then to his left. Recurring abscesses of a tropical variety had reduced both to relative deafness.

"Do we have a plea?" he asked.

Doctor Ricketts was staring at her. Maud gave him a weak smile, and he came forward to the dock.

"You will plead guilty, of course," he whispered. The spectators murmured to one another, heads turning to the side and inclining to the row behind. She gazed past the doctor and imagined what it would be like to sit among them. Had it been one of the Torte women, or any other planter's wife in the dock, would she have made the trip? She answered herself by shaking her head.

"But of course you must," whispered the doctor, watching her. "There were witnesses."

"Mrs Gow?" The Hon. Baxendale inserted two long fingers beneath his wig and scratched at his hot, itchy scalp. "Quiet!" he shouted, suddenly enough for the assembled to jump like the fleas on the runner. "We must have silence."

"Guilty." Maud struggled with the word. It came unnaturally to her. Once again, the judge had his hand at his ear.

"My client pleads guilty, Your Honour." The doctor turned to the judge. "But there are mitigating circumstances."

"Which are?" Baxendale was not looking at the doctor, but at the schedule on the bench in front of him. Intoxication, attempted murder, murder — natives and coolies. They were easily dealt with. But this case would be tricky, it could take all day. He looked over the throng in the court-house. It was always difficult to know which way they'd go, these Taveuni planters. At this moment they were all leaning forward, as thunder rolled above them, trying to catch the doctor's first words. There might well be a ground swell among them who'd like to see this poor soggy woman heavily fined. He sighed. Doctor Ricketts was pulling a sheaf of crumpled, damp papers from his jacket pocket. He cleared his throat.

"As Mrs Gow's physician," he was saying, "I have attended her in three confinements. Not one of the resulting infants survived more than three days. Since that time my patient has become addicted to tranquillising powders —"

Maud stared at the doctor. She had not thought him capable of lying, even for her.

"— administered in a tea by a faithful retainer. These Eastern medicines make it possible for Mrs Gow to go about her daily business, without the ever-present grief that previously overwhelmed her. It is my belief that on the day in question, Mrs Gow had over-indulged in this tea and lost control of her actions."

"You are saying," countered the judge, "that she was drugged?"

Doctor Ricketts nodded. "In addition, Your Honour, my client was further incapacitated by the large number of house guests at the Estate. House guests," here he turned to his audience, "who were, in the main, children. Having herself been deprived of the fruits of marriage, Mrs Gow does not enjoy the company of children."

Baxendale was leaning across the bench and poking Austin in the shoulder, but Austin's face had set into an expression of sympathy and his eyes were fixed on Maud.

"Would the Defence please face the Bench?" asked Baxendale himself, with exasperation, having failed to alert the Bailiff. The howling rain and his lack of hearing meant that he'd missed the last few words of Rickett's address, but he doubted they had any import. More and more, during the last ten years or so, doctors were called upon to defend aberrant behaviour, and Baxendale was one judge who would have none of it. The law was not subject to fashion, least of all fashions from Germany with scientific names. All reason dictated that if the Accused were insane, then she should be locked away. This planter's wife was fully in control of her faculties. He would fine her. And if she objected, the case could be taken to Suva and tried by jury. There was, he supposed, some merit in that idea. He could transfer the case himself, because of the woman's lack of a lawyer. And, anyway, brutality by a woman against a coolie was hard to excuse, women not being subject to the same passions and aggressions as men. God knows, worse things went on in the fields than a single slash to a child's face. He wondered what Ogilvy's reasons were for bringing this one to trial. He had to bring charges against someone every so often, Baxendale supposed, cynically, otherwise he wouldn't have a job. While these thoughts meandered through his mind, the judge's gaze lifted to the window above the spectator's heads. Something cylindrical and brown was rolling, high in the air, tossed around like a leaf. What the devil was it? A tree trunk? No, it wasn't. It was a dunny. The judge let out a sudden gurgle of laughter. The mission station dunny. Poor old Jamieson. Lost his church and now his vale lai lai. The doctor was gaping at him like a landed fish.

"Shall I go on?" he asked.

"No, no. We've heard enough." The judge turned to Maud, and she stood, by instinct. His cool eyes seemed to both instruct and expose at the same time. In that instant, Maud believed that Baxendale saw everything, her wasted afternoons with the teapot, her dark vigils by the little graves, the anguish of her loneliness.

Baxendale narrowed his eyes. He wished he could deliver a lecture on the futility of self-pity and on how women like Mrs Gow should pull together with their husbands to make Fiji a white man's colony, a productive part of the Empire.

"I find you guilty. This kind of behaviour rarely comes to the attention of the courts, which is not to say that it does not go on. Far worse cruelties than this are perpetrated upon the inferior races every day in this colony. It seems to me, as I travel around Fiji, that many planters are keeping themselves blissfully ignorant of the fact that the Indenture ended two years ago. The coolies that remain in white man's employ are merely serving out the last of their time. Your crime, Mrs Gow, and 'crime' is not too strong a word, does not help the black man in his endeavours to view the white man as his friend. I fine you five pounds." A cloud of dust rose with the bang of the gavel and the judge was already retreating.

"All stand." said Austin.

𝒥n the airless, dark room at the back of the court, Baxendale sank into a cane chair with half of its seat out, gazed out of the tiny, salt-frosted window towards the gaol, and commended himself on a clever verdict and sentence. The coolies would feel vindicated with Memsahib fined. To them, of course, five pounds was a lot of money. The planter community may well have quibbled about the issue, pleaded it was only discipline, that Mrs Gow had forgotten she held the piece of crystal when she slapped the boy and so the assault was accidental. But there had been none of that. They'd all sat as docile as lambs, as if they understood that by the nominated pittance the guilty verdict was only a sop.

By the time the women had gathered their bags and hats and joined the men on the porch, the coolies, now numbering over three hundred, had withdrawn to the other side of the road, in front of the Chinese store. The Europeans flung hats and jackets over their heads against the rain and the humiliating stares of the Indians.

"If Bernard Gow had married into his own class," hissed Annie Torte to Alphonse, "this would never have happened."

Alphonse took her arm and led her towards their tethered horses, but not before she'd glared ferociously in Bernard's direction.

"A whore's daughter with pretensions," spat Annie, "and no idea of how to control the servants." She was, herself, off a Colonial Sugar Refinery plantation in the Rewa and they'd never had this sort of trouble.

Suddenly, a round of angry yells erupted from the Indians. On the court-house steps stood Mrs Gow on the arm of her husband, with the two children behind her. From where the Tortes stood, the rush of coolies up the steps towards her was a bright, multi-coloured wave. Water splashed at muddy feet and ran clear from upraised arms. In a second, Bernard was pushed aside and Maud surrounded, her screams heard only faintly above the cacophony. The avengers shouted and screamed while Constable Moffatt blew his whistle and dealt truncheon blows. Running from the back of the court-house came Ogilvy, Austin and Fenn the gaoler. Between them they managed to restrain two of the older men who were not so quick on their feet. The constable meanwhile had collared a girl of seven or eight, but let her go as the coolies took flight, ruefully watching them disappear into thick forest. There was no point in pursuing them himself, a constabulary of one.

Maud had collapsed to the ground, her face scratched and nose bleeding. One eye was closed, but the other noticed groggily how a small brown animal had curled beside her. She reached out a hand. Was it dead?

Finding himself flung back against the wall, Bernard picked himself up and reached for his whimpering wife, pulling her to her feet. She was staring horrified at a large hank of her hair, ripped by its roots and lying bloodied in the dust. When she went to pick it up, he restrained her, and it took all the strength in his arm to lead her away, across the road, past the staring Europeans and natives, to the mission station.

After a while, when the engines of the last of the motorcars had faded away, two lonely figures came out from their hiding places in the dark of the court-house and made their way to the steps. Ralph was crying.

"When we get back to Aunt's place," Olive said firmly, wiping her little brother's nose with his shirt tail, "I will write to Mother and tell her we want to come home."

CHAPTER TWENTY-TWO

The Night's Brown Savagery

~ Elvira Gow ~

"The great essential thing is the Organized Chance of Living Again. We'll teach the whole damn World, that there's a better Heaven than the pale, serene Anglican windless harmonium-buzzing Eternity of the Christians, a Heaven in Time, now and for ever, ending for each, staying for all, a Heaven of Laughter and Bodies and Flowers and Love and People and Sun and Wind in the only place we know or care for, ON EARTH."
Rupert Brooke

The girl is here again with my food. I can hear her outside the walls, I can hear my ayah telling her to go away.

"Don't stay here," says Margaret, quiet, not quiet enough for me. "Just leave the food and go."

I have ears like a bat, hidden under my hair; my hair all matted now because my ayah has been too busy with all Adela's sons and that girl. Too busy to brush me. My ears prickle.

"Don't stay here."

The girl is crying, I think.

I have been so excited all day, I have been talking talking, since morning and Margaret is tired of me.

There she is. The girl. Coming in at the door. Quick. Pretend I can't see her, roll on to my back and hold Rupert's book to my breast, look up, up through the hole in the roof at the fast sky. Water came through, lots of it, the night after I showed them in the boat my bum. That was funny. Still giggle. Mean old Maud, I could see her eyes popping from the beach. Bernie had his back to me. Seen my bum before though, Bernie has . . . mustn't remember that now. Only remember at night, then it's nice.

Adela's girl is sitting beside me on the bed. There is water on her face. Touch it — tears.

I cried the night of the rain and wind. Bernie came back on the boat with Adela's boy. Watched them I did, I was at the graves talking to the babies and there they were, Bernie walking hard up to the house and Maud's mother. The wind came more and more 'till it blew me from my bure to the house in the dark. I peered through the slats, saw Bernie asleep in his chair. Bernie doesn't care about me. I danced on the verandah in the wind, laughing, then something white, it was Bernie's hat, flew up at me and Bernie was trying to open the door, so I ran again, ran to the servants' bures and hid with Margaret, cuddled up to Margaret till the morning.

I ask Olive, "What's the matter?"

"My mother," says Olive.

Adela. My friend Adela. Once she cut my hair. I sat on a chair brought from the dining-room, out by Maud's roses, and she cut my hair short. She said it was the fashion. I was beautiful, but not as beautiful as Adela.

"My mother is dead."

Now Margaret is here and there is a terrible noise, a howling and yooling.

"OOooo!"

"Hush now," says Margaret.

The noise goes on and on, coming from my belly, to my throat and out, into my hair, into the air around my head.

"Be quiet!"

It stops when I see the girl, squashed up against the broken wall on the other side of my big bed, eyes popping like Maud's when she saw my bum. Giggle. Still funny.

"Why is she laughing now?" asks Olive.

Margaret slaps me hard on my face part, so I hit her back. Fist. Margaret falls over. The table falls over, all the cups and plates, the lamp. Olive, crying, rushes forward, she's bending over my ayah.

"My ayah! Sega! Go away!"

Olive backs out, backs out the door. Stops, looks in. Margaret goes on her hands and knees after her. They wait outside. I lie down on my bed, still wet from the rain. Cough, cough. What's this? Cough.

Margaret still looking in.

$\mathcal{I}$ hit Margaret before, once. When Rupert was here. She told on us. I was beautiful then, Alabaster Queen. Bernie came. His face above Rupert's. Rupert loving me, his pale, thin body, his Englishman smell, soft English shirt, his yellow hair and pink cheeks. I didn't live in my bure then. I was part of the family, in the house. Bure was my hideaway.

Bernie said, "If you like it so much here you can stay for good."

That was later. Then it was words I'd never heard before, rude words that crackled in the air. Pulling, pulling Rupert away from me, throwing him out.

Then Margaret came. They've taken Rupert to Somosomo, she said. They've put him on a copra boat for Suva. Gone. Going on to Tahiti. Gone.

How did he know? How did Saka Gow know? You told him? You told him!

I hit Margaret. Once, twice, again. Margaret lay down, her face bleeding.

$\mathcal{N}$ow Margaret is outside, holding Olive's hand. She won't run for help. She knows better.

*A*fter Rupert left, they sent for Doctor Ricketts. He said to my brother, you mustn't. You must keep her up at the house. But Bernie said, no. Doctor Ricketts gave me morphia, then laudanum. He took me into the sea in his clothes and held me there 'till I quietened. I was given laudanum for weeks. Margaret stopped it. She said I was better, laudanum muddled me worse. I was grieving, she said. I was, for my Rupert, the things he told me, whispering in my ear that first night.

He came in from a storm. He said he'd nearly drowned, that he hated Fiji. Sitiveni Torte had rescued him, he was swept away by the river in full flood.

When he came in, into the parlour, I was in my white muslin, with my new short hair. He liked me better than Adela. He said she was disappointed, mannered, painted, her soul adulterated.

"What does that mean?"

He laughed. In the bure at dawn he took my shoes off and admired my strong feet. I promised him never to wear shoes again. He said I was like him, we were neo-pagans.

"What is a neo-pagan?"

He laughed. He said he adored me. I said I adored him. He asked me what I believed in, what made me like I am. I said I didn't know. I asked him the same question.

"Nudity and chastity," said Rupert.

So in the bure, at dawn, I took off my white muslin. He said if he were a painter he'd paint me, as a poet all he could manage were a few poor words. Alabaster Queen. Pale Savage. He kissed me and said I was to escape, to meet him and some other people — Jacques, he said, Margery, some others.

"Who are they?"

"You'd like them; we'll meet them on May first, 1933 at Basel Station."

"Where's that?"

"In Europe."

Europe, so far away, as far away as Death. Rupert will never live again. He has gone into the earth. Adela wrote to me, Margaret brought me the letter, Sitiveni told her what was in it. Rupert, dead, 1915. I don't know what year it is now. I grieve, still.

*O*live and Margaret, still holding hands, just inside the door.
"Is she asleep?"
Of course not. My heart beats in its box.
"What do you want?"
Olive says, "Me?"
"You."
"Tell me more about my mother. Was she your friend?"
She was my only friend. She was morphia, laudanum, wine. Her smell came from pretty bottles, her lips from a red tube. People stared at her. Mrs Hortense Torte couldn't believe her eyes. An actress!
But she had been famous and she told me it is hard to give up being famous. So she performed. She would play the piano and sing, recite poetry, speeches she'd learnt from plays. She'd toss her shining hair, she'd make sure people were watching. They were watching. They hated her . . .
Olive waits. I've said nothing. There is a sob. And another.
What can I say? Adela loved her children. When they weren't with her, she longed for them like she longed for an audience. She was clever and kind. She sent me Rupert's book. I try to talk, but cough instead.
Shouting, outside. A young man's voice, not properly a man's voice.
"Olive? Olive are you in there?"
I turn my eyes from her. The bure goes darker for a moment as she goes out the door. Light again. I hear her say to her brother, "What do you want?" And he says, "You've got to come up to the house. There's another telegram. From Dad."
They go away.

196

Margaret coming in. Pretend I'm asleep. She tucks my net around me, picks up the things we knocked when we fought. I listen to her moving around.

Dusk. Sweat, cold on my skin.

CHAPTER TWENTY-THREE

Reunion

A fortnight after the funeral, Hughie sent a telegram to Vuna Point to say he was on his way. The next day he and his three eldest sons set sail on *Vai* to Taveuni. Before he left, he tried to bid little Rosie goodbye, but she had turned her face away from his kiss, as if she sensed his despair and was troubled by it.

"Rosie?" he'd tried again, going down to her level, holding out his arms.

"Sega!" and Rosie had run for Elena. Something would have to be done about the child when he returned: she scarcely spoke a word of English.

It was Hughie's custom, whenever sailing with his boys, to name the skipper a day before pulling the anchor. For the first time, he'd named Eddie. A fine sailor in the McNab tradition, he moved nimbly and lightly around the boat. Now the boy, winding in a sheet, looked over at his father and grinned. It was a long while since he'd seen that smile, thought Hughie, at least not since the morning Elena's wails had drawn the household from the breakfast table to the bedroom to gaze at Adela, bewildered.

By being so much in the sun, Eddie was brown, his arms and legs strong and fibrous. Down beside Hughie now, he took the tiller and called to Tom to bring her about. They were through the reef. Tom hopped to and the boat swung around to the nor-east. At first, when Hughie had named Eddie as skipper, Tom had tensed and flashed him a look of wounded betrayal. The father then had keenly felt his first daughter's absence. She'd have made a joke and teased them out of it, run for her gear — the old shorts and shirt of Harry's she wore boating. Then she'd have helped the skipper organise the food for the overnight sail.

Hughie reached out and patted his son's hand, its smooth, long fingers on the polished wood of the tiller, and Eddie looked up, surprised, his green eyes searching his father's. Hughie smiled.

"Don't forget to keep an eye out for that copra boat," he said, "the *Tui Cakau*. She's missing."

"No hope for her. She would've gone down in the hurricane."

"Two ladies aboard, apparently," said Hughie.

Eddie shrugged. "Amazing, what some people will put to sea in."

"Where's Bill?" asked Hughie, after a pause.

"Below."

"You haven't made him cook?" Hughie hoped with all his heart he hadn't. The sea air was giving him his first appetite for days.

"Why not?" asked Eddie, as they ducked the boom. "You always said a full stomach gave you sea-legs."

"Not Bill. He's the worst cook in all creation."

The boy had resisted the idea of sailing to Taveuni at all. Hughie still had a bad taste in his mouth about it, from their argument on that day in the gauze-walled mosquito room, both of them drenched in sweat from the heat and nerves. It was a hot day, that day, the day they buried Adela. Hughie started to remember the busy cemetery, the ministers of every denomination interring, blessing, wherever there was a plot. Anglicans lay beside Catholics, Jews beside Methodists, the mourners mainly Fijian and all despairing and bewildered. The faces he'd seen that day, the faces of the dead and the living . . . he tore his memory from them and forced himself to go back to mulling over the bargain, the deal he'd struck with Bill. Come to Taveuni and then he could make his own way in the world.

"I'm going to America," he'd said, flinging himself into his mother's old chair and eyeing Hughie's glass of Scotch thirstily. "I want to work in the moving pictures industry."

Hughie had shaken his head, amazed. "And how do you propose to get there?"

"I'll work my passage."

"As a seaman?" He hadn't been able to keep the scorn from his voice. "You wouldn't last five minutes. I went off as able-bodied at your age, but at least I knew how to mend sails. Learn the trade son, and you'll have an easier time of —"

But Bill had interrupted. "I don't care if I go as galley slave. I just want to get out."

Then they'd argued, and Hughie had lost his temper. Who was this red-faced, loud-mouthed stranger? There was a moment of cold panic: why was he so different to the others? Was he mad? Then he remembered how Olive sometimes worried him. There was the occasion he'd found her hanging upside-down from one of the rain trees with her knickers showing, oblivious to the Indian horse-drivers looking up at her from the shade below. And Eric, his rare depressions were deep and bewildering. And Tom had his quirks. All of them. It was natural to feel like this. They were full of surprises, the whole bunch of them, as was their mother.

Tears filled his eyes suddenly and he turned away to blink at the rushing wake. He would never, until his last moments, understand why she'd done that, why with her last strength she'd transformed herself into a tragic, ridiculous clown. She was there whenever he closed his eyes, the thick paint, the pencilled eyebrows, the smudged linen. God help him — he mustn't cry in front of the boys. There was a trick of memory, if only he could find it, where you forgot the last glimpse, the deteriorating spirit and body of the last months or days and remembered instead the woman as she was. He'd done it with Rose, but surely to God he never missed her like this. He'd reined himself in, kept a stiff upper-lip. Narrowing his eyes at the last of the distant coast of Viti Levu, Hughie concentrated and fleetingly he had her, Adela at the piano at a party in Suva, not long ago, a year or two at the most, her lovely voice singing "Isa Lei". The strains of it, tiny, whispered, carried to him on the stinging wind beneath a sky, still battered blue and grey from the storm, and bruised his heart. The tears ran freely then, but mercifully without sound, so he could wipe them away without Eddie or Tom seeing.

The cabin door banged, and there was Bill with steaming mugs of tea all round.

"Thanks, son."

Bill, who must bend double to perform his galley tasks, was stretching his neck and gazing out to sea. Tom came down from the forward end and rolled a cigarette. Wordlessly, he enquired of his father if he'd like a durry too. Hughie nodded. The slap of wave on hull worked its old magic and the love of his sons warmed him. He felt a release, a softening in his spine as the boat bucked and flapped. Eddie smiled and Tom, looking from his younger brother to his father, chuckled, low in his throat. None of them were prepared for Bill's reaction, his misunderstanding.

"What is it now? What the bloody damned hell are you laughing at now?" he shouted, mostly at Tom because it was Tom who'd laughed.

Staring at anything but the others and certainly not at Bill, Hughie remembered an altercation between Olive and her eldest brother. Bill had blown up at her, bellowing with sudden rage.

"Bill Bull!" she'd yelled, "Bill Bull!" Then she'd run for her life. Hughie could see what she meant now, out the corner of his eye.

"Damn you all!" Bill muttered. He flung the dregs of his tea overboard and returned below decks, his feet on the boards as heavy as boarding cargo.

Tom shook his head at his father, but Hughie endeavoured to

love all five of his surviving sons equally and would not show any favours, especially not of intimacy or a closer understanding. Sighing, closing his eyes, he gazed once more on Adela's face, the painted mask of her. He'd done his best to wipe her clean with a damp cloth. None of the servants would touch her. When he'd finished, Elena came in, her arms full of hibiscus, orchids and peacock flowers. Weeping, she arranged them around her mistress. If the undertaker, when he eventually arrived, had wondered what the coloured streaks on the deceased's face were, he never asked. Hollow cheeked and dark eyed, the man was exhausted from a surfeit of business.

"You wouldn't countenance how many ayahs, garden boys and shop assistants are being treated to a real English-style funeral by their employers. As soon as this is over I'll be going in for a motor," he'd told Hughie, after his boy had shut the hearse doors on Adela. "It's a miracle."

A miracle for whom, wondered Hughie, as the black carriage rolled silently down the hill, the mares as gaunt and tired as their owner, their greying ostrich feather plumes as limp as palms after a hurricane.

Wearily, Hughie had climbed the steps to the verandah and turned for the view. Usually it was one that gladdened him, the dusty town below, the ships, harbour, the reef and the blue ocean beyond. That day, since the winds had departed, a thick pall of smoke from the Indian cremation fires obscured much of the immediate vista. The cutters and schooners close in to port pushed their masts above the grey cloud. In the spaces where the smoke cleared, he could see the ragged piles on the wharves. He'd known, without the aid of field glasses, what they were. Even now, two open trucks were disgorging their loads to add to them. Bending his ear, Hughie had heard the distant keening of the natives as they gathered there, hopelessly mourning their departed. Corpses were stacked as high as a man's shoulder.

He'd gone inside, closed the door and drunk himself blind.

They anchored for the night in Levuka Harbour, but were warned by a dinghy-borne, top-hatted official not to go ashore. The influenza, he shouted through a loud hailer, was rife.

There were fewer Indians on Ovalau, but even so pyres burned among the trees on the steep inclines of the island. For the rest of the town, the clapboard shops and hoardings, there was no movement. Ahead of its time, Levuka was a ghost town. Bill cooked them all something unpalatable, which they ate in silence on the silent harbour. As soon as it was dark, they turned in to their bunks. After a day's sailing, Hughie thought, he'd sleep like a top. He didn't. Each time he closed his eyes, Adela loomed, and though he longed for her, it seemed immoral to allow his dreaming self to go to her with open arms. His appetite for her had outlived itself. At length he lay on his back, his eyes wide open and his hands folded beneath his head. Once, he heard a seabird with huge wings flap past the boat and with its passing came the falling cadences of mourning from the land.

An hour or so before dawn of the next day, Eddie had them all up and pulling anchor. Beyond the reef, they met a stiff head wind, which worked them hard all the way to Taveuni. Summoned from his galley, Bill had emerged with bad grace and lent a hand as they tacked back and forth across the Koro Sea.

By the time *Vai* reached Vuna, it was well after nightfall and none of the crew was in a good temper. The closer to Taveuni they'd drawn, the more Hughie's ardent visions of Adela had been replaced by melancholy visions of Olive, her little face anxious and grieving. Bill's gloom had rubbed off on the other two boys, and as they rowed ashore, guided by the lit headlamps of Bernard's waiting Packard and the flickering windows of the custom official's house, all three glowered at each other. Bernard stood alone on the beach.

"Maud is with the children," he told Hughie, while the boys heaved the dinghy up and loaded their boxes into the motorcar.

"They're waiting up for you."

Hughie nodded, a lump in his throat. "Where's your driver?" he managed.

Bernard rolled his eyes. "We've had a bit of trouble. Don't mention it to Maud." But in the Packard, on the short journey to the estate, he told his brother-in-law about the court case.

"She always had a hot temper as a lass," Hughie offered when he'd finished, by means of comfort. Bernard grunted and the car was silent. Behind him, Hughie's three sons sat ranged along the hard seat, staring out at the slow, passing shadows.

"You'll stay for Christmas, of course," said Bernard. "No sense in rushing back to Suva with the way things are."

"I suppose not."

"First thing Maud said after she read the telegram — they'll have to stay for Christmas."

The telegram. Olive's face again, reading it.

"It was waiting for us," continued Bernard, "when we got back from Somosomo."

"And the children?" Hughie wondered suddenly what he looked like. Unshaven, haunted. He might scare the living daylights out of them. Rubbing his hand over his chin, he felt the stubble. "Are they all right?"

"Perfectly healthy, if that's what you mean," said Bernard. "That Olive . . ."

Bernard would have trouble with Olive, of course, thought Hughie. She was proud, blithe, high-spirited. But that's not what Bernard was saying.

"She was inconsolable, after Maud told her the news. Ah Jack gave her some laudanum and she slept for a day and a night. Since then, the last few days, we've hardly seen her. Disappears after breakfast, comes back for supper."

"Where's she going?" Hughie felt a rising anger. He'd expected better than this from Maud.

"Damned if I know. And that Ralph . . ."

Little Ralph. "What of him?"

"I'll tell you now, though it's probably the wrong time. I had the stick to him on one occasion."

"The stick?"

"You needn't look so horrified, old man. He deserved it. Cheek and disobedience."

Hughie watched Bernard's big head hunched over the wheel and thought how the man's mouth and chin, the lower lip curling, nearly meeting the hummock of his jaw, warned of violence and stupidity. He was mean, unreachable.

"Ralph is a good boy." The defence reached his ears as a hoarse whisper. He closed his eyes and there was Adela, pale, languid, pregnant with Ralph, lying on the daybed in the mosquito room. She looked up and smiled. Here was her gentle kiss, her soft, cool hands on his hot brow, the weight of her arm on his shoulder.

But it was Tom's hand on his shoulder, and he lifted his bowed head. They'd arrived. Old Ah Jack was hobbling down the steps towards the car, which Bernard had drawn up in the light from the open door. Behind Ah Jack stood Grandmother McNab, the angular silhouette of her head bestowed by the bombazine mourning bonnet, once again resurrected and supreme. Tom, Eddie then Bill were clasping her hand and kissing her cheek. She patted each one consolingly before they passed down the hall.

And she hated you, Adela, thought Hughie, she did her best to make your life unhappy. He got out and slammed the door.

Minnie, who'd been saying something comforting to Bill as he passed by her shoulder, snapped her head around. This gentle son rarely opposed her, but there was something in his tread, something in the way he and Bernard approached the stairs, that gave her a sense of argument, either recent or imminent. She took his hand.

"I'm so sorry, my dear," she said, bending her cheek for his kiss. Hughie shivered and would have pulled away, but Adela had drawn close. She was there, just behind him, urging him to be kind.

"Thank you, Mother," he said. "Where are the children?"

"In the parlour," answered Minnie, taking his arm.

And so they were. Tom had taken little Ralph on his lap, and the boy had his head on his shoulder. Sallow and impossibly thinner, Olive sat wedged on the ottoman between Eric and Eddie. Maud came forward to kiss him, her face badly insect bitten — or was it scratched? — and her head wrapped in a peculiar scarf arrangement. Behind her, the curtains billowed with the hot night breeze and around them the air filled with a rising wail. It was Olive. She rushed at him, clasping him around the hips as her aunt clasped his shoulders. There was an impatient, dry click of the tongue from his mother, as she did her best to prise the child loose.

"Mother!" It was sharper than he'd intended. In the struggle, Olive had intensified her crying. He bent to her, not such a distance now, lifted her in his arms and carried her through the open doors to the verandah. She was all bone and hair, her body not yet a woman's, but hard and light like a young boy's. Keeping his arms around her, he sat her on the verandah rail.

"Was it terrible?" Olive whispered. "Did she suffer?"

"I don't think so," Hughie said. "No, not at all."

Olive was staring at him. He looked into her wide, clear eyes and knew suddenly that she had changed. Her grief had given her knowledge of the world, there was a new light there. What was it? A kind of weariness? Perhaps it was just a necessary pragmatism. Or both. He sighed and held her close for a moment, before helping her down.

"Have you been looking after Ralph?" he asked, his arm around her shoulders. He wanted to smoke, so they sat together at Maud's table, in the wicker chairs.

"Margaret the ayah does," said Olive. "And Aunt Maud, especially since the hurricane last week, when Pepepeli flew away."

"Pepepeli?" Hughie lit up.

"Her bat. We stayed in Somosomo for Aunt Maud to go to court, and while we were away the bat disappeared."

"Go on. Never." Hughie took a deep lungful of smoke and gazed at his daughter. He'd missed her, he'd missed the discussions they had on the verandah at home. Late at night, when everyone had gone to bed, Olive would creep out, snuggle beside him on the bench seat and they'd talk and laugh. Olive always announced her arrival with, "I won't talk much, Dad, I know you like your peace and quiet, I'll just sit and keep you company."

"It's not funny," she was saying now.

"What?" He must have been smiling.

"The bat. It flew out of Grandmother's window in the morning, but the wind was so strong it blew away. Grandmother said it looked like an inside-out umbrella."

"Did she?"

"Aunt Maud still hasn't spoken to her. Did you see how the coolies have ripped her hair out?"

Hughie started. "Grandmother's?"

"No, Aunt Maud's. That's why she's wearing a bandeau. I think it makes her look as if she's got a goitre."

Hughie gave Olive his mock stern look, narrowing his eyes at her, and she giggled.

"And where is it you've been going, lass, every day on your own?"

Olive's mouth hardened. "It's a secret."

"What is it? Have you found some young Kaivitis to play with?"

"No." Olive thought how she'd never seen him looking so tired. In the dim light cast by the bulb inside, there were long, deep shadows and his pale eyes seemed crinklier than ever.

"I would like you to tell me, dear." He leaned forward and a bar of shadow fell across his face, making his nose appear long, like a shrew's. Olive smiled. Perhaps she should tell him. After all, if she didn't look after Elvira, who would?

"Olive?"

"I'm helping someone. She doesn't know how to look after herself and Ralph's got her ayah."

"Ah. Uncle Bernard's sister. Is that who you're talking about?"

"Yes, that's right!" Olive was pleased. Her father didn't seem at all shocked.

"I don't want you going to her anymore. As I remember her, she's very unpredictable."

"But she's got the influenza! She nearly blew away in the hurricane. And no one cares about her — I even have to take her her food!"

The child's tears were still close to the surface. Hughie decided to leave it now and take the matter up with her in the morning. He stood, grinding his cigarette underfoot.

"Bed time," he said, holding out his hand. "It must be midnight."

The others, they discovered, had gone up to bed already. The only footsteps downstairs belonged to Ah Jack, scuffing back and forwards from the kitchen with the cups and plates from the boys' late supper. At the top of the stairs Hughie kissed his daughter fondly and went to his bed. Grandmother, Olive remembered, was sharing hers now to make room for Hughie. At the thought of it her steps slowed, and as they did, Eric's voice floated out to her from the nursery. Peeking in the door, she saw him, lying in his bed across from Ralph's, telling him a story. The cradle was gone, the dusty canopy and cobweb-strung legs finally banished to a cupboard. Three canvas beds filled the floor, and in them the sailors were all fast asleep.

The story, as far as Olive could gather, concerned sword fights, noble horses, brave men and faithful dogs. It was very Henry Rider Haggardish and punctuated every now and then with a, "Are you still awake, Ralph?" to which sleepy Ralph would reply, "Immm," and Eric would continue. Olive was just about to turn away when a glint of glass and metal caught her eye. Hanging on the end of Eric's bed, on a piece of sennit, was her magnifying glass, not lost in the mud at Somosomo at all, but spinning slowly here, in a gentle draught. Just recently its loss had been superseded by the other greater one, and Olive had all but forgotten it. Now, the greater loss served to make the lesser more anguished, and she flung the door open, leapt in the light from the landing, snatched up the glass and ran.

"O — live!" Eric's bellow would wake the dead, though his sister heard only the explosive "O" before her swift door dulled the rest. The older brothers grumbled and moaned, shifting in their narrow beds, while little Ralph got such a fright, tears leapt to his eyes.

In what had been Minnie's room, Hughie was in the act of opening a window to let out the lingering scent of peppermint and peculiar odour of baking bread that always trailed his mother. Eric's yell propelled him out and into the nursery so quickly that, on arriving, he had no memory of leaving his room.

"What the dickens is happening?" he asked.

The scent of Tom's last cigarette lingered in the air, and gentle, even breathing ensued from all the beds, particularly from Eric's. They were miming sleep. He'd let it go, decided Hughie, resting his forehead against the momentary cool of the door jamb. His eyes closed, and there was Adela, on a bright Sunday morning, dressed for church in black feathered hat and magenta gloves, chastising Eric and Olive for fighting. As he took himself off to bed, Hughie smiled at the continuum of it, though his heart was breaking.

209

CHAPTER TWENTY-FOUR

A Cure, a Bath and an Ambush

Except for the morning after the night that Ah Jack gave her the laudanum, Olive had risen early since the return from Somosomo. Nipping downstairs barefooted, she'd run light as a leaf to the back of the house to the kitchen. It would be empty of chokras, the only occupant Ah Jack, packing a tin billy with food and filling a flask with cold tea. When it was ready, he'd give it to Olive and unlock the kitchen door to let her outside. The kitchen door never used to be locked, but ever since the business after the trial, Uncle Bernard had been nervous. It had happened on Laucala, Waiyevo, Lakemba; it could happen here, disaffected coolies breaking in at night and knifing the Sahib or the Sirdar. As an extra precaution, Winterson, the New Zealander, had been moved from his quarters to inside the house, where he slept on the sofa in the study.

On this morning, when Olive came downstairs, she could feel the heat of the kitchen from the hall and Ah Jack was not standing at the long, scrubbed table. With his back to her, stoking the roaring range, was Kalessar. Behind him, coming in the open door with a sloshing pail, was Mohan. Aiyaz, pristine in his white shirt and maroon cummerbund, sat at the kitchen table spooning up rice and milk.

"Hullo," said Olive, brightly, "have you come back?" Uncle Bernard was right, then. Two nights ago, when she'd stood with him and Eric on the verandah, watching the smoke rise from the cooking fires in the Lines, he'd said to Eric, "It'll be the kidglove approach. That'll get them working."

The men in the kitchen said nothing. Mohan nodded at her, but Kalessar had his head down, wrapping a thick slab of freshly baked bread in a cloth. He laid it gently in the billy. Today, the sahib would let the women out. That was the bargain, the deal. When he and Winterson had arrived down at the Lines yesterday, Winterson with a pistol, the workers were taken by surprise. Sirdar and Sahib had grabbed the nearest woman, a pretty young one kept by two warring brothers.

The coolies had expected her to be led away to the sirdar's cottage for the usual reason. But they hadn't done that at all, they'd gathered all the women, the twenty or so of them more precious than gold to the seventy-odd men, bound them together with rope and barricaded them into one of the Lines. Most of the men watched silently, frightened of the gun, but Kalessar had heard a group of young hotheads debate overpowering the sirdar and turning the gun on him. He spoke to them quickly, and they listened; he was one of the senior men.

"We will find our way in the end," he said, as Sahib held the gun and Sirdar took up hammer and nails. "Wait for Doctor Manilal."

The name of the great man soothed them like a drug. Gathering round him, the young men had asked, "Are you sure he will come?"

"He will come," said Kalessar, and Singh had nodded in agreement. "He will come."

The girl, Olive, picked up the billy.

"What are you doing?"

"I'm going to take it out to Elvira, of course," said Olive. Did he think she was stealing it?

"That is the job of Aiyaz. Put it down."

211

Olive did as she was told and wondered if she'd been disrespectful by referring to Elvira by her first name, rather than Miss Gow. Aiyaz's spoon was scraping on his empty plate. When he laid it to one side, he turned to stare at Olive and Olive stared back. The scar was healing purple and lumpy. Above it, the boy's eyes seemed sad and mourning. Olive reached out and patted him, comfortingly, on his forearm above the white cuff of his shirt. He glanced down at her hand, but did not move away. When he looked up again, she saw that his expression had not changed, but she had the impression he was staring at her with even greater concentration.

That is what she did before, Aiyaz thought, that's what made me drop the jug. Why does she do it?

Olive turned away, unnerved by the sudden antagonism in Aiyaz's eyes. Jiggling on one foot, she remembered her father was an early riser. If she wasn't quickly out of the door with Aiyaz and the billy, then Hughie would see her from the dining-room and stop her. If only the dining-room here was like the one in Suva, windowless. At last, Kalessar had filled the bottle and Aiyaz was climbing down from his chair. He took the billy, and Olive the bottle, and together they stepped out into the morning.

Against his custom, Hughie, after his sleepless night on board *Vai*, was still prone underneath his sheet. Grandmother McNab, who'd awoken several times in the night to anoint her itch and discern a sleeping child, fully clothed, on the mat beside the bed, now saw that same child flitting across the lawn with one of the chokras. As the girl's mother was dead, she supposed it would fall to her to instruct her in the mores of feminine conduct. Taking off into the wilds, barefoot and never mind the hookworm, this time not with a pair of suffragettes but a coolie boy, was not allowable. Planning an ambush on the verandah on Olive's return, she stood at the mirror, pinned up her hair and attached the bombazine bonnet. It was a beautiful morning, although it promised to be inhumanly hot later. She hummed under her breath.

Yesterday, she had intercepted Doctor Ricketts on his way down the stairs. He had been attending to poor Maud's cuts and scratches and healing scalp, and Minnie had taken the opportunity to whisper in his ear. She'd noticed over the past few weeks that the marks on her petticoat were now black, as opposed to green, and she'd wondered, several times a day, if she were dying. Her affliction, which she'd had well before even her turn of life, had only ever been treated with applications of witch-hazel. Perhaps, now she was seventy-one and God knows the undertaker would be packing that particular part of her anatomy with rags soon enough, perhaps it was time to see a doctor. And also, she told herself, now that Adela was dead she would need all her wits about her to control that unruly mob.

In her room, Minnie had lifted her skirts and lain back on the bed. Gonorrhoea now, she'd had that years ago in Levuka and then again, when she was virtuous, contracted off her lecherous husband. Both times she'd cured herself with splashes of strychnia and iodide of zinc, bought from the apothecary. This was different. Doctor Ricketts took a look between her legs, then drew her knees together again.

"You've allowed your condition to worsen beyond any I have seen, Mrs McNab," he'd said. "You must be in considerable discomfort." He'd reached behind the curtain and flung open a window. "If you will wait a moment in that position, I will prepare a syringe."

Minnie's heart pounded, but she gritted her teeth. Enough was enough. From his bag on the washstand, the doctor took a mortar and dissolved in it a half drachm of quinine with a little sulphuric acid. To this he added water, one drachm of golden seal and one of chlorate of potash, two drachms of sulphate of zinc and half a drachm of tannin. He knew the compound without referring to any book; *Fluor Albus* was a common ailment among white women in the tropics, especially the older ones who still wore flannel petticoats under the ubiquitous long skirts. The Aesthetic Dress Movement now, he'd read about that in newspapers from Home. If only some of the fashionable ladies here would champion that cause, he thought. Then the air could circulate freely in a refreshing and hygienic manner beneath the loose robes.

He filled the female syringe with the solution and cautioned his patient to lie still. Afterwards he placed her hand on a cloth over her ravaged vulva, so that none of the fluid would escape.

"Some relief will be obtained straight away," he told her. "But you must continue the treatment yourself. I will leave you the solution. Have you a syringe?"

Minnie shook her head and wondered why she suddenly felt as though she could weep. Shame. It was shame from lying there with her skirts rucked up, her hand over her quim. The doctor read her eyes and felt a rush of pity. All crumpled up on the bed, she was more like a cross, old, black hen than the proud virago with the razor tongue she was in legend.

"You can keep that one. I have another one in Somosomo and you can return that to me when you're better."

Minnie nodded. The doctor had left soon after, warning her to stand over the pot when she rose and to wash more regularly.

Today the itch was certainly better. On her way downstairs she felt almost girlish with relief and was debating whether or not she still had it in her to take them two at a time when Tom came from the nursery, hurried after her and offered her his arm.

"Morning, Gran," he said, gallantly. "Shall I escort you to breakfast?"

𝒯he bure, when Olive and Aiyaz reached it, was deserted. Loud splashings and yelling issued from the beach below. Leaving the food at the door, they went to the low cliff and peered down. There was Margaret, sulu tight around her breasts, up to her waist in the water. She was struggling with Elvira, who was naked and loudly resisting the ayah's efforts with the flannel. Wide-eyed, Olive turned to Aiyaz, but he had turned and was making his way back towards the house and his kitchen duties.

A loud sneeze broke over the waves below, and the two women came up on to the shore. Elvira sank down on to the pebbles in an attitude of exhaustion as Margaret wrapped a dry sulu around her trembling shoulders. Uncle Bernard's sister was sneezing and coughing in great shuddering gasps. Olive scrambled down to join them.

"Bula!" she called, as Margaret turned to the crunching of her feet on the stones. "Good morning, Elvira."

"Bula," said Margaret, her hand on Elvira's head, turning it to see the approach of her friend. "See who has brought you your breakfast."

Elvira's eyes were bloodshot and watery, perhaps from the salt water, thought Olive, and she was shivering in the heat. For a moment, Olive thought she hadn't recognised her.

"You help me, eh?" said Margaret.

They went either side of her and lifted her to her feet. Her hair, as it passed Olive's nose, smelt of smoke and something else, something wrenchingly familiar, although she hadn't smelt it for a long time now; the sour, panicked sweat of difficult breath. And she was at least as heavy as Ah Sam's box of fireworks. They turned her towards the bure and bent their backs, stumbling and slipping on the stones to the path, where Elvira coughed harshly and made to sink to the ground again.

"Sega!" said Margaret, roughly, hauling her upright. Even though Margaret was so much taller than Elvira, she was not nearly so strong. Her bulk was soft, while Elvira's small square body was hard, like a horse, or an ottoman, thought Olive. On the path, Margaret went ahead, pulling on Elvira's arms, and Olive went behind, pushing her pebble-dented bottom. At the top, with the bure in sight, Elvira shed her sulu altogether and lowered her head before propelling herself forwards like a lumbering, top-heavy cart. The other two had to break into a run to keep up with her. The billy and bottle scattered at her feet and from inside there was a crash of bed-springs as she fell into her four-poster. Olive picked up the billy and handed it to Margaret.

"Are you going to stay here all the time, now?" she asked. Margaret nodded, three threads of silver in her black hair catching the morning sunlight.

"Too many up there now," she said. "Too many big boys in the nursery."

"But aren't you frightened? Elvira has the influenza."

"Elvira is my girl." Margaret was smiling and shaking her head.

Whose girl am I? wondered Olive. Her Dad's she supposed, and he had asked her not to come here. She suddenly felt guilty, that dull, new feeling. Maybe she could say she'd come to say goodbye. She took one last look inside the bure, to Elvira on the bed. The red book of poetry was clasped to her chest and her eyes were closed. With each breath she rattled. Maybe she would die, too. Olive started to cry, and Margaret squeezed her under one arm.

"Don't worry. Elvira is strong. She'll get better."

"Will she?"

"Yes. Soon. You go now." Margaret picked up the bottle of cold tea and brushed it off. "Who made this? Ah Jack?"

"Kalessar."

Margaret nodded approvingly, and put the bottle under her arm. If it had been Ah Jack, then she'd have tipped it out. She wouldn't trust that tiny, banana-backed man. She didn't want Elvira stumbling around, more confused than she was already.

The girl hadn't moved.

"Moce," she said, and waved her away.

But Olive knew suddenly why she had come again. It wasn't just to see Elvira, because Elvira had frightened her a lot in these past few days with her mad, sweat-soaked ramblings. It had seemed more likely that she would turn on her suddenly, attacking her with those broad, swinging arms and man's hands. Fury had flared and extinguished in Elvira's tiny, hard eyes, green and blue, again and again, throughout the day, until it was too dark in the bure to see. Olive had come because she wanted to ask a question, the same question she'd asked two days after the first telegram, when she'd refused the laudanum and escaped out of the house.

"Did my mother really send her that book?"

"Yes, she did." Margaret smiled at the memory of the gift.

"But — how did Mother know Elvira? Did she visit her like I do?"

"In those days, Elvira lived the days here and slept at night in the house. Before the poet she was not so sick. Then, Saka made her spend the nights here as well. Your mother, Adela, and the doctor, they tried to tell him no — let her live in the house — but he was made up in his mind."

From inside the bure, Elvira's cough rasped and shook. Olive saw she had turned her head and was watching them, her thumb in her mouth, her eyes glassy and reflective.

"Now you go," said Margaret, firmly. "Kua ni leqa. You will have a good life."

"Goodbye, Elvi —" Olive began. But Margaret had brought her finger to her lips, in the same gesture Elvira had used when they first met.

"No farewells."

Margaret seemed to know, somehow, that she'd been forbidden to come again. With heavy feet, Olive turned towards the guava and nut trees and the house beyond.

By the time she passed through to the other side of the grove, Olive was musing on how Providence had sent no spectacles since before the court case, and how only three weeks had passed since the departure of Miss Prime-Belcher, and how it seemed at least a year, and how lovely it would be if she got back and Dad said there had been a terrible mistake and that he'd just got a telegram from Suva saying Mother hadn't died after all. Surely it was possible. It seemed much less likely, now that she'd seen Dad, that Mother wasn't at home making soup for the influenza victims, or playing the piano, or nursing a new baby. Besides, who was helping Elena look after little Rosie? Dad loved to play tricks, he was always playing them on the older boys. Once, for a dare, Harry stole a tin of Park Drive from a Chinese merchant in Suva. It went undetected until Ming Lo told Dad. Dad had got a Chinese letterhead off Ah Sam and written a letter, pretending it was from the merchant, demanding that Harry pay for the tin or he'd talk to Stanlake, the real Stanlake, the Head of Police. Harry had flown down the hill, the money in his pocket, as if the Devil was after him. Maybe this was another trick . . .

But no. Nobody made jokes about that kind of thing. Her heart dropped suddenly, heavily, enough to make her sigh and lift her head to see she'd veered off course, walking all that way with her head down, and that she'd come close to the three little graves. She could hear voices, a man's and a boy's. They belonged to Dad and Ralph, as did the yellowing panama and cloth caps she could see through a gap in the ixora hedge. They were sitting on the other side, looking out to sea.

"So, shall we do that then, sonny? Sail to Savusavu Bay and visit the Molloys, the lot of us? Tom and I'll measure up for their sails and we'll sail home for Christmas."

"When?"

"Monday morning. The weekend here, then we'll go."

There was a silence while Ralph considered. Olive crept around to the back of the hedge and peeped around. Neither of them had heard her careful feet. Hughie had his hand above his eyes, peering out to sea. He pointed at the blue shape of Vanua Levu, across the Strait.

"It's not far — " He was interrupted by a wild, swooping yell, and Olive flew through the air. She must have grown, or gained in strength since she hadn't in weight, for she knocked him over on to his back, and that had never happened before.

"Olive! You near startled me out of my wits!" He pushed her off.

"Did you think I was one of Aunt Maud's dead babies come back to haunt you?" The words were out before she could consider them. Fleetingly, Hughie looked as though he might slap her or, at the very least, raise his voice. He did neither.

"That's enough of that, dear," he said mildly, picking up his hat from where it had rolled under the hedge.

Olive sat down beside Ralph. He had that mouse smell again, the smell boys get if they sit too long in the sun.

"What's this about Savusavu?" she asked.

"I want to go home," said Ralph, sullenly.

He hopes Mother is still there, thought Olive. He's so little, he doesn't understand. She took his hand.

"Mother never approved of the Molloys," she told her father, although surely he knew. Hughie was turning his hat round and round, between thumb and forefinger, before clamping it on his head.

"Dad?"

"Yes, dear?"

"Did you hear me?"

"Your mother never even met them. She was used to bright lights and towns and cities. Never felt the same loneliness as poor Maggie."

"Is that Mrs Molloy?"

"There is no Mrs Molloy," said Hughie. "Maggie is a Miss." He stood up, dusted himself off, and held out a hand to each of his children. "Time to go up and find Tom, eh? Then we'll all go and clean up *Vai.*

$\mathcal{T}$om was on the verandah with Grandmother, and Grandmother had her eyes on them as they came up the steps.

"The coolies are back," she told Hughie, and to Olive, "Come here, lass."

Although the child stood still enough, eyes on her filthy toes, and made no attempt to run after her father and brothers until they called her from the front of the house, Grandmother McNab could not help but feel her ambush was inconsequential to the ambushed. When once she'd paused to draw breath, Olive asked a question about those loose Molloy women, and she was compelled to silence her with a rap on the legs with the cane. Tears had smarted in the girl's eyes but not fallen.

"You can go," Minnie had said, after Hughie called a second time. Watching her retreat, she remembered how she'd been like that herself as a girl, never wasting a tear on anything so predictable as a scolding. Perhaps her life would have been different, happier, if she'd learnt humiliation earlier. A wave of malice filled her and she called the girl back.

"You heard about the *Tui Cakau*?" she asked, looking up at the girl's face. It was in shadow, with the sun hard behind it. Olive shook her head.

"Copra boat, with that hussie Perkins-Green aboard. And her friend. It went down in the hurricane."

Minnie heard the girl take a deep breath. Her arms came up in front of her as if she would push her grandmother over.

"It did not!" she was shouting. "It did not! You're lying, you're a horrible old witch!"

Grandmother made a half-hearted attempt to get at her with the walking stick, but Olive was gone, running through the house to join her father and brothers.

CHAPTER TWENTY-FIVE

The Dead

*T*he Hon. Baxendale leaned down from the bench and peered at her. His face was red, dripping. In one hand he held the gavel and in the other a handkerchief, sopping with a load from his brow.

Standing before him, Olive held her mother's dear hand, the long, double-jointed fingers curled around her smaller version of the same. Both tilted their faces bravely to meet Baxendale's enquiring eyes, although Olive longed to turn her head sideways to see who was in the dock. She seemed to have been forbidden to do that. Mother's face, at any rate, was set straight on to the judge.

Behind them, the court-room rustled, there was a cough and a sneeze. As Baxendale banged his gavel, Olive and her mother turned to the spectators and saw they were among the Dead. There was Harry and his mother, Rose, side-by-side in the front row. Lolling in the aisle was Grandfather McNab, as whisky-sodden as ever. They were all that Olive recognised. Harry looked just the same and Dad's first wife Rose the same as her photograph. Grandfather McNab she only just remembered. He had died when she was three. Her mother, though, was intent. Olive watched her eyes flicker over everyone there, giving little gasps of recognition or shudders, depending on whether or not she was pleased to see that particular Deceased. Suddenly, with a small cry, Adela flew from Olive's side and ran to a man standing alone by the door. Olive didn't recognise him either, although he looked a bit like Bill, only older: the same florid cheeks, deep-set eyes, bull neck and *yellow hair. Sweetly, he kissed her mother on the cheek and opened the door. Before leaving, Adela turned and waved farewell to her daughter, standing alone before all the Dead with the judge's rank breath hot on the back of her neck. Then she stepped out into the white light beyond the door, the big man with her, and the door swung shut. It swung shut again. Bang. Then again. Bang. Bang.*

It was the lali and Olive was leaving the court-room without ever seeing who it was who stood accused. She flung her head back over her shoulder to see, and there were two familiar female figures, dripping with water, a smell of the sea on them, one older and square, one light and tall, but they were not fully there yet, they were just shadows, they had not yet arrived, they were not yet properly dead.

Disturbing though the dream was, Olive spent the first few moments of consciousness listening to the lali calling in the coolies and debating whether or not it was a spectacle sent by Providence and her mother together, and if it was, why had it been sent so late? It was Eric who had foreseen, all that time ago on the steamer, that Mother would never get better. How did he know? Olive was sure he'd never had visions, otherwise he would never have been so scathing about the Lunaria. She wondered again if, in giving the stone away, she'd given away all future communion with Providence. Then again, life without it, just lately, had been peculiar enough.

Beside her in her nightgown and cap, Grandmother took a deep, rasping breath. Beside the door, Olive's bag was packed and ready to be taken to Vuna and rowed out to *Vai*. She pulled the net free, slipped carefully out of bed, pulled off her nightgown and slipped on her oldest dress. Better to have Harry's old shorts and football jersey, but they were still in Suva. As she took her magnifying glass from its hiding place in the lining of the suitcase and hung it round her neck, there was noise and movement from the nursery. They boys were up, dressing, dismantling their canvas beds.

Grandmother took another rasping breath, although there had been no exhalation since the last intake. Why didn't she die? Why had God deemed it time to take Mother and not her? The heat of Adela's hand was still on Olive's and the daughter brought her hand to her face to see if there was any change in it, a mark on the skin, a lingering perfume, but there was none. She pressed the hand to her chest, against the ache, returned as strong as it had been after Aunt Maud read her the telegram. In dreaming of the company of the departed, there is a comfort, thought Olive, but on waking you lose them all over again. She took hold of the magnifying glass, feeling its cool, steel rim dig into her palm, and wished she could sit for a while with Miss Prime-Belcher, wherever she was. Her lovely, dead mother, the vine at Tagimaucia — she'd tell her about it all.

There was a light knock on her door, and she opened it to Hughie. His fine, brown and grey hair was greased and slicked, his canvas bag drawn tight and slung over his shoulder.

"Ah, you are up, lass. Get some breakfast into you and we'll get moving."

*T*here were seven McNabs in the Packard and Vishnu to drive, so Uncle Bernard and Aunt Maud, who'd risen early especially, while Grandmother slept on, bid their farewells on the steps.

"It'll be very quiet without you," said Maud, as she embraced her niece, the lump in her throat formed partly of disappointment. She had hoped for so much more from Olive: companionship; talk; complicity. There had been none, no sympathy even, for her torn hair and the loss of Pepepeli. When she went to kiss Ralph, he turned his face away, so her lips met with the rubbery curl of his ear. His arms gave him away though, she thought, stealing up to her waist and giving a quick squeeze.

"Goodbye, Maud," said her brother. "Thank you for everything."

"Will we see you for Christmas?" asked Maud. "It would be

nice." That Hughie was not only going to the Molloys but taking the children was to be kept a secret from his mother, so Maud felt bound to disapprove enough for both of them. "It would be more . . . suitable for the little ones," she continued.

"We'll see," said Hughie. "We'll see."

Maud watched the Packard pull out, pasted on a smile, waved, and worried about her brother. It was as well, in a tragic sense, that Adela's last child had never seen the light. Otherwise Hughie would feel compelled to marry again. This way, with little Rosie already five, Hughie would not be making a fool of himself with a third wife. He was fifty-one years old, for goodness' sake.

"Winterson!" bellowed Bernard, as he strode away down the side of the house towards the Lines. Winterson's cottage was too far away for the man to have heard him, thought Maud, as she turned inside, unless the man had ears like a bat. Bernard never missed an opportunity to bellow.

Ah Jack had been instructed to leave her tea in its usual place, and Maud made her way there now. There was the table, the teapot, cream and sugar, and a slice of paw-paw under organdie. As she pulled her chair out, she heard a flutter and familiar chirrup.

Pepepeli! Could it be? At her arrival, the bat's little eyes had opened blearily, and it was surely her bat because it knew to sidle up the weave of her chair to her arm and swing to her back, keeping its wings folded. This morning, after so long an absence, Maud stalled the bat in its progress by dandling it from arm to arm, wincing at its claws through the voile of her blouse, but marvelling at its return before stopping short, with a small gasp of pleasure. There was something wonderful — a second, smaller head, snuggled into Pepepeli's copper fur, its tiny claws buried at its mother's side and wings as soft as kid leather. Pepepeli did not seem to mind her stroking her baby, but made to nip her when she tried to disengage it.

224

Maud allowed the animal to crawl to her back, then ate her pawpaw and drank her tea. The sea shimmered and leapt, hot and bright beyond the graves where, as she could see, Bernard had set two coolies to clear the ixora. Soon the little ones' view across the Strait would be unimpeded. With the house quiet, her bat returned and the graves tended, all was right with the world. At least, it was as right as it ever would be.

CHAPTER TWENTY-SIX

Savusavu Bay

On the other side of the Strait, Maggie Molloy banged the teapot down in front of her three uncles, side by side at the table in the long kitchen. Hot light flooded in at the old men's backs, through the salt-frosted windows set high in the pit-sawn walls. None of them thanked her for the tea, they never did, although George nodded. As younger men, strangers could never tell them apart, but now they were seventy it was easy. George had smiled more than the other two, so his crowsfeet and the lines at the side of his mouth were deeper.

All his life resigned to his place as underdog and scapegoat, Wallace's hunched posture had made him the shortest. If it wasn't for his identical, sparse, grey hair he would have appeared younger because, at first glance, his face was smoother. On closer inspection, the lines were there all right, fine fractures come of worry and sorrow.

Uncle Howard was the one Maggie had always tried, in her thirty-four years, to avoid. Having had, for most of his life, a furious and ready temper, his face had set in an expression of full-blown rage, just as the same fury had lodged in the weather-beaten face of his unmourned father before him. For the last decade or two, though, Howard's face had spoken more of pique and pettish annoyance.

Life had not gone well for the brothers, at least, not in the way their father had anticipated. Old man Molloy had broken in the land, built the kauri house, the copra sheds, the Lines, driven his miserable and sickly wife to an early but welcome grave and kept a firm hand on his triplet sons and Ellen, the only daughter. His children had never been allowed to visit the Planters Club in Savusavu town, or go to the dances, or the Christmas parties, or weddings or christenings. By the time the old man died, the surrounding Europeans had forgotten they existed, except for in legend.

"I'll send you up to old man Molloy," they said to errant children.

One man had discovered they were real though, and he'd come calling long enough to get Ellen with child. Their meetings were clandestine, in remote corners of the estate. How many times they'd fallen into one another's arms the brothers did not know. It only took once after all; at least, it did with the cattle and pigs and dogs, and that's all the brothers had to go on. Eight years ago the details of the affair and identity of the lover had died as secrets with Ellen. All that was for certain was that the result of the man's endeavours was Maggie and that the man must've been tall, with red hair, because Maggie was and Ellen hadn't been. Had the brothers ventured into Savusavu town at the time and listened to the gossip, they may have heard tell of the captain of a visiting schooner, a wild and bearded Scandinavian with a taste for adventure and women of all colours and creeds.

George was glad Maggie was with them, for her laughing and her singing and not least her hard work over the heavy coal range. He was frightened for her when for the first time history repeated itself and her belly grew bigger and bigger until one dreadful, screaming night a native woman came from the neighbouring village and helped Ellen in delivering Maggie of a Fijian daughter.

For the first five years of Florrie's life, Howard spoke not a word to mother or babe. Seated between his two brothers, he ate with an air of disgust while they tended to his need for salt, or milk, or sugar. The other great uncles couldn't help but take pleasure in the child, with her reddish curly hair, and bright all-seeing eyes. It's father, a widower, visited occasionally and dandled the child, too, staring beseechingly at Maggie, but she refused to marry him. She already knew what it was to be an outcast. Marriage to a native would mean no one of her own kind, except her two gentler uncles, would ever speak to her again. It never occurred to her that that's how it was for her already. The association with the Fijian continued for a while, until threats from the man's second wife put a stop to it. The brothers were glad, as their niece was not as discreet as their sister had been, and even their heaviest, most drunken sleep could be disturbed by the raging and squalling of her bedsprings. She must have taken precautions though, because there were no more children.

Florrie grew tall and bronzed, like her father in every way except for the red in her hair, which deepened to garnet. Briefly, after Ellen's death, when she was eight or nine, the brothers talked of sending their grandniece away to a native school, but Maggie would have none of it.

Watching Maggie now, as she laid out the three heavy white cups, the last remaining three of old Molloy's wedding set, which compelled the brothers to use them not only for tea-drinking but also for shaving their spindly whiskers, George wondered if Maggie regretted it. Her eyes strayed occasionally to Florrie, languorous on the backstep, sixteen and giving her breast to a tiny girl with the fine-boned features of her Hindu father. The brothers had heard the Labour talking to one another, the Solomon Islanders and few remaining coolies in the Lines.

"White people soon all gone in the Big House," they said. "Soon no white people left."

On the rare occasions Wallace was well, and happy enough to walk out of the house and round the place, he often thought, "The sooner the better."

Only one of the Lines was still habitable, the other had no roof and one wall fallen in. The copra sheds were dilapidated and scarcely functional. Rain fell regularly through the holes in the roof and ruined the crop. The cutter they used for conveying copra from this side of the bay to Savusavu town needed new sails and patching. At low tide it listed in the sand like a ghost ship. Over a year ago now, Howard had taken the cutter into the timber merchant in the town, loaded it up with enough to mend the outbuildings, but nothing had happened. It seemed, as copra prices slumped even lower and the rapid decay of their sur- roundings accelerated impossibly faster, that nothing on the Molloy Estate should ever improve.

That was why it was such a surprise on this particular morn- ing, as Maggie was on her way back to the range to stir the bub- bling porridge, and Florrie was switching her baby to the other side, and Wallace and George were stirring sugar into their tea, when Howard, scowling, said, "The sailmaker is coming today, with his boys, from Suva."

Maggie and Florrie looked first at one another, then at Wallace and George, but they were just as nonplussed as they were.

"Why'd you go doing that, Howard, getting the sailmaker in?"

Howard leaned back in his chair and fixed his rheumy eyes on George, whom he considered not to be the full pound, although Maggie, he knew, had more affection for that brother than she did for himself.

"To measure up for sails for the boat, what do you think?" Howard's voice sharpened. He was talking through his nose, which he did when his brothers' stupidity irritated him.

"How many boys?" asked Maggie. She would have to find somewhere for them all to sleep.

"I don't know." Howard pushed his chair out from the table with a prolonged squeal. The baby whimpered at the sound, and Florrie noiselessly got up from her seat at the door, glided over the rotten step and went around the tank stand to sit with her in the sun. At her back, she heard the three old brothers come one after the other carefully over the decaying threshold and away round the other side of the house. They were off to inspect the Labour, the father of Florrie's baby among them, and Great Uncle Wallace was going too. Perhaps the prospect of visitors made him festive, thought Florrie. Her own spirits had lifted and so had her mother's. Behind her, in the kitchen, Maggie was singing, in her deep rich voice, "Kathleen Mavourneen". For Florrie, her mother's hair and voice had always gone together, they were somehow the same colour. She leaned back against the cool wood of the tank. Sons, Great Uncle had said. She hoped Ahmed wouldn't get it into his head to get jealous. She'd go down to the Lines at sundown to explain.

*V*anua Levu, it seemed to Olive from her position high in the bow as they sailed into the bay, was a kingdom of mist and cloud. At the edge of the bay, the fabled hot springs sent up their billowing steam against the forested backdrop of dakua, vesi, yasi and bua bua. Deeper inland, pushing up through clouds as white as the steam, the island's spine of mountains showed, here and there, dark and distant valleys. Mist rose from them to mingle softly with the mountain cloud. Olive wondered if mist as pure as that would have a perfume, like the fine miasma her mother sometimes had allowed her to spray from the cut-glass bottles, with their little rubber pumps, on her dressing table. For a moment, her mother's hand formed in the clouds in the sky, long and white, more gentle than breath. Grief clutched at Olive's throat. She dropped her eyes to the shore, where currents of air tangled and caught in the curlicues and wisps of steam and sent them across the water. In places the steam gathered so thickly that it looked as if the sea itself was boiling.

Keeping Nawi Island to starboard, Hughie had his crew of sons turn the yacht to the north-west side of the bay, to anchor off the Molloy's plantation. He hoped Olive wasn't sulking, but with this many boys aboard it hadn't been necessary to engage her as a sailor, good at it though she was. As *Vai* hissed and flew into the shallows of the bay, Ralph clambered up to join her. They lay down on their stomachs to watch the bright fish. Olive was in the hope of seeing a nuqu, a fish more terrifying than a barracuda, with teeth that could tear the flesh from an arm or leg in seconds.

"Maybe there will be an octopus, too," said Ralph. "A giant one which will crawl up the anchor chain and grab us."

"Silly," said Olive. At the corner of her eye there was a waving arm — Hughie's — and she sat up to see a group of people coming down from the grass to the sand. The plantation behind them, with its rows of nut trees and low buildings, was duller than the Taveuni one. No bright hibiscus or wildflowers frothed under the trees. Beyond the white sands all was either green or brown. Slow brown cows lumbered among the tree trunks, a couple of them staring moronically as Eddie threw out the anchor.

There was colour in the people though, the three old men, a woman with flaming red hair and a Fijian girl who was carrying a baby. One of the old men walked ahead while the others formed a knot behind him and talked among themselves, heads inclined, as if they were a family.

"I know these people," Olive thought, suddenly, "I've been here before."

It must've been a long time ago, she decided, because she couldn't remember the voyage, or who she'd come with. Perhaps it was when she was tiny, because there was a glimpse of a memory of being elevated, as if she was being held high in an adult's arms in a clear, rushing wind and watching Florrie boil the copper. In the dinghy, as they rowed ashore, Olive realised it couldn't have been a memory at all, at least, not the usual kind. The Fijian woman and her baby, they looked the same now as they had then, whenever it was, and the three old men, dour and sour and alike as three old lemons . . . She must have dreamt them.

"D'you feel ill?" Tom asked her, leaning forward as he rowed, to where she sat in the stern seat. "You're an awful colour all of a sudden."

Olive put her hands to her cheeks and felt them cold; the chill crept into the bones of her fingers. They were arriving at a place of great unhappiness for a great many years. The eyes of that old man Dad was calling Howard, who'd come into the shallows in his shoes to shake hands were cruel, terrifying. She clutched Ralph's arm and watched Eric and Eddie shake hands with the old men and nod shyly to the women. The one with the red hair was coming towards her.

"Hullo," she said, "I didn't know we would have female company as well." She smiled, creasing her long, green eyes, and Olive began to feel reassured. It was the woman's voice that comforted her, deep and sweet.

"This is my daughter," she was saying, bringing forth the Fijian girl, "Florrie."

And Olive knew then, why Grandmother didn't like the Molloys, why nobody did, much. It wasn't just the three old men, the disturbing trinity, the one who acted as clerk in his rusty black suit and a pencil behind one leathery ear, the other two in regulation white duck. It was these new generations of women, the fearlessness of them. Coming to rest as rarely as they did on the judging eyes of others, Maggie Molloy's eyes were undulled, a brilliant, glittering green. They were unlike any other eyes Olive had ever seen, pure and proud. Her mother would have liked her if they'd met, Olive decided, she wouldn't've been able to help herself.

Tom had rowed out to *Vai* again, to pick up Bill and their bags and boxes.

"Shall we go up?" asked Maggie, taking one of Olive's arms. Florrie took the other, and with the baby gazing at her intently from the crook of its mother's other arm, they began the stroll to the house.

"Did you come from Suva today?" Maggie asked her, kicking

a stray cocoa-nut out of the way. Olive looked down and startled: Maggie, a grown-up white lady, had bare feet! Her eyes travelled slowly up her long skirt and blouse, patched and worn, to Maggie's lovely eyes, which smiled into hers.

"No," answered Olive. "Two of my brothers and I were at our uncle's, on Taveuni."

"Ah," breathed Maggie. "The Gows."

Olive could tell by the way Maggie said the name, giving it an explosive "G", that she didn't much like her relatives.

"Do you know them?" she asked.

"No," said Maggie, and pressed her lips against the desire to say more.

As the women approached the house, a shadow slipped from the door, and ran behind the creeper-covered water tank. It was a man, a coolie. The sound of his feet died away quickly on the coarse, sandy grass. Maggie sighed.

"Go after him," she said to her daughter, "I don't want any trouble while we've got visitors." The last word was said in such a tender, longing way, that Olive saw the other woman's loneliness as clearly as if it were a sore, like the ones on Ralph's legs, that she'd examined with her magnifying glass. Florrie had dropped Olive's arm and stopped short, sticking out her lower lip.

"Florrie!" said Maggie, warningly. "Here. Give me Lily."

The younger woman handed the baby over before running, as fleet of foot as whoever the man was. Ahead of Olive now, with her granddaughter in her arms, Maggie stepped into the house.

"Watch the step," she said, and continued on as though Olive had asked a question although she hadn't. "That was Ahmed, who was here before. He is Lily's father. Uncles won't have him in the house, and Florrie won't live in the Lines."

"Oh," said Olive, climbing up into the house behind her. She liked the way the old men were called "Uncles".

"Hold her for a moment for me, would you, please?" asked

Maggie, pushing the baby into her arms before hurrying outside again.

Olive held Lily and gazed around the room. It had a kitchen at one end of it, under a lean-to. This was occupied mainly by an enormous old range, which pushed its flue up through a ragged hole in the iron roof. There was a dresser with some chipped cups and plates and a jar full of dried, flowering grass heads from the beach. In the room proper, near a line of windows, was a long, scrubbed wooden table, with an assortment of chairs and stools and boxes around it. On the wall were two portraits, one of a thin, wizened woman and the other of a man with a white beard and fierce eyes. Every now and then a large piece of tapa cloth, which had been nailed over a doorway, lifted in the breeze and obscured the old man's gaze. When it fell back into place the old man seemed fiercer, as if he resented this continual eclipsing. Some fans and an old war club were nailed into the walls as well, to hold up the scrim, which was sagging, as much as any attempt at decoration. Away from the table were two old, brown armchairs, with the seats bellying out beneath them, and a low cupboard.

The baby was about six months old, Olive thought, having carried out the experiment of putting her on the floor and finding that she could almost sit up. She was lovely, plump and smiling, with eyes the same shape as Maggie's, but dark brown. With one tiny hand she reached up to Olive and grabbed the cord of the magnifying glass swinging at her neck. Olive picked her up again, wandered over to the windows and gazed out towards the beach. Sometimes, beyond the low dunes, one of her brothers' heads, or her father's, bobbed as they unloaded the dinghy. Nearer to the house, Maggie was wielding an axe, splitting cocoa-nut husks and wood. Beyond her and behind some trees, the Lines were just visible. There were two, and one of them was a ruin. No wonder Florrie didn't want to live there, thought Olive. She kissed the baby's cheek and it gurgled. It smelt of cocoa-nut oil, its skin and hair were shiny with it. With the warmth of the little body in her arms, the ache that had sat heavily in her chest since the arrival of the first telegram, the one about Mother, began to ebb away. She squeezed Lily tight and sniffed the lovely baby smell at the back of her slender neck.

From behind her came the sound of Maggie's bare feet on the bare boards of the floor. She was bending her head over the iron range, hooking open the fire door and feeding in husks.

"You must be hungry," she said.

"We had some sandwiches on board," said Olive, not that she'd eaten any of them.

"Sit down if you like," offered Maggie. "Take the weight off your feet. Lord knows where Florrie has got to."

Olive sat, balancing the baby in her arms just as she had when Rosie was smaller. She considered herself to be pretty good at looking after babies. For a while there was no sound but the crackling of the fire and the buzzing of some drowsy flies against the smeary windows. Olive's mind filled with a picture of her mother as she had been the last time she'd seen her, thin and pale against her pillows, surrounded with a bleak aura of fear of what was to come. The heat of the afternoon and the sight of Maggie before her, warm and alive, took away some of the anguish of the memory. Her mother had died and that was all there was to it. Her father was still here and so was she, and so were all of her brothers except Harry. And Miss Prime-Belcher. It was impossible that she was dead. She wasn't the kind of person just to die. Maggie sat down at the table with a dalo and a small sharp knife to pare away its thick skin.

Then there were voices outside, and the men came in, the room filling quickly with their voices and the smell of their sweat, the leather of the uncles' boots. Ralph came straight to Olive, pulling out the stool beside her. From Olive's lap, Lily stared at his earnest, sunburnt face, his gap-toothed smile and pink ears. Her little face opened up in a wide grin.

One of the uncles opened the low cupboard and took out a bottle of gin. He proffered it to Hughie, who nodded. Another old uncle, the one in the dark suit, fetched three thick china cups from the dresser, half-filled them and passed two to his brothers. He took a draught from the third one himself.

"Lucky you didn't call in to Savusavu then," said one of the other uncles, who had a fatter tummy than the other two and a mouth that seemed more given to smiling. He passed his cup to Tom.

"Why's that, George?" Hughie patted Olive on the head and leaned against the table beside her.

"They've quarantined it. Dreadful. Natives and Indians dying like flies."

"You haven't seen it here, then, this side of the bay? The epidemic?" asked Tom, handing on the cup. He wiped his mouth with the back of his hand and took a breath. The gin, Olive could tell, was strong.

"Not yet," answered the one in the suit, with the pencil.

"Don't go on saying that, Uncle Wallace," scolded Maggie. "We'll not see it at all."

The pale-grey eyebrows in Uncle Wallace's pale-grey face rose towards the roof, as if he were offering up a prayer, but Olive watching through the afternoon, saw it was something he did often. It was a kind of nervous tic. At its strongest it drew up the corners of his lips, into the only kind of smile anyone had ever seen from Wallace since his boyhood.

Lily was not at all perturbed at the absence of her mother. Thumb in mouth and her long lashes against her cheek, she snuggled into Olive and went to sleep. Olive wished she had bosoms to cushion her little head. The baby's breathing and snuffles made Olive feel soft and sleepy herself. With her eyelids lowered, she watched Maggie with one of her strong, freckled hands intercept one of the three cups on its rounds. She drank deeply before handing it on to Hughie, who took his sip watching Maggie over the rim.

Such eyes; he caught himself admiring her and shut his own. Maggie smiled at this, wondering at him, but he had turned away, offering the cup to Howard, to hide himself from her. That time, when he'd closed his eyes, Adela hadn't been there, he'd seen nothing but a deep-red dark, his ear had not caught even the ghost of her voice. It was too soon for her to leave him. The gin had burnt his throat. He coughed.

"Not my tipple, gin," he said.

Howard flicked his eyes over him. Gin was all he had.

At the door, Tom, Bill, Eddie and Eric stood looking out towards the beach. It was growing dark. Olive wished Florrie would come back. Her dress was wet. Beside her, Ralph had put his head down on the table, on his bony freckly arms, and gone to sleep. Once, when Maggie stood and came away from where she'd sat with Hughie, Olive hoped it was to take the baby from her, or get them all something to eat, but it was only to take a kerosene lamp from a nail in the lean-to, trim the wick and set it down on the table. As she lit it with a taper from the stove and the glow filled the room, Olive looked up at her father. In his shadowy face his eyes gleamed and his mouth worked as if he were eating.

Olive struggled to her feet, keeping the sleeping baby against her, and stepped over the legs of Uncle George and Uncle Wallace who were asleep in the armchairs. Her own brothers had vanished through the open door into the night. At the end of the room, the tapa cloth was lifting and rasping its soft edge on the floor. Olive lifted it at one side and saw it covered the entrance into a dark, hot, corridor, which at first, until her eyes accustomed themselves, Olive thought was perhaps just a large cupboard. Then, slowly, faint oblongs of pale grey showed themselves as doorways into other rooms. She went carefully forward.

The first room was Uncles'. Moonlight from a narrow window showed her three narrow beds, ranged against the walls. A clothes-horse in one corner had a jumble of shirts thrown over it, and the door, when she'd thrown it open, clunked against something china. Peering around, she saw it was a washstand, with an enormous, chipped white jug and basin, big enough to bathe triplet babies. Above it, high on a shelf and as wreathed in dust and cobwebs as Aunt Maud's cradle, was a toy outrigger. If she'd still had her Lunaria, she could have held it in the hand free of the baby and she would have heard the boys' voices, three identical chirruping voices more excited than they'd ever been. Then the excitement would turn to argument; Howard even then was the possessor. Their father, savage voiced, would come to take the canoe away and place it on the shelf. He would forbid his boys to touch it, ever again, on pain of a taste of the coolie whip.

There was a sudden, old, sour smell in the room, malevolent, yellow and thick, rising from the walls and the beds and the discarded clothes. Olive backed out, panic welling in her chest into the dark, until a pair of warm arms clasped her from behind.

CHAPTER TWENTY-SEVEN

Love

*H*er scream had brought no one running. The level on the gin bottle was too low for that. She only woke the baby and scared Florrie half out of her wits.

"Hush!" said Florrie. "It's just me. Your dress is all wet."

Olive handed the child over. "From the baby," she said, miserably. "I'm so tired, Florrie. Can I sleep somewhere?"

"My bed. Come with me."

Florrie and Maggie shared a room at the end of the hall. The net that hung over the one big bed had holes big enough to let a bird through. There was a washstand like Uncles' but smaller, a netted cradle for Lily and a door that led outside. There was also one window, with no glass, which gave out to the night and the nearby gentle surf. Its shutter leant against the wall beneath it. Florrie lit the lamp that hung in the centre of the room while Olive, past talking, pulled off her sodden dress and climbed into bed, hauling the sheet over her head before the night insects discovered the open window. She didn't wake even when Florrie returned with the baby and a dish of mashed bananas and sago for its supper. The mother opened the door that led outside and sat cross-legged, feeding her daughter, looking out into the dark and soft stars, as she did every night. Then, as soon as the baby was fed and changed, she laid her in the cradle, dimmed the lamp and slipped out through the open doors, back to her lover and the Lines.

In the early hours of the morning, Maggie fell into bed beside her and Olive stirred. The older woman's red hair spread like a landscape on the pillow, rivulets and hills, hollows and plains, here and there a silvery thread picking up the moonlight and flashing with pale fire. On the other side of the wall, beyond their sleeping heads, footfalls bent the grass and turned towards the beach.

When Maggie had said goodnight, she'd bent to kiss Hughie on the brow. He'd been talking, his tongue loosened by the gin, about his loss, about how Bill wanted to leave, about anything. Hughie knew, as he scuffed across the sand, that he'd talked too much. He lay down against a bank of sand and tussock and pulled his panama over his eyes. Dawn was on its way. If he could just snatch some sleep, away from the snoring old men and Ralph's head on the table framed by his thin, freckled arms, which somehow, in the dim glow of the lamp and with too much gin inside him, had seemed unbearably poignant, this time Adela would come. He needed her solace, her forgiveness for another woman's kiss. Had he come to depend on these waking dreams? Within Hughie's wiry frame, the pragmatic tradesman did battle with the superstitious sailor. Surely it was not really a spirit, this wandering remnant of his wife who came to him, but memory enriched by sentiment, the colours brightened by grief.

In the end, as he slipped away, it was not Adela who loomed but Keizo, his face under water, his eyes closed and expression blissful. Clutched in his hands and held against his chest was a lacquered box, black and gold. The gold shivered in the green water, like carp. Nudging up against his submerged shoulder was the prow of his little boat. Then the shoulder rolled, taking with it the rest of Keizo and he began to sink. The black and gold box broke free from his hands and bobbed to the surface. When Hughie reached for it, he found the smooth embossed surface to be warm. Of its own accord, it opened in his hands and showed its contents: a glowing coal, an ordinary ember from a brazier.

The water's surface showed no image of Keizo now, he was gone for ever.

Hughie woke in a sweat. The sun was high and he was itching like the devil all over. Close by, her back to him, sat Adela in a silk wrap, pink with red chrysanthemums. He reached out a hand and touched her. A breeze from the bay lifted her dark curls, and without turning she said, "Are you awake, Dad?"

It was Olive, in fancy dress.

"How'd you come by that get up?" He hunched up, rubbing sand from the back of his pounding head.

"It's Maggie's."

Maggie. Her name quickened his heart. Silly old fool, he told himself. What was he thinking of? Marrying her? He tried to picture her in the house at Waimanu Road, looking after the children, coping with his mother and going out into Suva society. No. It wasn't possible now, never would be.

"How about a cuppa?" he said to his daughter. That, and a tot. Something that could be relied on to clear this awful head.

Olive, grinning, hauled her father to his feet, and he hooked his arm around her shoulders.

𝒯rom the Lines, as they passed them, came the ring of hammer on hard wood and the dry, laughing sound of a saw.

"Look — it's Tom!" said Olive.

Hughie watched his eldest son with watery, aching eyes. The Labour, the eight men that remained, had gathered around and were watching him as well. Tom was a natural craftsman — in cloth or wood, in the sewing of sails, the construction of boats from the inside out, the building of houses from the outside in. Working beside him was one of the Indians, perhaps it was Ahmed, the one Maggie had told him about, the father of her grandchild. Tom had set Eric and Eddie to work repairing the fallen wall, making good the timber that had lain stacked for who knows how long. A flash of match and puff of cigarette smoke drew Hughie's eye: Bill, standing to one side, his arm around Ralph, with Florrie and the baby. The sight of him made Hughie's head ache more. He turned and stumbled towards the house. Olive, a Chinese princess in her robe, wrapped it tightly around her and went to help her brothers.

Waiting by the window for Hughie's return, Maggie had stoked up the fire and set the kettle. She'd covered a thick slab of yesterday's bread with tinned New Zealand butter and guava jelly she'd made herself. It wasn't in her nature to serve a man like this, she provided only the basics for Uncles who in turn provided a roof for her. The old men were asleep in the kitchen when she'd risen, and she'd chased them off to their beds. When they were younger, they could drink all night and work all day, but now, she knew, it took the stuffing out of them.

"Good morning." She offered Hughie the bread.

"Thank you." His hand, he noticed, was shaking. He sat down at the table. "How are you this morning?"

Maggie stared at him. Nobody ever enquired after her health.

"Box of birds, eh?" continued Hughie.

She nodded and smiled then, before going to the kettle and filling the teapot.

"Uncles are still asleep." She was dunking two of the cups in a bucket of water. "Best thing for them."

He nodded.

"Your Tom is a good boy. He's got going on Florrie's house."

He nodded again and wished he hadn't. His eyeballs felt as though they could fall out of his skull. Maggie came back to the table with the teapot in one hand and the cups in the other.

"Sugar?"

"Yes, please."

She handed him his cup and he took a scalding, sweet mouthful.

"Eat the bread. You'll feel better," she said, sitting opposite him.

If he picked it up, she'd see his hand shaking again. How could she be as unaffected by the night's revelry as she was? Surely she'd sipped from their shared cup as much as he had. Now she had picked up the bread and was holding it out to him. Did she want him to take it from her? He leaned forward, instead, and took a bite. Laughing, she held it closer. He growled like a dog and her eyes danced. Taking the crust between his teeth, he pulled at the bread, tearing it away in clumps, so she had to stand to feed it into his mouth. With the last bite she leant her body across the table and kissed him. They stared at one another, he with surprise, she with an air of challenge, before she came around the table and led him past the armchairs, between tapa cloth and wall, down the corridor and into her room. She kissed him again there, pushing her tongue, sweet with the tea, between his teeth. When she stepped away to shutter the window, he stumbled backwards into the cradle, and the sight of it, with its rumpled damp linen, the impression of the child's body in the kapok mattress, made him falter. If he could only close his eyes to see if Adela was there . . . but the name that formed on his lips was Maggie's, as were the hands that now closed about his own and led him closer to the bed. As she bit and sucked at his neck, her mouth drew from him a rage of grief and longing. Her skirt tore as easily as the bread, its poor fabric coming away in his hands until he cupped her smooth hot flesh. The mosquito net parted with their weight, her legs came up from the floor and she lay herself back, her strong calves crossed over his buttocks, her neck and breasts open to his mouth.

Maggie was like nothing Hughie had experienced in either of his marriages or on his few visits to the brothels of Levuka and Suva. He hadn't even imagined her. The feet he felt against the pearly skin of his rump were calloused and rough. She was taller than him and perhaps as strong. When she flipped him over on to his back, he was uncertain, suddenly shy. He could scarcely look at her. There was something frightening about her concentration, her breathing belly and breasts above him, her gripping thighs at his hips and hands on his shoulders, slipping now to press flat against his chest. She seemed to be watching him closely, and he noticed now, as she rode him, that one hand had slid from his chest across his sweat-slicked belly to move between her legs.

As he approached his climax, fast, too fast, she did too, silently and quickly, with three convulsive shudders before flopping over, lying her long white body against his and filling his mouth and eyes with her red, smoke-scented hair. His arms came up from the bed to hold her, and as his lips found her hot, flushed cheek, it was Adela's face he kissed. She was taking a final bow against the red curtain of Maggie's hair, her eyes twinkling, knowing, almost congratulatory, before she faded away.

Maggie sat up and lifted off him to lie on the cool sheet. She kissed the round of his shoulder and murmured something he didn't hear. Hughie's ears were full of a sudden, thundering panic. Why had Adela gone like that?

Although it was beautiful, the Chinese silk wrap was hot, and Olive, having handed up hammers and held planks steady for sawing in the full glare of noon, decided to return to the house. It was cooler there, quiet and still, except for the occasional whistling snore from Uncles in their triplet room. Her suitcase was piled up with her brothers' canvas bags just inside the door. She pulled it to the floor and opened it. Carefully folded on top was the white broderie anglaise, which she ignored, rummaging beneath it for her plain blue smock. There was a frilly pinafore that went with it, she remembered, but thankfully it had been left behind in Suva. She pictured her room there with its high white bed and wardrobe full of clothes that she mostly hated. She hoped Ming Lo was looking after Stanlake, whom she sometimes allowed to clamber on her snowy pillows like a scaly Scott of the Antarctic, dipping his mournful head and little black eyes between the linen folds. Perhaps Alfred had learned to talk. It was Adela who had named the mynah, one afternoon, during a rare, precious couple of hours Olive spent alone with her mother. Mother had been almost giggly that day, remembered Olive, more like a big sister.

"Quite a performer, isn't he?" she'd said, stopping beside the bird's cage as he'd hung, screeching, upside-down from his perch. "Has he got a name?"

"Well," Olive had begun to explain, "I thought I'd call him Champak because mynahs, as you know, are from India and I think it would be as well —"

But her mother interrupted, "Oh no! You mustn't do that! Champak may be insulted. I think you must call him Alfred. He is, after all, a dreadful hack," and at this she laughed and laughed until her tears left streaks in her powder. The bird himself objected to the name and still more to the hilarity. Righting himself, he put his head on one side, fixed Adela with his mean little eye and gave out a series of ear-splitting shrieks.

$\mathcal{O}$live's stomach rumbled. On the table lay a fly-laden crust of bread and two cups of tea. She cupped her hand round one and took a sip. It was strong, but very sweet and lukewarm, just the way she liked it. Feeling like a thief, she drained the cup quickly and put it back on the table. She wanted to change now. Nobody was coming from outside, she saw through the salty window. Florrie and Ahmed were going in and out of their new home, dragging mats and pallets out into the sun. What if one of the uncles was to wake and totter out into the kitchen just as she was slipping out of the silk robe? Perhaps she should change in the same room she'd slept in. Hooking the smock neatly over one arm, she lifted the tapa cloth and stepped out into the dark, close corridor. The whistling snores were louder there and the smell that had frightened her the night before was thick, brown, over-layed with the sharp scent of gin. Olive bowed her head to a rush of nausea but steadied herself, bringing the end of the robe's sash to her nose.

She took a step and stopped. There was another noise, one beneath the snoring, from the room at the end of the corridor, a rasping and creaking, the same as when Elvira had bounced on her old four-poster. A voice, her father's, strained and groaned as he did when he lifted a heavy sail in the loft. Then there was a long sigh and a breath, before silence. In the silence was the moving of bodies and the shifting of bed linen. It was broken by Maggie's voice, murmuring.

It was time, Olive decided, to ask Tom about all this, or maybe Florrie. She realised she'd been biting her tongue and that moisture teeming from her armpits had darkened the sides of the robe. It would be a release to cry, as she had done at the lake, after watching Miss Perkins-Green and Constance. Tears sometimes gave a kind of company, she thought, and it was worse when no tears would come, like now. She felt desolately dry and alone. The smock dropped to the floor, and on tiptoe she turned back through the tapa cloth, across the living-room, over the rotten step and away, running through the grass and sand of the dunes to the beach, holding up the long hem of the wrap. The magnifying glass bumped and flew on its tether, knocking at her chest and chin, its hard metal edge brought welcome tears to her eyes, its glass flashed and glared. Beneath her feet the white ground slithered and hindered. She fell twice, picking herself up and running on, elbows and knees prickling with sand. Faintly, from a long way behind her, she could hear not only the hammering as Tom made good the roof, but also Uncles' whistling snores. Crossing down to the hard sand, she shook the sounds from her head, running as fast as she could, the wrap pulled up to her waist, her khaki bloomers displayed to the waves and the birds. There was no one else around.

A little way ahead, the beach curved to a point, and when she reached it Olive stopped, panting. Here the sands curled away again, in long, shallow bends before they reached the heads of the bay. So intent was she on the glittering, open sea beyond, that it was a while before she realised that standing beside her, quite near, was a shelter of some sort. It was behind a row of cocoa-nut trees, set back enough so that its occupant would not be at risk from falling nuts. Four posts, now on unstable angles, supported a roof of mangy thatch. It was a summerhouse, built of native materials. Inside it, also on four wobbly legs, stood a tattered, white, wicker chair.

Olive took herself between the trees, inside the structure, and sat down carefully. There was a wide view of Savusavu Bay, its islands and calm, blue waters. Far away, on the other side, was the cluster of buildings that made up the port and town. The magnifying glass hung heavy and hot against her bare chest, and she took it in her hand, lifted it over her head and held its lens to the arm of the chair. The wicker was home to many tiny, burrowing insects, minute and white, like the peeling paint. When she held the glass away she couldn't see them at all, at least, not individually. There was a slight seething, only just detectable.

A sudden gust of wind blew her hair across her face and for a moment she saw nothing at all, but a thick, textured black. It was when she sat back to push the hair from her eyes that she had the first inkling of who had sat here before: a lonely, loveless woman, a woman who'd kept silent and waited. Much of the waiting had been done here, for a skiff-borne man who was Maggie's father. If Olive narrowed her eyes at the stretch of water between the beach and clustered islands he would have to have navigated, she could almost make out the shape of his boat and discern an echo of his strong, hailing voice. But he was nowhere as clear as the poet on the beach had been. It was the first spectacle since Somosomo, she realised, but it was clouded. As the loneliness of Maggie's waiting mother flew in at her through the open walls, Olive once again took up the cool weight of her magnifying glass, the handle worn smooth by Miss Prime-Belcher's palm. Prisms of colour shifted at the edge of the glass. The lens showed her how the insects had made a nest in the wooden frame of the chair. There were worlds within worlds, in nature and in Providence, one leading into another with more or less detail and colour. Olive felt tangled, as tangled as she'd been in the embrace of the vine. She wished for the same sense of separation from the world that she'd experienced while she threw stones into Lake Tagimaucia, that sense of standing apart that allowed her to make deals with Providence, or whatever it was that made the world animate.

It didn't come. Instead, she felt herself dispersing from the sandy flesh of her arms and scabbed knees, flowing out into the air around her. The waiting woman drew close to one side, and Olive knew that if she turned to the other her eyes would rest on her mother's face. Her heart eased its thudding. She felt easier, calmer. There would be no more visions, she knew, now she had this new understanding. There was no need for the world of surprises to stand separate, it was all part of the same. On either side her feys nodded their ghostly heads. When Olive stood, she felt them bless her and watch her all the way along the beach to the house.

$\mathcal{E}piloque$

"$\mathcal{G}$oodbye Bill! Good luck!" The wind blows Olive's voice away, and Bill, a lonely figure on the service deck of the San Francisco-bound *Niagara*, waves for the last time as the vessel passes through the Suva reef. Hughie brings *Vai* about and she bucks and rolls in the big ship's wake. Olive is a triumphant skipper. With her grandmother's tongue, she captains Eddie and Eric on the sail back to the mooring.

While the tiny yacht is turning for home, Tom, with little Rosie on his shoulders, has already begun the walk from the wharf, side by side with his youngest brother. He stops at the bottom of Waimanu Road to give Ralph his handkerchief. The boy mops his tears, and Tom, before putting it back in his pocket, has a surreptitious wipe of his own.

$\mathcal{A}$n hour or two later, unseen by any of the McNabs and least of all by Grandmother, who snores in her dark room, two other crafts breech the reef. The first, although dark-sailed and storm-battered, is brave and seaworthy. It hails from India. On board is Doctor Manilal, lawyer and political activist, an emissary of Gandhi. By 1921 he will be banned from not only Fiji but other neighbouring dominions. For now, for the next few months, the Governor and his administration will turn a collective blind eye. Everywhere he goes, Manilal will draw crowds of coolies and ease the anguish in their hearts with his simple words.

The other, a gleaming yacht with Alphonse Torte at the helm, bears two women rescued from a shipwreck of some months' duration. The younger supports the older as an official from the Colonial Office escorts them to a car to convey them to the hospital, a facility much improved since the influenza epidemic. Agnes will recover more quickly than her companion and embark on her passage home in a matter of weeks. Then, the following Christmas, coming in from visiting Johnny's memorial plaque and chilled to the bone, she will find a card waiting for her in her father's hall: "With warm regards from Constance and Brigid." Hope will flood her heart, not for her lover returned, but for friendship. She will endeavour, in her ensuing association with the card senders, not ever to remember the magnificent sensation of Constance's whiskers on her nipple. This will be especially difficult during their co-operation on a book dealing with their shipwreck and miraculous survival. However, Agnes will comfort herself, falsely perhaps, that a *ménage à trois* with the muse is a greater intimacy than that of lovers. She will even agree that the fly-leaf bear the inscription: "For Olive, Whose Gift of Her Lucky Stone Was Our Comfort And Salvation During Our Long Island Isolation."

*H*ughie McNab sits on his verandah, whisky in hand, thinking that the faint plume he can see to the west may just be the last of the *Niagara's* head of steam as it disappears into the sunset. He takes a sip of his drink and casts an eye sideways at his daughters. Olive, still in Harry's shorts and football jersey, sits beside him with Rosie on her knee. Ralph leans against a verandah post, his hair a golden fuzz in the last of the sun. Tom comes through and pours out a nip. All would be peaceful if it were not for Alfred the mynah, shrieking in his cage under the eaves. Olive stands up, and Hughie sees how much she has grown. She can reach Alfred's cage.

"He's never going to learn to talk," she says in Adela's voice. It happens now and again, and startles Hughie, the ghost of her in Olive's pronouncements. He never sees Adela anymore. After that first time with Maggie she disappeared.

Maggie will be a comfort and a joy to him. As the boys get older and take over at the sailroom he will, more and more, if the weather allows, sail to Savusavu to see her. Sometimes he'll take Olive because she so loves the sail across, just herself and him, tolerating the interlude of a few days with the Molloys only for the sake of the return voyage.

But for Hughie and Maggie they will be golden times. He will watch her as they sail alone in the bay, her strong thighs bracing under her thin skirt as she brings *Vai* about, her red hair flying behind her like a stay-sail, her broad grin in her freckled, creased face as she looks up at him, her delight in him . . . and at night, in bed, the love they'll make because they owe each other nothing. It will be a perfect, strangely innocent love.

He will come to think of Maggie as a gift from Adela to warm his last years, a love somehow sent by her. She had taken her leave so gently that it will be years before he can summon her face to memory again without the aid of a photograph, and years before he understands why. Then suddenly, when his children are all scattered to easier lives in cooler colonies and he is a long time between visits to Maggie, Adela will come to offer him company. He will find himself greeting her without grief. Quite probably, on that morning, he will decide to go with her, grateful for her presence on that long, final fade from life.

"Is he, Dad? What do you reckon?"

Olive unhooks the little door and holds it open. Alfred comes to the threshold, cocks his head and gives her a long, unblinking stare. His wings spread and ruffle in the evening breeze. Then he remembers the wider world beyond this small one, and takes determined flight.

Glossary

Fijian

Mata-ni-waitui — Eyes like the ocean
ayah — nanny
Bula — hullo
bulu makau — beef
bure — Fijian house
cassava — a green vegetable (Manioc)
cava — what
curu yani — go inside
dakua — species of Fijian tree
dalo — taro
gunu — drink
ika — fish
i-lavo — money
i-talanoa — story
Kaivitis — Fijians
kalou — God
kua ni leqa — don't worry
kula — species of parrot
lali — drum
liku — short grass skirt
lotu — Christianity
Marama — Lady
"Like a Mbuan drinking nut" — Fijian expression meaning
    someone or something unsuited to the task

253

meke — dance
moce — goodbye
ngone ca — bad child
nuqu — species of dangerous fish
Pavavalagi — European
reba — Fijian name for grey goshawk
Rotuman — person from Rotuma, a Polynesian island near Fiji
Saka — Sir/Madam
Sa malumalumu talega na i rogo ni lali — The bell sounds
   weak
Sara quqa na mataivalu ni Peretania — The war has been won
   by the armies of Great Britain
Sara vakadrukai na kai Jamani — The Germans have been
   beaten
Sa yadra — Good morning
Sega — No
sulu — length of fabric wrapped around as a skirt
tapa — cloth made of beaten cocoa-nut fibre
tinana — mother
vale levu — big house
vale lai lai — toilet
vale ni cula laca — ships chandlery/sailroom
vavalagi — European
vesi — species of Fijian tree
vinaka — thank you/yes
wai — water
yasi — Fijian hardwood

Hindustani

chokra — Indian servant, usually a child
Jai — Hooray!
Memsahib — Madam/lady
punkah — ceiling fan

roti — Indian bread
Sirdar — overseer
wallah — servant

French

The French on page 172 translates as:
   "Once we are in the open sea, it will not be so uncomfortable," he said . . . "And I'm sorry about the bilge-water."
   "Is the ship safe?"
   "This is only a south-easterly gale, nothing to worry your little head about" . . .
   "I'll fetch another chair."